The Solace of Denim

by
Kathy Otten

A Young Adult Mystery from
Dragonfly Publishing, Inc.

* * * * *

THE SOLACE OF DENIM

Young Adult Mystery
Released in 2023

Paperback Edition
EAN 978-1-949187-46-5
ISBN 1-949187-46-2

Published in the United States of America by
Dragonfly Publishing, Inc.
www.dragonflypubs.com

* * * * *

Dedication

Amanda: Thanks for letting me use your laptop way back in 2005 and for creating my first email account for me. Hopefully, this story won't embarrass you.

* * * * *

CHAPTER 1

SCHOOL sucks!

Joey Kowalski kicked the bedroom door shut and tossed his backpack in the general direction of the closet. The weight of his books inside dropped the bag to the hardwood floor with a thud.

Pinching the zipper tab of his winter jacket, he pulled down. It jammed halfway. He jerked the tab, but the zipper didn't move. Reaching behind his neck, he grabbed the back of the collar and yanked the nylon coat over his head. He left the sleeves to dangle wrong side out and flung the useless jacket toward his book bag.

He limped to his bed, flopped face down, and sighed into his pillow. He'd survived another day of whispered name calling, a stolen lunch, and guys knocking into him. He'd made it through another gym class struggling to play basketball, waiting to shower last so no one would see his scars.

He'd endured another lecture from Mrs. Brolin, who told him: "This circled F at the top of your math test is there because you're being lazy. Your grades at the beginning of the year indicate you can do better. You just aren't trying."

His math book was in his backpack. He had homework, but without Luke to explain the A's, B's, and negative numbers, Joey just didn't get it. Besides, even if he aced every quiz and test from now to the end of the semester, he had so many zeros and F's he'd still be failing at midterms. So why bother? It was like falling out of a plane without a parachute. If you're going to die at the end, you might as well enjoy the fall.

"Joey!" Lorraine's sharp voice rose up the stairwell and penetrated the bedroom door. Usually, he ignored her. If he waited, her voice would rise an octave with each failed attempt to gain his attention. Sometimes he wondered how high her voice could go before shrieking into nothingness. Today he just wanted her to shut up.

He lifted his head off the pillow. "What?"

"Frank and I are going grocery shopping. We're taking the little ones with us. We'll be back in a couple of hours. Before you do your homework, I want you to come down and help Allison decorate her gingerbread men."

He'd rather do his math.

"Do you hear me?"

They'd be gone for a couple of hours. Maybe he could get out of here for a while. He rolled off the bed.

"Joey!"

Her voice had jumped all the way to a high-C.

"Coming!"

"Don't take too long. I want the kitchen cleaned up by the time we get back."

Whatever. He shivered and massaged his right thigh, waiting for them to leave.

Even with a long sleeve T-shirt beneath his flannel shirt and hoodie, he was cold. The old farmhouse was drafty, and Frank was too cheap to keep the thermostat above sixty-five.

The shrieks and squeals of little kids faded as the back door slammed. Soon gravel crunched beneath the weight of the minivan as it rolled down the driveway. A minute later the faint, low southern tones of Elvis singing *Blue Christmas* drifted upstairs.

Every Christmas was blue. Fa-la-la and ho-ho-ho was for stupid kids who still believed.

He walked over to the closet to find another sweater or sweatshirt. He was sick of always being cold. It made his leg ache and his chest hurt. Maybe when summer came, he'd feel better.

He turned the knob and pulled open the door. He had a blue Penn State sweatshirt in there somewhere. He reached out to sift through the shirts and froze.

A faded denim jacket hung slightly apart from the other clothes.

His heart skipped a beat. He swung around, searching the corners of his room. For what, he didn't know. Everything remained exactly the same as it had been a moment ago. He turned back to the closet. The jacket was still there.

Joey hugged himself, rubbing his hands over his biceps. He squeezed his eyes tight and then opened them, but the jacket hadn't vanished. His pulse thudded inside his ears, muting all sounds of Elvis.

Both afraid of the jacket and drawn to it, Joey reached out and pulled it from the hanger. It looked the same as it had the last time he'd seen Luke wearing it. Band logo patches decorated the denim across the shoulders, back, and front: *Tool, Nine-Inch Nails, Manson, Slipknot,* a skull, and a peace symbol.

He couldn't fathom how Luke's jacket had gotten into his closet after all these months, but there it was.

Should he put it on?

He glanced around the room once more. It was stupid to look. Luke wasn't here.

He swung the jacket over his shoulders, shoving his arms into the sleeves.

Originally, the jacket had belonged to Luke's dad. It had been a little big on Luke and was even bigger on Joey, but for the first time in a long while he felt warm.

He pulled the hood of his sweatshirt from beneath the jacket, leaving it to drape between his shoulder blades, and buttoned up the front.

An overwhelming need to escape the homey scent of gingerbread sent him striding across the room. He opened the door and made his way down the stairs. Maybe he'd head out on the railroad tracks for a while, just walk away from this place, away from the memories and the pain of Christmas. Walk until his head cleared and there was no place left to go.

He stepped into the kitchen.

Allison stood at the island, a faded green apron enveloping her gangly frame. A plastic container filled with plain gingerbread men sat beside a bowl of white icing and a decorator bag. Her phone on the counter blared the annoying twang of *Grandma Got Run Over by A Reindeer.*

That song would probably be stuck inside his head all night. If he still had his ear pods and phone, he could block out the annoying melody with some Rammstein cranked loud. He could block out everything.

Allison's off-key singing stopped.

Even with her music blaring and him wearing only socks, she seemed to sense his presence.

She whirled around, her ponytail swinging over her narrow shoulders. "What are you doing?"

"Nothing."

"Where are you going? Mom said you're supposed to help me."

"She's not our mother."

Hurt flashed in Allison's large brown eyes, and she dropped her gaze to the floor.

Maybe Allison felt that affection for Lorraine, because Allison had lived here for three years. He'd only been here since January and couldn't imagine ever feeling that way.

"But my 4-H party is tomorrow night."

"Not my problem." Joey limped past the island, his right heel scuffing across faded green and gray linoleum tiles that looked like they belonged on the floor of the old-time diner from *Back to the Future.*

Allison looked up. Her brow furrowed. "Isn't that Luke's jacket? Where'd you get it?"

"None of your business."

He grabbed his insulated lace-up boots off the newspaper that had been placed by the back door.

"How can you stand wearing that thing? It's *sick*."

At the table, he pulled out one of the chairs and lowered himself onto the vinyl padded seat. Most likely an antique, the green Formica table with its chrome legs and matching chairs had been purchased by Frank's parents back in the day, and Frank was too stingy to get something newer.

"Mom and Dad think there's something wrong with you."

Joey glanced up at this new bit of information. "They are not my mom and dad. Yours neither." He stuffed his feet into the boots.

"Ms. Allen called. They had some meeting with the school therapist." Allison's chin tilted up. "They say you're failing all your classes and you don't talk to anybody."

"So?" He leaned over to tug the laces tight before tying them. He stood and lifted a black knit cap and a pair of gloves from the shelf above the overcrowded rack of coats and jackets.

Allison followed him to the back door, crossing her arms. "What am I supposed to tell Mom when she asks me where you went?"

"Whatever you want." He opened the back door. A wave of colder air blew in from the enclosed porch. "And she's not my mother," he called just before the door swung close and the latch clicked in place.

He tugged the sweatshirt hood over his cap and hunched his shoulders against the cold. The warmth and sunshine of the previous day had flipped like the page of a book into a day of chilling damp and gray sky. The slush along the edge of the road had frozen into dirty clumps of ice that crushed into tiny beads under the weight of his boots. His hair fell to the bridge of his nose and lifted slightly with the damp breeze.

He cut through the heifer pasture, navigating the intricacies of two barbed wire fences in order to reach the high gravel bed of the railroad tracks. He turned and headed west.

His pace slowed. With his bad leg, it was an effort to keep from stumbling each time his boots punched through the thin layer of crusty snow.

Endless miles of track stretched before him, luring him toward the horizon. Sometimes the pull was so strong it was hard to make himself stop and turn around, especially lately. Maybe he should keep walking and never look back, all the way to California.

Patches of brown grass, exposed by the warmth of yesterday's sun, dotted the landscape. Elsewhere, clumps of weeds poked through the snow in shades of muted gold and rust. Snow and clouds blurred together into a backdrop of sameness broken only by a line of distant trees, their gnarled limbs outlined in stark contrast against the bleakness of the day.

He didn't mind the desolation. He liked the aloneness of it, away from prying eyes and people who made judgments.

On his right, Branch Creek meandered alongside the tracks for half a mile and turned left. It then wandered south toward the next creek and the next. Eventually, it flowed into the Allegheny River.

Where the tracks crossed over the creek, Joey stopped to watch the water pass below. He and Luke had climbed down there many Saturdays to fish or lie on the bank to watch clouds and talk.

Ice now edged both banks, but periods of warm weather kept the narrow creek from freezing solid. Today the water was higher than usual and moving fast, swollen from yesterday's snowmelt. Joey found himself staring down for several minutes, mesmerized by the silver flicker of water over rocks.

Luke had refused to stand here and watch the water. Looking down had made him dizzy, even though the distance was less than ten feet. While Joey often lingered to watch the water, Luke had kept to the center of the bridge with his eyes fixed on the horizon. He had somehow managed to place his feet on the ties without looking off either side.

As Joey stared at the flickering shimmer of light on water, an image formed like those found in clouds moving across the sky. The reflection of a train trestle bridge wavered in the surface.

Abruptly, the water turned black. As though he were pulled inside some science fiction vortex, the current shifted and swirled. The distance between the water and the bridge seemed to grow, until the whirling stopped. Joey stood, looking down from the precipice of a trestle bridge ten times higher than where he'd been.

His chest squeezed so tight he could only breathe with short panting gasps of air. Black spots floated before him. He squeezed his eyes shut. Wind roared in his ears.

Words echoed inside his head. Except the voice wasn't his. It was Luke's!

No! Luke cried. *Don't! Please!*

At that moment the Earth seemed to tip, and Joey felt himself pitch forward. He opened his eyes to find himself plummeting toward black water, falling and falling, except some part of him knew that he was still standing on the tracks. A scream ripped from his lungs. His own or Luke's, he wasn't sure.

Numbing terror choked him, the way it had six years ago when a bullet had torn though his right lung and he'd frantically struggled for his next breath. Except this time there was no pain.

He squeezed his eyes tight and pressed his hand against his chest.

Breathe!

Gradually the ability to suck in gulps of air returned. When his heart quit its incessant hammering, he opened his eyes.

The world was as it had been before, white and gray and brown. With caution he peered down at the creek. Silvery gray water sparkled below.

What the hell just happened?

A sudden ache blossomed behind his eyes, and he took a moment to rub his fingers against his temples. He drew a deep breath, turned, and hurried the rest of the way across the bridge.

The jacket. It reminded him of Luke. That was all.

His mind was just playing tricks. There were no voices. Hallucinations weren't real, unless he'd finally cracked from the pressure of his silence, from the stress of not knowing what actually happened that day.

The thing was, Luke had been terrified of heights. They'd told each other stuff like that. Things they shared with no one else.

Joey even told him how if someone in the house dropped a plate or slammed a door, he could feel again the tearing pain through his right thigh, the impact of the bullet through his back. It would be hard to move, hard to breathe, just as it had been six years ago on that night two days before Christmas.

Had Luke felt that same kind of pain?

When his body was found in the river below the trestle bridge the second week of October, he'd had a bullet in his back.

Whether what Joey felt moments ago had been his own memory or Luke's, it didn't matter. Everyone looked at Joey, as though he was supposed to know what happened. In his grief and pain, he'd ignored them all, which only isolated him in a way far worse than when he'd started school as the new kid nearly a year ago.

Things grew worse after Investigator Kraus from the State Police came to school with his partner to talk to the principal, Ms. Allen, and to all of Luke's teachers.

Kraus and his partner had even come twice to Frank and Lorraine's house to ask Joey more questions.

But he'd refused to say a word.

Now whispers floated behind his back and fingers pointed when he passed.

Losing Luke had been as painful as losing his brother Kyle. Though he and Luke had known each other less than a year, they had somehow connected and grown closer than brothers. Joey closed his eyes and rubbed his temples. Life sucked. It wasn't fair.

He ran, his gait awkward and clumsy as he tried to distance himself from memories he couldn't escape. He pushed harder and faster, until he felt like an exhausted marathon runner stumbling toward the finish line. Now at least he could blame the tears burning in his eyes on the wind.

His left foot dropped through a deep patch of snow. He pitched forward onto his hands and knees. Shards of icy snow dug through the worn denim of his jeans. He pushed back to sit on his heels and then swiped at his eyes. Bits of snow clung to the sleeves and front of Luke's jacket. Carefully, he brushed it all away.

The pounding in his head eased. Lethargy settled into his limbs. The grays of late afternoon had deepened into shades of charcoal.

A car door slammed somewhere below him and then another.

Confused, he glanced around. Somehow, he'd made it as far as the overpass, where the tracks crossed over the narrow road which headed northeast, past Frank and Lorraine's house, past Luke's house.

One more door closed with a thump. Three doors. Three people. White light of headlights illuminated each end of the road from beneath the overpass.

Joey peered beneath the rusty pipe railing, over the edge of the railroad ties. On the road below a shiny black car, partially obscured by shadows from the overpass, sat on the west bound shoulder. Idling on the opposite side was a navy-blue late model Chevelle SS with a dark green hood and a maroon door, its faulty muffler giving a distinctive clatter.

The acrid bite of cigarette smoke wafted up on the damp air, but Joey resisted the urge to shoo it away.

Recognition rolled through Joey's stomach, as if he'd just slammed back a large glass of cold water.

Nathan Kelly. A big guy who'd played football in high school and still kept in shape, Nate now worked at one of the local mini marts.

Wherever Nate went, so went his younger brother Greg, an offensive lineman on the high school football team.

Between the rumbling engine and gusts of wind, most of their words were distorted mumblings. Then the breeze stilled. Nate's car idled down a few RPM's and the deep, modulated tones of a voice he didn't recognize echoed through the short concrete tunnel. The man must belong to the black car.

"I won't risk anyone, especially not your nosey neighbor, spotting us together," Black Car said.

Joey was tempted to stick his fingers in his ears. The less he knew the better, but fear kept him from moving even that little bit.

"I got two G's here," Nate said.

"With all the college bowl games, I expected at least another grand."

"It's almost Christmas. People want to buy presents."

"Well, I'm not Santa Claus."

Beneath Joey's knees the snow warmed, soaking the front legs of his jeans, but he remained rooted to the spot.

"A few paid the juice and owe the rest, but they're regulars. They're good for it."

"You're in collections. Collect. I expect it by Friday night. And I warned you to stop placing bets for kids."

"We stopped."

"Well, someone boo-hooed to Mommy and Daddy and set the cops to poking around." Black Car's tone was reasonable, yet an underlying threat hung in the moments of silence that followed.

"There are two who still owe me."

"Hey," Greg interrupted. "None of 'em would dare call—"

"Shut up," Nate snapped.

"I don't want excuses," Black Car said. "Just take care of it. And whatever happens with the cops, it's on you. Anything leads back to me, and I'll cut you loose."

"Yes, sir. Got it."

Tiny prickles raced like ants through the muscles of Joey's right leg. Before it went numb, he eased his weight onto his left and straightened his right. He bit his lip against the pins and needles.

Beneath his foot under the snow, a few pebbles dislodged. They sifted down the incline, over the edge of the concrete bridge, and pinged off the roof and hood of Nate's car.

Joey froze.

Silence.

He imagined them looking up, wondering.

Greg stepped from beneath the overpass. "It's gimpy boy!"

The words slammed into Joey with the impact of a shotgun blast.

Greg dashed to the end of the sloped retaining wall and scrambled up the embankment.

Joey jumped up to run, but his aching leg hindered his escape. As he dashed forward, hands grabbed him from behind. A palm landed on his shoulder, as fingers yanked the hood of his sweatshirt and dragged him backward.

Off balance, Joey fell. Arms and legs tangled together, and the pair tumbled off the tracks into the frozen snow.

Joey thrashed beneath Greg's weight and kicked out, catching the toe of his boot against Greg's chin.

"Sonofa—" Greg's hold loosened, and he clapped his hand to his mouth.

Joey tried to scoot backward up the hill in a weird imitation of the crab walk they'd done in gym class when he was a kid. Greg grabbed his foot and pulled him down the embankment toward the retaining wall and the road, toward Nate and the quiet stranger so out of place in an overcoat and hat.

Twisting away, Joey made a last-ditch effort to escape by latching on to clumps of grass and scrub brush, seeking purchase on the slippery slope. It wasn't enough. A second hand wrapped around his ankle above his boot. His leg was jerked from under him. His cheek hit the frozen snow, scraping raw over the icy crust.

Greg dragged Joey down the embankment to the place where it met the angled concrete wall and sloped to the road.

As soon as Joey was within reach, Nate twisted his fingers into the neck of Luke's jacket and dragged Joey into the shadows beneath the bridge. "Well, lookie who we have here."

Joey gulped.

Greg stepped up beside his brother. He slapped his black knit Penguins hat against his left thigh knocking off the snow before slipping the cap over his head. He laughed. Rather than humor, malice underscored the tone in a minor key.

Nate twisted the denim fabric of Luke's jacket a little tighter. "Doing a little eavesdropping, Gimp?"

"N-no," Joey croaked through his dry throat and shook his head.

The stranger from the black car turned to Greg. "Get up there." He jerked his head toward the slope. "Stand where he was and let me know what you hear."

The next instant, Nate slammed Joey's back up against the concrete retaining wall. The air in his lungs rushed out in one big *oof*. Several seconds passed before he was able to catch a normal breath.

"You better not be lying, Gimp."

Nate pressed his opposite forearm against Joey's throat. "You won't like what happens to gimps who lie to me," he warned in a menacing tone and then stepped back.

Joey rubbed his throat and swallowed.

Black Car stepped closer, crushing the icy snow beneath the weight of his feet. A curling Grinch-like smile pulled up the corners of his mouth. His cool gaze roamed over Joey.

Joey's nostrils flared at the earthy scent of the man's cologne.

Black Car curled his black gloved fingers into a fist and drove it straight into Joey's stomach.

Oof! Joey folded in half, and his knees buckled. He planted his palm in frozen slush to keep from pitching face-first onto the road.

The man leaned over. The hem of his topcoat brushed the toes of his shiny black, wingtip shoes.

A shiver rippled through Joey's insides.

"You will stay out of my business, Mr. Gimp," he said quietly. "Or next time I won't be so forgiving."

Joey sat back on his heels, his thigh aching to be rubbed.

Greg slid down the embankment and jumped from the wall to the road. He shook his head, joining them under the overpass. "Can't make out nothing up there."

The stranger nodded. The chilled air warmed a bit.

"Car coming," Greg said.

The three of them exchanged glances.

"Later," Nate said, as he and Greg headed to their car.

The stranger with the powerful punch strolled across the road and slipped into the driver's seat of his black sedan. A moment later the vehicle eased forward and continued west.

"And you," Nate snapped at his brother across the roof of the car. "I told you he'd find out about your friends."

"I don't know how he—"

"What the hell's it matter? He knows. Lean on those kids. Get me that money. Then we'll destroy the evidence."

They climbed into the car. If they both slammed their doors with a little more force than necessary, what did Joey care? He pushed to his feet and leaned against the support of the graffiti-covered wall.

Nate's car roared and sped off, spraying salt and slush across the front of Joey's legs. He assumed they were heading home to their rusty white and gold single-wide trailer about a mile and a half up the road past Frank and Lorraine's.

With deliberate effort he stepped away from the retaining wall and brushed off bits of dirt and snow that clung to Luke's jacket. He pressed his arm against his trembling stomach. His cheek burned and he shivered in his wet jeans.

Could this day, could his life possibly get any worse?

He started walking.

A vehicle approached from behind and reduced speed for the curve. The engine grew louder as it passed under the tracks, and then the SUV slowed to a crawl alongside Joey.

A premonition of dread rippled through his body. He kept walking.

From the corner of his eye, he saw the dark glass of the passenger window lower.

"Joe?" called a familiar masculine voice.

Yes. His life could definitely get worse. Only one person ever called him Joe.

Still walking, he turned his head and met Detective Marek's gaze across the passenger seat. Each exhale of breath increased the tension between them. He hadn't seen Detective Marek since the funeral, and he wasn't sure what to say.

The man studied him. "Are you okay?"

Joey hadn't expected concern. "Yeah. I fell climbing down from the tracks." He gestured back toward the underpass.

Their gazes came together again. Detective Marek was no fool. Multiple boot prints pock-marked the slope. Chunks of snow lay scattered across the pavement.

"Get in."

The last person in the world he wanted to deal with was Detective Marek.

Joey stopped.

The SUV stopped.

Shivering, Joey opened the door and climbed inside the big, warm vehicle.

They rode in silence. Marek continued to shoot covert glances at Joey, as though poised to fire off a question.

Joey looked toward the man several times. Between the dark interior and the navy peacoat, Joey couldn't make out the weapon worn at his waist. Marek was right-handed. As long as he kept that hand on the steering wheel, he couldn't reach for his gun.

Trying not to think about it, Joey replayed the lyrics of that stupid reindeer song in his head. He wished he was back at the house.

"What were you and Luke fighting about the day he disappeared?" The question hung in the air like an anvil in a cartoon, heavy and dangerous.

The blood drained from Joey's face, leaving him both cold and sweaty. He hadn't thought anyone had seen that fight. Odd, because not only had it been their only fight, but it had actually gotten physical.

Who had seen it? Why after all this time had they even reported it?

He clenched his teeth. The hairs at the back of his neck prickled. Had someone been watching them that day?

Who had told Marek?

Investigator Kraus from the State Police had only asked Joey about it yesterday when Kraus and his partner stopped by the school.

Joey crossed his arms against the waves of cold that rippled through his body. He shifted on the seat. When had the heat stopped blowing? Staring out the window, he pretended he couldn't feel Detective Marek's piercing gaze boring straight through him.

"Joe?"

Absently, he kneaded the knot of scar tissue in the muscle of his thigh.

"A witness said you threatened Luke." Intensity radiated from the man. His tone demanded truth. "You know something about my son's death, don't you? Don't you?"

Joey cringed. His pulse thudded against the back of his jaw. He stared at Detective Marek's right hand, making sure it stayed on the wheel. As inconspicuously as possible, Joey popped the seatbelt free and held it in place. He moved his other hand to the armrest. His fingers wrapped around the door's release lever.

Angry silence pulsated inside the vehicle. Joey didn't know what to say, and Detective Marek's jaw clenched as though he were trying to keep his accusations locked behind his teeth.

Tires crunched against ice and gravel as the car pulled into Frank and Lorraine's driveway and looped around past the old cow barn to the back porch. The headlights swept over a large blow-up polar bear and snow globe before the car stopped.

Exhaling a sigh of relief, Joey opened the door and hopped down. He turned for a moment and met the gray-blue eyes of Detective Marek. Bitterness glared back. Joey clamped his lower lip between his teeth and focused on the pain of his top teeth pressing deep into the muscle. He stepped back to close the door.

"Joe."

Joey lifted his gaze, hoping in that millisecond of time that Detective Marek would say he was sorry. Sorry he'd doubted him.

"Give me back my son's jacket."

Joey blinked, confused for a moment. He gave the briefest of nods and slipped off the jacket. He held it for several long seconds, loath to surrender it, loath to part with the last piece of Luke.

He fought the sting of tears, as pulled wide the door and laid the jacket carefully on the seat, making sure the sleeves didn't drag on the wet floor mat.

Moving back, he closed the door and watched Detective Marek drive away.

For an unnerving moment he swore he could hear Luke's voice calling to him from that jacket.

* * * * *

CHAPTER 2

JOEY limped up the shoveled pathway.

Someone had tossed rock salt on top of the glazed surface, dotting it with tiny gray holes.

Yellow glow from a bulb over the back door illuminated the steps of the enclosed porch. Colorful lights traced the eaves, and electric candles shone from the windows of the house. They should have been a beacon of welcome, but Joey exhaled a resigned sigh, feeling unwanted as he walked through the porch and opened the back door into the kitchen.

Lorraine stood at the stove, stirring something in a pot. Steam rose from a second, larger pot beside it.

Behind her at the kitchen island, Frank wrapped each decorated gingerbread man with plastic wrap while Allison tied the gathered ends with ribbon and slipped a miniature candy cane beneath the knot. Next to her, Benny stood on a backward-facing chair. White icing coated his face and hands. He held a butter knife, caked with frosting which he had apparently used to decorate three broken cookies in front of him.

They all looked up as Joey stepped through the door, even baby Carrie watched from her playpen, a puffy red plastic stacking ring shoved against her mouth.

"Where have you been?" Frank asked.

Joey closed the door and pushed back his hood. "Nowhere." He tossed his gloves and cap into the basket on the shelf above the coat hooks.

"Whose car was that?"

Joey turned and met Frank's gaze across the room. Was the guy really going to pretend he hadn't spied through the window the minute he heard the crunch of tires in the driveway? Detective Marek lived in the next house down the road. Frank knew whose car it was. What Frank really wanted to know was why Joey had been with him.

"You were supposed to help Allison today."

Joey didn't bother to reply. He pulled a chair from the table, allowing it to scrape across the linoleum tiles, and sat to untie his boots.

"Look, we're trying here," Frank said, "but you have to make some effort."

Joey set his boots on the newspaper and pushed in the chair.

As he turned back to the table, he caught the exchange of glances between Frank and Lorraine.

"I'm making your favorite," Lorraine said in that perky voice she used when she talked to Benny. "Hot dogs and macaroni and cheese."

He looked toward the stove but didn't see the usual blue box.

"I'm making homemade," she said, as though able to read his mind. "The cheese sauce is nearly done. I just have to drain the pasta and bake it for twenty minutes."

"I'm not hungry."

"But you love it."

"I only like the box kind. I hate that homemade shit."

"Joey, don't speak to your mother in that manner."

"She's not my mother. You're not my father. None of you are my family."

Frank stiffened. "That doesn't give you a reason to speak—"

The loud jangle of the green, wall-mounted phone interrupted Frank's lecture. He moved to the end of the counter near the archway to the dining room and lifted the receiver.

"Hello?" He twisted the cord around his finger and nodded. "Just a minute." Frank extended his arm toward Joey, the receiver in his hand. "It's for you."

No one ever called for him. Curious, he limped toward Frank and took the receiver. "Hello?"

"Hi, Joey. It's Mary Custer."

His case worker paused, waiting for him to exchange a greeting. Since she never called to talk to him, suspicion swallowed his response.

"I don't know if Frank or Lorraine mentioned it or not, but I stopped by this afternoon to talk with you."

A visit *and* a phone call.

"I would rather have discussed this in person, but I won't be available now until after Christmas." She heaved a sigh, either because he wasn't responding or because she had to rally herself to tell whatever was so important it couldn't wait. "Your father's attorney contacted me. It seems that not only has your father been a model prisoner, but he's been going to counseling. The court is allowing him to contact you."

The impact of Mary's words slammed into his abdomen like one of Black Car's sucker punches. Cold washed through him, leaving him numb. He managed to maintain his grip on the receiver, but the printed bowls of fruit on the wallpaper blurred into multi-colored blobs.

"Of course," she continued, "he can only send letters or messages through his attorney who passes them to your court appointed attorney. He will never be allowed your address or phone number."

After six years what was he supposed to say?

"Joey?" Mary prompted from the other end of the line. "Just think about it. I understand he has cancer and he—"

Joey's mind went blank. He returned the receiver to the metal cradle and moved like a zombie through the dining room into the front hall. Gripping the banister, he pulled himself up the stairs to the second floor.

When he reached his room, he eased the door closed. Darkness swallowed the room. He squeezed his eyes tight and leaned against the solid brace of wood.

Fighting a whirl of memories, he pressed the heels of his hands against his eyes. He wished he still had his phone, his computer, his game system, anything that he could use to block out the spinning reel of images.

His mom used to sprinkle crushed corn flakes over the top of her macaroni and cheese before she slid it in the oven. She would laugh and say he and Kyle loved her mac-and-cheese so much that she could never make enough for them.

Why would he ever contact the man who took that away?

He slid his back down the length of the wood panel, until his butt hit the floor. He extended his bad leg and swiped tears from his eyes.

Why did it suddenly hurt so bad after all this time?

Because stupid Luke went and got himself killed. His death had ripped open all the old wounds and made them bigger.

Maybe if Joey could figure out who killed Luke, it would ease the constant fear that gnawed at his gut.

"Supper!" Frank called up the stairs.

Joey ignored him. A few minutes later the murmur of voices rose from the kitchen. While he'd never felt as though he were part of that whole happy family thing Frank and Lorraine tried to create, lately he felt as if he were Damien, the demon child from the *Omen.* It seemed they neither wanted him nor knew what to do with him.

His stomach rumbled. He'd grab a bowl of cereal after everyone was asleep. He rolled to his feet. Flipping on his bedside light, he grabbed a clean pair of flannel bottoms from his dresser and headed into the bathroom between his room and Benny's. While the Grinch tried to steal the joy from Christmas in the TV downstairs, Joey stripped and stepped into the shower. The hot water and soap stung his abraded cheek, but he didn't care. He let the water beat down on his head and shoulders, washing away the soap and tears, until Frank yelled up the stairs to stop using all the hot water.

After pulling on his clean T-shirt and flannel bottoms, he wiped the mirror and checked his cheek. Not too bad. The thin scratches would heal in a day or so. He squeezed a couple of zits on his forehead and ran a comb through his hair, letting his bangs cover the spots. The fine hairs on his upper lip were visible again. He lathered up some hand soap and rubbed it over the area in lieu of shaving cream.

When he'd asked Frank to buy him some shave cream and razors, Frank had told him he didn't have anything to shave. But Joey could see the shadow, the start of a dark moustache. He pulled open the bottom drawer and reached behind the disposable underwear Benny wore to bed and grasped the razor he'd found in the garbage in Frank and Lorraine's bathroom. Carefully, he wiped away all traces of soap and hair. He nicked the curve of his chin with the dull blade, but he didn't care. When he finished, any hint of dark shadow was gone. Washing all evidence down the drain, he wiped off the sink, turned out the light, and closed the door. In his room he tossed his clothes in the hamper and crawled under the covers to wait.

Downstairs the dishwasher hummed and the Whos down in Whoville began to sing.

Half an hour later, Lorraine and Benny came up the stairs.

He rolled toward the wall and pulled the pillow over his head, yet he could still hear their routine in the adjoining bathroom.

A bath, pajamas, and *brush your teeth*. It was then time for a bedtime story. *Whose Mother Are You?* Lorraine read aloud.

The tears returned, burning Joey's eyes. He fought them back. He'd toughed it out alone all this time. Why cry about it now? He wasn't a baby anymore. It had been six birthdays, six school grades and soon to be six Christmases. *Daddy* sure as hell hadn't cared then, why should Joey care about him now? Let the son-of-a-bitch rot from cancer.

He heard Lorraine kiss Benny night-night, tuck him in, and turn out the light.

Joey's mom used to come in his room every night to give him and Kyle each a kiss before she went to bed.

Though Lorraine must have seen the light shining beneath Joey's door, she walked down the hall without peeking in to whisper good night. Her footsteps didn't even pause.

* * *

"I want him out of this house." Though Lorraine's voice wasn't loud, the sharpness of demand carried through their bedroom door.

Joey stopped on his way to the kitchen. What had he done now? Had Lorraine found the kitchen knife he kept under his mattress? He made his own bed every day and changed the sheets on Saturday, so she probably hadn't. Besides, Frank sounded too calm.

"Now, Lori," Frank murmured. "All teenagers can be moody and disrespectful."

"Do you know what Benny asked me when I gave him his bath? He wanted to know if he could sleep in the closet like Joey. Did you know about that?"

Joey leaned against the wall to better listen without the fear his shifting weight would creak a floorboard.

"No," Frank replied, "but you probably should mention it to his therapist tomorrow when you tell him about his father."

"I'm also calling Mary in the morning. He's a bad influence on Benny, and Allison doesn't like him."

"Allison was molested by her father. She has an issue with men in general."

"I don't care. He scares me."

"Lori, we don't know for sure that he did it. The State Police don't think so, or they would have arrested him by now."

"That investigator Kraus was here yesterday, asking him about a fight he had with Luke. They must suspect something. Maybe they don't have enough evidence yet."

"Believe me, I have doubts, too. Everyone wonders. But unless we have a valid reason, Mary isn't going to come and just take him."

"Why are you taking his side?"

"I'm not."

"New placements take time. Why don't we hold off 'til after the holidays? Let the kid have Christmas."

Joey didn't wait to hear more. His appetite gone, he eased away from the door.

In his room, he lined up pillows down the center of the bed and pulled the covers over them. Slipping his hand under the mattress, he pulled out his knife. He grabbed an extra pillow and a blanket, pulled open the closet door, stepped inside, and dropped to his knees. Closing the door, he curled onto his side and pulled the blanket over him.

Joey lay awake with the knife clenched in his hand and stared at the narrow line of light beneath the door.

Now that Frank and Lorraine knew, he wondered where he would sleep tomorrow.

* * *

Joey slouched in the club chair in a corner of the office, arms crossed over his chest, the ankle of his good leg crossed over the knee of his bad.

He stared out the window between the long thin panels of vertical blinds, watching people come and go from the parking lot two stories below. Absently, he rubbed the place where the bullet had torn through his thigh.

His psychologist, Doctor Mercer Something-or-Other PhD., who specialized in childhood trauma, sat in silence waiting for Joey to say something. The doctor wasn't good with silence though. Every once in a while, he would ask Joey what he thought about his teachers, or the new paint color on the wall, or the light snow falling outside. But Joey didn't say a word.

He hadn't spoken to any of the doctors or therapists over the years who'd wanted him to play games and draw pictures. Why would this weasely little man, with his elbow-patched jacket and his bifocals slid halfway down his nose, expect anything different?

"I see you're rubbing your leg. Your medical records indicate it's completely healed. Why do you think you still limp after all these years?"

Joey didn't even bother to glance his way. He'd heard it all before. Unresolved survivor's guilt. Repressed anger. Selective mutism. What did any of them know? Had they ever been shot? If he'd hurt his leg playing football, no one would say a word.

"If you could choose just one word to describe your father, what word would you choose?"

Where the hell had that question come from?

This time Joey couldn't help but look over at the man seated in the other chair.

Notepad in hand, pen poised, the psychologist sat with his legs crossed, peering at Joey over the tops of his glasses. "He wants to write to you."

Joey curled his fingers into a loose fist and pushed the heel of his hand hard against his thigh. His old man could write all the damn letters he wanted. Joey didn't have to accept them.

Doctor Mercer Arrogant-Asshole watched him in that creepy way he had, as though poised to pounce at the slightest reaction from Joey just so he'd have something to analyze.

"Does that surprise you?"

Joey turned back to the window. Of course, it surprised him. And the man knew that.

"Your mother called me this morning and mentioned it."

Joey clenched his teeth against the urge to shout: *She is not my mother!*

"Your case worker stopped by the house, but you were out."

The muscles at the back of Joey's jaw tightened. Lorraine had a big mouth. And wasn't Mary Custer supposed to keep things confidential? Not that he had ever trusted her. Or Frank. Or any of them.

"I understand he's sick. Cancer."

One by one, the streetlights blinked on. Hopefully, the cancer was the long painful kind, so the man suffered for years.

A woman holding the hands of two small children approached a blue minivan. The taillights blinked and she slid the side door open.

"Perhaps it would be good to hear what he has to say. Find some closure before it's too late. The first step in the healing process, the first step toward forgiveness."

Forgiveness?

Joey shot from the chair. In three strides he was across the room.

"Then you write to him and tell him to go screw himself."

He yanked open the door and stalked past the receptionist's desk, past Lorraine flipping through a magazine. He pushed through the glass door and strode into the corridor.

He'd forgotten his coat, but he'd be damned if he'd go back for it. The zipper was broken anyway.

He hit the button for the elevator, but it was taking too long. Instead he just took the stairs.

Outside, he lifted the door latch on the minivan. When it wouldn't open, he leaned against the hood. Hands jammed in the pockets of his jeans, he waited for Lorraine.

By the time she'd exited the medical building and approached the car, his teeth were chattering. She handed him his coat and pressed the unlock button on the key fob. As he slid into the seat and closed the door, he wondered what she and Doctor Mercer Big-Mouth had been talking about for so long, but she didn't say, and he didn't ask.

They rode in silence through town, beneath the garland and giant bells which had been strung across the streets. Tiny white lights twined their way up light poles and flickered in the branches of the giant Christmas tree which filled the bandstand in the town park. The quiet should have evoked a sense of peace, but as Lorraine drove past the elementary school and the shopping plaza filled with cars, the fingers of both her gloved hands seemed to wrap tighter around the steering wheel.

He was tempted to yell *boo.* Would she scream?

She cast him a few sidelong glances, as they drove by empty fields, past a couple of dairy farms, and followed the S-curve beneath the train tracks where Joey had tussled with Nate and Greg the day before.

A few minutes later she turned the car into the driveway and parked in the detached garage.

Allison and Benny looked up from their plates, as Joey followed Lorraine into the house.

"How did it go?" Frank asked from where he sat beside the highchair, helping Carrie scoop food into her mouth.

Shrugging out of his jacket, Joey glimpsed Lorraine as she pressed her lips together and shook her head.

Parka in hand, Joey turned toward the coat rack—and froze. There, draped over Benny's red snowsuit, hung Luke's denim jacket.

*****

CHAPTER 3

JOEY snatched the jacket from the coat rack and whirled to face Lorraine. "Where'd you get this?"

She hung her coat over the back of the nearest chair and stepped closer to Frank. "Why? What's the matter?"

Joey extended his arm, his fingers gripping the heavy denim so tight the curved edge of one of the copper buttons dug into his palm. "I gave this to Detective Marek yesterday."

"There's no great mystery," she said in deliberate calm lathered with condescension. She lowered herself into the chair beside her husband. "Will Marek's mother stopped by this morning." She turned to Frank. "What's her name?"

His brow furrowed for a moment. "Sandra."

Lorraine nodded and switched her attention back to Joey. "She was cleaning and found it. She thought Luke would want you to have it."

Blood rushed from Joey's face leaving him light-headed. "How did it get into my closet yesterday?"

Lorraine shrugged. "I found it behind the washer, so I hung it up. Luke must have left it in your room. You probably mixed it in with your laundry, and it accidently fell back there."

That made no sense. Joey did his own laundry on Saturdays. He would have seen it. He looked toward the washer and dryer in the far corner of the kitchen. A basket of clean clothes sat on the floor and more clothes had been heaped in a pile on top of the dryer. If the jacket had fallen, it would have landed behind the dryer, not on the top-loading washer.

He hung up his coat and then slipped his arms into the sleeves of Luke's jacket.

"You're not going to wear that again, are you?" Allison asked from the end of the table. "It's creepy."

He shot her a poisoned, mind-your-own-business glare.

She stuck out her tongue and resumed eating.

His stomach growled. He glanced at the plates. Hamburger, pasta, and sauce, again. He assumed if a person was going to make a career out of providing foster care, they'd at least take a few cooking lessons.

"Why don't you grab a plate and help yourself?" Lorraine suggested in that fake cheerful voice.

He pulled out a chair to sit and untie his boots. "I'm not hungry."

Frank turned. "You can't keep eating cereal in the middle of the night."

"I want cer-al," Benny said.

"Cereal is for breakfast, sweetie." Lorraine reached out a finger and nudged Benny's plate half an inch closer to the little boy.

"I want cer-el."

She sighed. "See the nice food Frank made just for you?"

"I want cer-el."

"No, Benny. You're not having cereal."

Benny leaned back in his chair, dropped his chin to his chest and started to cry.

A moment later, Carrie began wailing.

Allison shot Joey a smug smile. "Now see what you did."

Joey stood, leaving his boots untied, and grabbed his old blue coat from the rack.

"Where are you going?" Frank demanded, coming to his feet.

"Out." He grasped the denim sleeve ends between his fingers and palms to keep the material from bunching as he shrugged his own coat over Luke's jacket.

"Sit down! You can't run off every time things don't go your way."

The sharp words cut through the room, muting the noise with eerie silence. Benny and Allison swung their gazes toward Frank, their mouths agape. Even baby Carrie in her highchair turned her head and stared at him with wide eyes.

Frank locked his glare on Joey, as if daring him to disobey.

Without acknowledging any of them, Joey yanked open the door.

"I can't see how that doctor is helping," Frank said, as Joey slammed the back door.

His stomach rumbled, as he limped down the driveway.

What did they want from him? Did they think that after eleven sessions he would suddenly declare 'Dr. Mercer Asshole is fantastic'? *Thanks so much for forcing me to go to him. My life is going to be perfect from here on out.*

When he reached the road he turned east, away from the underpass.

Did they expect him to start crying 'my son-of-a-bitch father is dying'? *His last wish is that I forgive him. Please, can we go see him right now?*

Or did they keep their unspoken fears hidden in silence and exchanged glances, the fear that one night Joey would find a gun and use it.

He sucked in a deep breath of cold that hurt his lungs.

The road ahead was clear, washed in pewter moonlight. He ran. His untied boots clumped against the pavement, the noise emphasizing his gangly, uneven stride.

A car approached. He darted into the opening of Detective Marek's driveway, careful to stay outside the circle of light cast by the lamp atop a black pole at the end of the drive.

The car passed.

Instead of continuing up the road, he found himself walking up the length of driveway toward the house.

The house sat back away from the road. A row of cedars followed the boundary between Detective Marek's property and an empty pasture.

He didn't know why, but he trudged forward. The faint notes of a piano drifted through the evening air. Skirting the illumination of the porch and garage lights, he stepped onto the porch which spread across the front of the house.

Despite the cold, he stood in the deepest shadow and leaned against the wall. He closed his eyes and savored each note from the piano, visualizing Will Marek's fingers as they moved over the keys.

Joey had always been drawn to the baby grand in the corner of the living room. Luke warned him not to touch his dad's piano. When Luke's grandmother was there, she would let Joey play it. Luke had mentioned once or twice that back in college his father had been in a rock band.

Tonight was the first time Joey had heard Marek sing or play. His deep voice seeped through the walls with that rough, rocker edge that people paid money to hear. He sang the old Bob Seger song, *Turn the Page,* as if he performed it on stage for an audience.

Inside a dog woofed. A moment later the blurry head of Luke's golden retriever, Cody, appeared in the narrow length of window glass alongside the door.

Joey shrank farther into the shadows. The music stopped. The front door opened, and a wide beam of light rolled out like a carpet runner.

Will Marek's shadow spilled out with it.

Cody trotted across the porch, tail wagging. The retriever shoved his cold nose against Joey's hand. Reluctantly, he reached out to pet the dog's silky head and ears.

"I can see you shivering from here." Marek held open the door. "You might as well come inside."

Joey hung back, telling himself to leave before Luke's father regretted the invitation.

Instead, the man just stood there filling the doorway.

Joey's feet seemed to inch forward of their own volition. He moved out of the shadows and into the house.

Until Luke died, Joey hadn't realized how much time he'd spent at the Mareks' and how much he missed hanging out here.

Everything looked the same as it had the last time he'd visited. Framed photos hung on the wall above the couch. Luke's prom picture was the newest one. Luke hadn't wanted to wear the tux, but he looked handsome standing next to Jessica Bickman, who wore a long blue dress with her blonde hair all done up on top of her head.

There were other photos Joey had seen many times. Luke at various ages with his mother. Luke standing beside his father, his dad's hand on his shoulder. All three of them together fishing, at a ball game, at a family picnic.

There were trophies, too. Joey had always admired them. Three with batters on pedestals for Little League. One karate fighter atop a faux marble base for second place in a martial arts competition.

He glanced toward the staircase. He could almost see Luke bounding down the stairs, pulling on his denim jacket. *Joey, my man. What's up?* They'd fist bump, and Joey would follow Luke out the door into whatever escapade Luke had planned for the day. If the weather was bad, they'd hang out in the basement family room and play video games.

Without Luke, the house felt hollow and strange, like walking through a cemetery expecting to see a ghost. Joey turned. He shouldn't be here.

Luke's dad blocked the door, his arms crossed over a dark green Henley with the sleeves pushed up, a navy T-shirt visible at the base of his throat. A black holster on his right side held his gun.

In the past when Joey had seen him, he'd been going to or coming from work, his sports jacket concealing the ever-present sidearm.

Now standing here, casually dressed in jeans, the gun was in plain sight.

One time Joey asked Luke if his father had ever shot someone, but Luke had only shrugged and said 'when he was in the Marines'.

That Luke hadn't elaborated nauseated Joey more than the chilling revelation that Marek had pointed his weapon at a person and pulled the trigger.

"What are you doing here, Joe?"

The question wasn't harsh or demanding. Still, Joey had no idea how to answer. He shrugged and looked down, studying the darker tones and lines in the sand-colored floor tiles.

Staring at them without blinking caused a dull throb to pulsate at his temples. The lines in the tiles blurred and shifted, until he stared at what appeared to be a gun. The barrel pointed to the right, the thumb and fingertips of a left hand wrapped around the grip.

His heart raced, thudding wildly against his breastbone. The image looked almost real as if he could lean down and pick it up. A chill ripped through him, and he shuddered. He blinked and rubbed his arm across his eyes, trying to ease the ache behind them. When he peeked at the floor again, the tile appeared perfectly normal.

"Joe?"

The impatient edge of Marek's voice brought Joey's head up. Had the man been talking to him? Intense gray-blue eyes stared at him for several seconds, drilling him with unasked questions.

"I asked if Frank and Lorraine know you're here?"

Joey shrugged again. At least Luke's dad hadn't said *your parents.* But then he never had.

Joey wondered if he should leave, but he wasn't even sure he could get past the man to open the door and go.

Even if he could, he didn't want to return to Frank and Lorraine's. Walking in the dark and the cold wasn't high on his list of fun activities, so he stood there not saying a word.

Cody whined and shoved Joey's hand. Unable to resist the dog's request, Joey stroked Cody's shoulder and ruffled the scruffy fur around his neck.

"Leave your shoes by the door and hang up your coat." Luke's dad stepped around him and walked past the stairs toward the kitchen at the back of the house. "What's the number for your place?"

"It's 555-5621," Joey called, as he toed off his insulated boots and opened the closet. Once filled with coats, sweatshirts, and windbreakers, it was now empty except for white plastic hangers and a large cardboard box on the floor, the logo for a popular brand of paper towels across the front. He slipped off his blue jacket with the broken zipper, hung it up, and closed the door.

He trailed Cody to the kitchen where Luke's dad leaned against the peninsula, cell phone in his hand.

Joey almost expected to overhear the kind of conversation one had with a neighbor after their dog had gotten loose, knocked over the trash cans, and dug up the flower beds. Could they please come and get their messed up foster kid and make sure he didn't come over here again? Instead, he heard something else.

"Just wanted to let you know Joe is with me."

A long stretch of silence followed interspersed with a few uh-huhs.

Was he talking to Frank or Lorraine? Judging by Marek's lengthy pauses Joey assumed whoever he was talking to was listing every sin Joey had committed since the day he arrived in their care.

"Didn't want you to worry. The van's going where? Oh, a 4-H party. Yeah, I can bring him home."

Luke's dad pressed his finger to the screen. After setting his phone on the counter, turned toward Joey. His brow furrowed and the muscles at the back of his jaw bunched, as his narrowed gaze fixed on him.

Tiny hairs on the back of Joey's neck lifted. The same condemning scowl that had etched Detective Marek's expression yesterday, now stared fiercely at him from across the room.

Joey swallowed and then slid his foot backward.

Luke's father turned and strode to the table where file folders, papers, and photos lay in stacked neat piles beside a closed, silver laptop. He lifted his navy pea coat off one of the chairs and laid it over the back of a second. He studied the empty seat for a moment, and then leaned over and looked under the table.

Joey retreated another step, his elbows pressed tight to his side. He swallowed. Could he make it to the front door, grab his boots, and get outside?

Marek wouldn't shoot him, would he? No, he was a cop. Cops didn't just shoot people.

Sometimes they did.

Heart racing, Joey eased back a few more inches. He bumped against the wall.

This was Luke's dad. He wouldn't.

Then again, sometimes people said *I love you* and the next day pointed a gun at your back and pulled the trigger.

Detective Marek straightened. From the other side of the table, he locked an angry stare on Joey. "How the hell did you get that jacket?"

*****

CHAPTER 4

JOEY flinched, as though shocked by a jolt of electricity. His mind urged him to run, but his feet had frozen in place.

In two quick strides, Detective Marek moved around the table and stood looming over Joey.

Not that he was so much taller, but the anger and pain which radiated from him created an intimidating aura of power that caused Joey to cringe. He opened his mouth but couldn't make a sound.

Marek gestured toward the table without turning. "I left it on that chair. Except for yesterday, I haven't seen you in months and yet here you are, lurking on my porch, wearing my son's jacket. Again."

He swung away and paced to the end of the peninsula. Turning, he crossed his arms over his chest and came back. "Are you a thief? Is that why you hung around with Luke?"

"N-no, sir."

"Strange, don't you think, how many things in my house turned up missing after you started hanging around. Video games, cash, my gold watch, and my SIG P220. Can you explain that?"

"No."

"Can't or won't?" He swung away driving his hands through his short brown hair, clutching the back of his head for a moment. "Damn it, Joe." He exhaled, exhaustion lacing his words. He lowered his hands to his sides. "You shouldn't be here."

Joey turned and headed back toward the foyer.

"Leave the jacket."

He nodded. A few sizes too big, he easily shrugged it off. Opening the closet, he swapped it for his blue coat and stepped into his boots without tying them.

Reaching out he pushed down the front door lever, but it wouldn't move. He turned the locks and tried again. The door still wouldn't open.

His stomach twisted, as he made several more attempts, moving the locks this way and that, pressing and pulling on the door handle. Panic grew with each failed effort.

"Joe, wait." Marek's voice traveled down the hall.

Joey released the door lever and stepped back. He stared at the slightly curled length of gleaming gold. His aching head pounded.

"You eat yet?"

Joey shook his head. Whether in response to the question or in denial of what had just happened, he didn't know. Somehow standing next to Will Marek seemed like a good idea.

He hurried to the kitchen, scooted to the end of the peninsula, and wedged himself into the corner farthest from the door.

Luke's dad sent him an odd look. He pulled a red and white can from one of the cupboards, popped the top, and dumped a blob of red into a pot. "I haven't eaten either." After adding milk, he grabbed bread and cheese. "You can stay, Joe. It's okay to take off your coat."

Leary of the front hall, Joey hung his coat over the back of the nearest stool and toed off his insulated boots, while Luke's dad fried sandwiches on a griddle in the center of the stove.

The ache in his head eased as exhaustion weighed him down. He slid onto the stool, fighting the urge to lay his head on his arms and sleep.

A few minutes later, Marek poured soup into two mugs and set a couple of hot sandwiches on plates for each of them.

Marek said nothing, as he took a seat two bar stools away. He picked up his grilled cheese sandwich, tore it in half and dunked it in his soup.

Joey lowered his gaze to the food in front of him. Steam rose from the mug to tickle his nose. A growling sound rumbled from his stomach. "I didn't take Luke's jacket," he said softly, focused on the blackened edges of the bread.

"Eat."

"Lorraine said Luke's grandma brought it to the house. She said she wanted me to have it."

Marek grunted.

Did Detective Marek think he was lying?

"Eat. It's getting cold."

Joey's mom used to cut the grilled cheese diagonally into two triangular pieces, but Luke's dad had just fried them and slid them onto plates. Joey picked up his sandwich and bit off the corner.

Then with a quick glance at Luke's dad, he tore his sandwich in half and dipped it into the soup before taking another bite.

From the corner of his eye, he watched as Luke's dad removed his wallet from his jeans and pulled a small photo from one of the plastic picture sleeves. He set it on the countertop.

Using his pinky, he slid it toward Joey.

Instead of picking it up with his greasy fingers, Joey leaned close. He recognized Luke's blue eyes and dimpled chin, although in the picture he was just a little kid. He had on the jacket, his arms lost in denim sleeves that brushed the floor and a waist band that reached to his ankles above a pair of black and neon-green sneakers.

"He was four. His mother thought it was cute, him wearing my jacket, so she took the picture." He pulled it back and returned it to his wallet. "Once he started school, he pretty much wore it all the time. He'd almost grown into it."

Pushing to his feet, he carried his dishes to the sink. He nudged up the faucet lever and remained for several seconds, his hands braced on either side of the sink, his head hanging as water streamed from the tap.

Unsure what to do, Joey set his mug on the plate and wiped his hands down the thighs of his jeans. He rose and shoved his hands in his pockets. Cody rolled to his feet and trotted over. Joey gave the dog's ear a tug.

"Thanks for the sandwich." He glanced around, wondering if he should take his dishes to the sink, but hesitated to intrude. "I guess I'll be going now."

The water turned off. "No. I don't want you walking home in the dark. It's better than a half mile to your place. Give me a few minutes. Go downstairs. Watch some TV. Play a video game. You know where everything is."

"Okay." He headed toward the basement stairs. As he left the kitchen area, he glanced back to see Luke's dad still at the sink, staring at his reflection in the black glass of the window.

* * *

"Come on, Joe. Wake up." The raspy edged voice of Luke's dad carried down the stairs. "I've got to get to work."

Joey groaned and opened his eyes. Work? Was it morning? He pushed back the blanket and sat up. Blanket? Where had the blanket come from? When he stretched out on the couch last night, he'd only intended to close his eyes for a few minutes.

Now it was morning? He hadn't realized he'd been so tired. His headache had disappeared, too. He rose and stretched, happier than he'd felt in months. Cody jumped up from beside the couch and followed Joey into the bathroom. When he finished, he washed his hands and splashed water on his face. It seemed like years since he'd slept so sound.

He raced Cody up the stairs, the double-time cadence of their footsteps thumping against the treads. For a moment it was as if he and Luke were racing, when his grandma called them for lunch. He laughed as he burst into the kitchen behind Cody, last as usual, but he didn't care. He ruffled Cody's fur and looked up to find Luke's dad watching him.

The smile which tugged at the corners of Joey's mouth faded.

Marek leaned against the counter, a stainless-steel travel mug in his hand. "I don't have much in the house for breakfast anymore. Some bread if you want toast."

Joey shrugged. His light-hearted mood dimmed. "That's okay. Lorraine has cereal."

Marek nodded, gave the dog a pat, and stepped to the table where he scooped up his coat.

Joey's gaze skimmed across the pages of notes, pictures of the trestle bridge and the bank along the river. Though Trooper Kraus was officially investigating the case, it was no surprise to see Detective Marek looking into it on his own.

The picture that caught his attention was of a black handgun nestled in the gray foam of its case. He suspected it was like Marek's stolen gun, but wasn't positive. Luke had only shown the Sig to him once.

Two bow hunters had been deer hunting before Thanksgiving and found the murder weapon below the train trestle bridge near the river. Whether or not it was Marek's missing gun, the state police hadn't said.

But what caused Joey to squirm and the back of his neck to tickle, was that it looked exactly like the image he'd seen on the tile floor last night. The barrel of the gun was even pointed to the right. The only things the photograph lacked were the thumb and fingers of a left hand wrapped around the grip.

He jammed his hands into the front pockets of his jeans. He looked up and met the intense gray eyes of Detective Marek.

They stared at each other across the width of newspaper clippings and scattered photos. Why was Detective Marek watching him like a cat with a mouse? Did he believe the rumors? Was he now judging Joey's reaction to having seen the gun?

He needed to leave. He glanced around for his jacket and boots. Not seeing them he whirled and limped down the hall to the closet in the front foyer. He yanked open the door and grabbed his coat so hard the hanger flipped onto the floor. He jammed his feet into his boots.

With one arm in the coat he tried to open the front door. Nothing happened. Flicking the lock back and forth, he pressed down on the handle. Denial swelled inside his chest, hurting his heart as if someone were squeezing it inside a giant fist.

"It's locked."

Joey flinched, recoiling against the closet, but the door was open, and he fell backward tumbling into the large cardboard box.

"Relax, Joe." Marek extended his hand. One corner of his mouth quirked upward for just an instant. "I'm not going to hurt you."

Their gazes met.

The teasing light in Marek's eyes faded. "Ever."

Joey wanted to believe, needed to believe that there was someone in this world he could trust. But there was no point in wishing. The naive little boy who would have readily grabbed that extended hand had died six years ago.

Marek's hand dropped to his side, and he stepped back.

Joey braced his hands on the sides of the box and pushed, but one side of the box buckled, rolling him and the box to the side. Joey fell against the door jamb and grabbing the frame he scrambled to his feet.

His cheeks burned as he sidled away from the closet. Avoiding Marek's gaze, he focused on his jacket and slowly pulled the zipper up, hoping the two sides would stay together. But halfway up the teeth separated. He tried wiggling the tab back to the bottom, but it was stuck.

"Is that the only coat you own?"

Joey glanced up.

Frown lines stretched across Marek's forehead. Without waiting for an answer, he stepped to the closet and dug into the box. A moment later he pulled out a black jacket. A cool one like snowboarders wore, with zipper pockets and a neon green design that swirled through one shoulder.

"Here." He tossed the jacket to Joey. "A few people dropped off stuff for the department's toy and clothing drive, but I kept forgetting to bring this box to the station."

The logo of the high-end company on the upper left side was easy to recognize. Joey didn't have to look at the tags hanging from the sleeve to know the jacket was expensive. Not too many kids had coats this nice.

Marek gave a shrug. "We only collect new stuff. Take it, Joe. Merry Christmas."

Joey laid the jacket on the floral cushion of a nearby bench and yanked his old one over his head. Marek took it from him and hung it in the closet as Joey grabbed the new jacket and slipped his arms into the sleeves. He smoothed his hands down the front. Extending one arm out in front of him, he admired the sleeve. Like the denim jacket, this coat was a little big on him, but he didn't care. It was the nicest thing he had ever owned.

With his other hand he reached over and snapped off the dangling tags.

He shoved them into an inside pocket and lifted his gaze.

Marek gave him a curt nod.

For a half a second Joey imagined Marek's wide hand coming to rest on his shoulder with an affectionate squeeze, the same way he'd done with Luke so many times.

Instead, Marek bent and picked up the box. "You might as well take all this stuff. Keep what you want. Give the rest to the other kids."

Thrilled to own a jacket that didn't label him a loser, Joey didn't bother to see what else was in the box. He met Marek's gaze. "Thanks."

Marek nodded and started back toward the kitchen, pressing his key fob.

Joey followed him through the laundry room and into the garage. The SUV was already running, as Marek pushed the garage door opener and then locked the house.

Parked on the other side of the SUV was Luke's green, late model, half-ton pickup. Luke had explained once how he'd saved his wages from his job at the mini-mart for half the cost of the truck and his dad had matched the other half.

Was Luke's dad going to keep the truck or sell it?

Had he tried to sell it?

Joey's empty stomach knotted into an uncomfortable lump. The truck couldn't be sold without the title, which Joey had. He'd always intended to return it and the watch, but hadn't had the chance.

So much time had gone by. He had no idea how to fix things. Will Marek was a nice guy. Wasn't it better to have him think badly of Joey rather than taint the memory of his son?

Marek stowed the cardboard box in the back of the SUV and slammed the hatch.

Maybe Joey could think of another reason to come back here. He could get upstairs, put back the title and watch, and Luke's dad would never know the truth.

"You coming?" Marek opened the driver's side door and slid into the front seat.

Neither spoke as they backed out and headed down the road to Frank and Lorraine's house. Pink and gold highlighted the silhouette of the eastern hills and tree line.

The lack of breakfast gurgled in Joey's stomach.

He glanced over hoping Marek hadn't heard rumbling, but the man stared through the windshield, his mind seemingly elsewhere.

The blinker softly ticked as he slowed and turned the wheel, swinging the car into the driveway and pulling to a stop near colorful pools of nylon, the blow-up holiday polar bear and snow globe now deflated.

Joey reached for the door latch, reluctant to leave the warmth of the car.

"They can't force you to have any contact with him."

Joey's gaze snapped to Marek, who seemed focused on some distant point beyond the windshield.

He shouldn't be surprised either Frank or Lorraine had blabbed on the phone last night. They seemed determined that Joey should allow his father to contact him. Did they think that reading his father's letter would turn troubled teen, failing tenth grade Joey into some happy-go-lucky honor student?

What surprised him was having the support of Luke's dad.

He shot Joey a sidelong glance. "I don't think I'll ever forgive the bastard who killed my son." His voice caught on itself, and he cleared his throat. "If I ever get my hands on the guy who shot Luke and threw him off that bridge, I'll rip—"

His stormy-blue gaze searched Joey's face.

Joey knew Marek wanted to ask 'do you know something'.

Despite the warmth of his new winter coat, a shiver rippled down Joey's spine.

"Thanks," he mumbled and hopped out of the car.

He closed the door and limped up the path toward the side porch, but it wasn't until he went inside that he heard the SUV drive away.

*****

CHAPTER 5

JOEY sighed. Once again someone cut in front of him in the lunch line.

The period was nearly over and as usual he was the last one to get his food. If he could summon enough energy to be angry about it, to stick up for himself, maybe they wouldn't be so quick to take advantage of him.

Sliding his orange tray along the rails, the servers set out the food for him to take. A grayish hotdog cradled in a bleach white bun, a scoop of soggy broccoli, limp microwaved French fries, a plastic cup of applesauce, and a small carton of milk. A meal hardly worth fighting for. If he wasn't so hungry, he would have tossed it all in the garbage.

The tables were full of people he knew, but didn't know well. Cliques of friends laughed and talked. Most days he ate alone. Head down, he walked toward the only table not surrounded by kids.

Their silent disdain, their unspoken accusations followed him with their gazes as he moved toward the only empty spot, a table in the center of the cafeteria. He scanned the room again, hoping to find an empty space in the corner, but there remained only one place to go.

Jessica Bickman and four other pretty girls sat at the table right before it. At the end Greg Kelly and a group of his friends stood talking, blocking Joey's way, forcing him like a funnel toward the center table.

They stopped talking as he approached. Joey tried to sidle past them, but something caught his ankle and he tripped, falling forward as he and his tray of food crashed to the floor.

Laughter and applause erupted throughout the room. The sounds echoed off the painted concrete walls. His left wrist throbbed. His knees hurt. He pushed himself up to sit for a moment as cell phones came out, all aimed in his direction. Without a doubt, in moments a video of his humiliation would be shared and tweeted across every social media site on the internet. Good thing he'd sold his phone and his laptop. He'd never read their nasty comments.

He climbed to his feet and then limped over to pick up his scattered lunch.

"Killer," someone whispered.

"Here now!" a male voice rang out. "That's enough."

Joey glanced up. Mr. Dresdan strode toward him.

"Get to class. The bell's going to ring anyway."

The kids headed toward the door. Someone shoved against his shoulder, knocking him into a table.

The rest of the students walked by giving him a wide berth, flowing past him like water around a boulder in a stream, their cell phones capturing new pictures as they passed.

Mr. Dresdan set his tablet and water bottle on the nearest table and hunkered down to scoop up the scattered fries and broccoli.

"I've dealt with a few bullies myself over the years." He stood and set the tray on the table.

Joey nodded in thanks and rubbed his sore wrist.

"You and Luke were close, and the police have been talking to you. It makes things awkward. Most of these kids have been Luke's classmates since kindergarten. They don't know how to act around you, so they lash out. Things will get better once this guy is caught."

Mr. Dresdan meant well, but he didn't know that somehow the other kids had also found out about Joey's father. He'd been called Killer, Fish, and Gimp since he first started at this school, and those were the nicer names. At least when Luke was alive, he'd kept the taunting in check.

Joey carried his tray to the return area, and Mr. Dresdan moved his tablet and water bottle to the head table where the lunch lady had just wiped it down in preparation for the next period study hall.

"Joey."

He turned toward the English teacher who reached into the inside pocket of his corduroy jacket and pulled out a banana.

"You didn't get any lunch. Here." He extended his hand.

Joey shifted his gaze from the banana to Mr. Dresdan's face. The corners of the man's mouth weren't curled up in a smirk. His brows didn't arch in a condescending manner. The teacher seemed sincere.

Joey stepped forward and accepted the fruit with a nod.

"If you have any more trouble with bullying let me know."

The bell rang indicating the end of lunch. Didn't Mr. Dresdan know tattling would only make things worse? The knot in Joey's stomach twisted. He turned away and pushed through the cafeteria door.

Algebra was next, and he needed his book from his locker. Chomping off a large bite of banana he hugged the wall as he made way through the congestion of students toward the nearest staircase. His knees and thigh hurt, as he grabbed the handrail and pulled himself up, one stair at a time. The other kids bumped into him, shoved him against the rail and muttered curse words. He could have taken the elevator, but he didn't want to give them satisfaction.

He grabbed his algebra book and a notebook from his locker, and then turned the corner to head down the hall to Mrs. Brolin's room. Ahead, Greg Kelly stood beside his open locker, holding court with a group of kids, his arm draped over Jessica Bickman's shoulder.

Roger Wade, a senior Joey had seen in halls a lot last year with Luke, separated himself from the others and moved closer to Greg. The two whispered for a moment. They bumped fists and slid their palms together in a handshake that obviously transferred something from Roger's hand to Greg's.

Greg slipped his hand into his pocket, and Roger continued on his way. Joey hadn't heard that Greg sold drugs, so it was probably the gambling money Greg promised Nate he would get by Friday.

Greg was an arrogant bully and Joey's worst enemy.

This morning he and his brother had driven past Frank and Lorraine's driveway while Joey was waiting for the bus. Their car had stopped and backed up.

"Hey, Gimp. Where'd you get the new coat?" Greg called through the open window.

"That coat's too good for you," Nate said as he and Greg climbed out of the car. "My brother could use a new one. Give it to him."

Joey tried to stop them, but Nate was strong and had held Joey's arms while Greg pulled it off.

"Lukey-boy owed me money." Nate gave Joey a shove that landed him in the snowbank next to the mailbox. "This jacket should cover most of it. And remember, you tell anyone about yesterday and I'll kick your ass so hard, you'll think your dear ol' daddy was back to make your life hell."

"Hey, Gimp, how was your lunch?" Greg called. Laughter filtered down the hall with the chuckles of the students who walked past.

Joey started past the group, trying to ignore them. He glanced into the open locker and saw his new jacket hanging there. He stopped.

Damn it, that was his jacket. Marek had given it to him. And Joey wanted it back.

Heat washed through his body. He dropped his books and charged. Muscles quivering, he planted both hands on Greg's chest and shoved.

Wide-eyed Greg stumbled backward.

Joey reached into the locker and grabbed his jacket. Heart pounding, he ran back the way he'd come.

"Get back here, you little shit!" Greg's voice rose above the cheering of his friends.

Rather than head down the stairs, Joey turned the corner and ran, as fast as his awkward gait allowed, away from the mob pounding down the hall behind him.

Why he thought he had a chance to outrun Greg, Joey had no idea, but suddenly beefy fingers grabbed him by his collar jerking him back as Greg's fingernails raked down the skin of Joey's neck.

Greg whirled Joey around and slammed him up against the wall of lockers. His shoulder and the side of his face absorbed the impact.

"Son-of-a-bitch, give me my jacket." Greg tried to wrest it from Joey's grip, but he dug in his fingers and clenched the nylon tighter. Why did Greg want it anyway? The jacket was at least a size too small.

The tug-of-war pulled Joey around and Greg drove his fist into Joey's stomach. He folded in half, the jacket pressed against his abdomen.

Around them students cheered.

Greg pulled back his foot and swept Joey's legs out from under him.

Joey fell onto his side, forced to use the hand that held the jacket, the hand he'd already hurt, to brace himself. He expected Greg to grab the jacket at that moment. Instead, Greg drew back his foot to deliver a kick.

As the toe of the insulated boot came toward Joey, he threw his free hand up and shoved away the foot.

Off balance, Greg fell. The back of his head cracked against the tile floor. Eyes closed, he lay still.

The crowd went silent.

"What's going on here? Break it up."

Mr. Carlson pressed through the crowd.

Joey pushed himself upright to lean against the lockers, cradling his wrist, pressing his arm against his sore stomach.

In the center of the hallway, Mr. Carlson knelt beside Greg who uttered soft moans.

"Stay still, son. You might have a concussion." He looked up, meeting the gaze of Ms. Reed. "Call 911."

She nodded and pushed back through the crush of students, as Mr. Breen wove his way into the center of the ring.

"Is he alright?"

"Not sure," Mr. Carlson replied. "He was out when I got here."

"What the hell happened?" Breen turned and his gaze fell on Joey.

Jessica stepped forward and pointed. "He started it. He stole Greg's new jacket right out of his locker."

Several students supported her statement.

"Kowalski just shoved him and took it."

"I saw Greg wearing that jacket when he got to school."

"Yeah, he came at him right out of the blue."

Slowly Joey pushed to his feet, keeping his arm pressed to his stomach. Stupid, stupid, stupid. Why had he ever believed he'd be able to get his coat back? He'd just wanted it so bad, and he was so Goddamn sick of being picked on and teased. He just wanted it all to end. His life wasn't getting better, it was getting worse. Tears burned his eyes as Mr. Breen grabbed him by the arm and yanked him away from the lockers.

"Let's go. Down to the office."

Joey stumbled forward. With a quick glance over his shoulder, he took one last look at his brand-new jacket laying on the floor.

* * *

Lorraine and Frank were probably on their cell phones, which was why they hadn't come to get him. Joey slouched in the chrome and gray padded chair of the vice-principal's office. Extending his bad leg, keeping his arms crossed, he stared at the pattern in the dark brown carpet. The light-colored shapes looked like a flock of seagulls taking flight.

Creating images in the carpet kept him from having to look at Officer Gonzalez who guarded the door. It was easier than allowing his gaze to roam over Vice-principal Wheaton's desk, which was covered with framed photos of his stupid smiling family and his goofy-looking girls, whose crappy artwork hung in frames on the walls. Joey clenched his hands into fists to keep from throwing it all on the floor.

His cheek bone and eye hurt. The back of his neck stung, and his stomach ached. He gnawed his lower lip as the sore knee of his good leg bounced up and down.

Frank was likely telling Mary Custer that she needed to find Joey a different placement. They couldn't handle him anymore. Not only was he rude and belligerent, now he was fighting and stealing. And Lorraine was probably on her cell phone looking for advice from Dr. Mercer Friggin' Tree Hugger Why Can't We All Get Along.

There was a quick double-beat knock on the door.

The school-assigned police officer stepped aside, allowing principal Allen into the room along with Mr. Wheaton and the school therapist, Mr. Dunham.

"I spoke with your foster parents," Ms. Allen began as she crossed the small room and stood in front of the desk, her hands clasped at her waist. "They tell me your winter coat is blue, not black and green, and certainly not one so expensive."

Hadn't Frank or Lorraine even noticed what he'd been wearing when he got back this morning? He'd sat right at the table, with his new coat on, eating cereal. But conversation that morning had revolved around Allison, her nine o'clock dentist appointment and her middle school Christmas concert tonight. Guess they hadn't even noticed him.

"Can you explain why you suddenly felt you had the right to steal Greg Kelly's new coat from his locker? While he stood right there? It's no wonder he chased you down the hall and grabbed you."

If only Joey had been able to run faster, he might have gotten away.

Should he even bother to explain the jacket was too small for Greg? Had no one seen the Kelly brothers drive up, while Joey waited for the bus?

"Where'd you get the new coat, Gimp?"

Had no one noticed that it was twenty degrees, and Joey had gotten on the bus in his shirtsleeves?

The only time anyone in this town thought about him was when new rumors about Luke's murder case circulated. Last month when Detective Marek's stolen gun was found, everyone seemed to notice Joey. No one ever said anything to his face, but he heard the whispers behind his back. They all thought he did it, thought he was crazy.

"Detective Marek gave it to me." He wasn't sure if the surprised looks were because he'd actually spoken or because of what he'd said.

Ms. Allen frowned. Mr. Wheaton and Mr. Dunbar exchanged glances with slight shakes of their heads. Officer Gonzalez even snorted in disbelief.

Joey sighed and switched his gaze to the wings on the carpet. Why even try? They didn't believe him. No one ever did. They weren't going to call Luke's dad. After all, why would Will Marek give a brand-new snowboard jacket to the prime suspect in the murder of his son?

Ms. Allen frowned. "You are very lucky Greg's brother decided not to press charges. By all rights you should be sitting in a jail cell tonight, but Nathan reminded us that Greg should have told a teacher instead of chasing you down and continuing the fight.

"However, beginning the day after Christmas vacation, you will report here to Vice-Principal Wheaton's office immediately after school, where you will sit and do your homework until five o' clock. You will do this every day until your grades have reached a C average. There will be no more stealing and no more fighting. If it happens again, you will be expelled. Are we clear?"

Was Greg Kelly getting detention? Did Greg Kelly have to do his homework in the principal's office? No. Greg Kelly got a new coat.

"Are we clear?"

"Whatever."

"Since it is already so late, and your parents—"

They are not my parents!

"—Are unable to pick you up, Officer Gonzalez will take you home."

Joey forced his aching body from the chair and limped to the door. His leg had stiffened from sitting for so long, but he'd be damned if he'd rub it in front of them.

Officer Gonzalez pulled on his short, dark blue jacket and gestured for Joey to move into the hallway ahead of him.

If anyone in town had been asked, they probably would have said Joey had ridden in the back of many police cars. In fact, this was his first time. He slid into the seat and waited with his arms crossed for the officer to buckle the seatbelt, close the door, and slide in behind the steering wheel.

He looked up to meet the officer's steady gaze in the mirror. The thick divider which separated him from Gonzalez wavered in front of him. Joey blinked against the burning in his eyes afraid that maybe, like father like son, this was his future.

The officer pulled his car out of the parking lot and headed down the street. Gonzalez didn't ask which way to go, and Joey didn't tell him.

He shoved his hands in his pockets and wondered how long it took for the heat to reach the back.

* * * * *

CHAPTER 6

"I suppose you should put some ice on that." Lorraine's disapproval was evident, but what could he do, tell her he was only trying to keep the new jacket she didn't know he had?

She sat on the corner of the couch, trying to thread white tights over Carrie's kicking legs. The toddler squirmed, arching her back, as Lorraine finished with one leg and started pulling the tights up the second leg.

His foster mother heaved a sigh that sounded like one of Cody's soft growls. She glanced up, meeting Joey's gaze and frowned.

"There's a bag of peas in the freezer. Just wrap them in a dish towel."

He shivered at the thought of putting something cold on his face.

"Mary Custer called for you again. Why don't you call her back?"

Sure, like that was going to happen. He didn't even want to remember he had an old man, let alone exchange cards and letters like they were family. He smoothed his palms down the front of his thighs several times. Had Frank turned down the heat again? Shoving his hands in the front pockets of his jeans, he returned to the kitchen.

Benny stood at the island, his blond head not even reaching the lip of the countertop.

"Your supper is in the microwave," Lorraine called.

Joey walked over and popped open the door. A plate of fish sticks, French fries, and green beans sat in the center of the glass turntable. With a sigh, he pressed the button to reheat his meal.

"See." Benny held up a blue-masked, turtle action figure.

Joey reached out and accepted it. He'd never seen that toy and wondered where the little guy had gotten it. A long time ago, Joey and his brother Kyle used to lay on their bedroom floor and play with turtles just like this. Kyle even had a storage case for his turtles with a compartment to store extra weapons.

Joey glanced around the floor and table, wondering if this turtle had come with any accessories the little guy might swallow. He didn't see anything.

The microwave beeped.

"Cool." He passed the turtle back to Benny. "Where'd you get it?"

He pulled his plate from the microwave, set it on the counter, and then grabbed a bottle of ketchup from the fridge.

Benny pointed toward the washing machine.

Joey grabbed three soggy fries off the plate and glanced across the room. The fries froze halfway to his mouth.

Detective Marek's box sat on the floor in front of the washer. Joey didn't know why he should be so surprised. Marek had probably dropped it off after his shift.

Unconcerned, Benny ran over and peered inside as though double checking the contents before reporting. "Toys," he said.

Joey stepped close and braved a look. He wasn't sure what he expected to find, but all he saw were gloves, hats, fashion dolls in pink boxes, cars, puzzles, and board games. He breathed a relieved sigh. "Nice." He held out his fist and Benny bumped his own small knuckles against Joey's.

Benny grinned and followed Joey back to the island. Joey handed him a couple of droopy fries before he snagged a few more for himself to eat on his way to the living room.

"When was Detective Marek here?"

Lorraine stood and set Carrie in the playpen. "He came by about a half-hour ago. Said he forgot to drop off the box this morning."

Had Frank and Lorraine told him about the fight?

"There's not much in it for you, maybe some gloves. There were some video games, but Frank took them out." She picked up the overalls Carrie had been wearing and approached Joey at the archway to the kitchen.

He stepped back as she passed.

"You know how we feel about violent fighting games." She sent him a pointed look and continued toward the washer, where she tossed the dirty clothes into an empty, white plastic basket. "Allison had to be at the school an hour early, so Frank took the games. On his way home he's going to drop them off for those nice boys who live up the road."

Sure, why not?

He carried his plate to the table and picked up a fish stick.

"Frank and I discussed what happened today. You're grounded for a week." Lorraine watched him from the other side of the counter, her arms crossed. "You will stay home tonight and do your homework. No TV. No video games. No going out with your friends."

Did she forget who she was talking to? This was Joey, not Allison. His best friend was dead. There was no one else.

He'd sold his video games and system, along with his phone, laptop, skateboarding sneakers, and boards.

"You must have forgotten your denim jacket when you were at the Marek's last night."

"What?" A wave of nausea rolled through his stomach, sending the burn of acid and fish up the back of his throat.

"It was in that box. Detective Marek must have found your jacket and put it inside."

Joey shook his head. No way. Detective Marek couldn't have, wouldn't have. No. That wasn't possible.

"I put it on your bed."

Joey shoved away from the table and dashed up the stairs, taking them as fast as his bad leg would allow. The jacket must have fallen off the hanger and into the box. Luke's dad just hadn't noticed.

He hesitated in the doorway to his room, almost afraid to actually step inside and see the thing. Drawing a breath, he entered.

The jacket lay on its side in the center of his bed, as if Luke had carelessly tossed it there, the logo patch for KORN visible on the upper sleeve. Joey shivered. If he turned, would he would see Luke sitting at the desk, chair tipped back with his feet on top crossed at the ankles?

He avoided the desk and stepped forward. He picked up the jacket. Holding it in front of him, he checked it over, front and back. He lifted each sleeve and looked inside. Every patch, every stain, each frayed thread was exactly as he remembered.

He slid one arm into the sleeve and flipped it around his shoulder to push his other arm into the second sleeve.

Warmth enveloped him. Luke's presence was so strong Joey swore he heard him laughing.

Joey swung around, but no one lounged at the desk. A twinge of pain pricked his temple. He rubbed at it with his fingers.

Grasping the hem of the jacket, he held it out from his waist and studied it. The denim had faded over the years to light blue with a deeper blue etching the corners and crevices along the seams. Nothing remotely spooky.

He flopped backward onto his bed. The tension of the day escaped his body on the breath of a shuddering sigh. Stacking his hands behind his head he closed his eyes.

Detective Marek would want it back.

* * *

"Does Benny have any mittens?" Frank's voice floated up the stairway, mixing with Lorraine's as they talked and hurried around the house.

"They should be hanging from his coat sleeves."

"Where?"

"Inside the sleeves. They're connected through the coat from one side to the other. If he pulls them off, he can't lose them."

"Oh. Got 'em. Did you turn off the tree?"

"It's artificial."

"I know, but I don't like to leave it on when no one is home."

"Joey's in his room."

"Oh, right. Well, turn it off just in case."

"Joey, we're leaving," Lorraine called up the stairs.

"And remember," Frank added, "get that homework done."

"Yup," Joey yelled back. He hadn't had any books with him when he'd gotten hauled into the office. Nor had he arrived home with any books or a coat when Officer Gonzalez dropped him off. Aside from English, math was the only subject he had homework in, and it was way harder than it had been last year. He was never going to catch on and it just made the rest of his classes seem pointless.

When Joey came to live with Frank and Lorraine back in January, he'd quickly fallen behind in all his subjects, especially geometry. He'd only had basic geometry at his old school. If it hadn't been for Luke's help, he never would have passed with a B. This year he had algebra. He could barely divide and multiply numbers, let alone letters with tiny numbers attached to them. With Luke's help Joey had done okay. Now it was hopeless.

The back door banged closed, and the house went still. Joey rolled off the bed and headed downstairs. His supper was still on the island. He frowned at the golden-brown lumps and tossed it all in the garbage before sticking the plate in the dishwasher.

He filled a bowl with cereal, poured in some milk, grabbed a spoon and carried it into the living room. He dropped on the couch across from the Christmas tree. Lorraine had turned off the lights, but Joey had no desire to turn them back on.

Picking up the remote, he flipped through the channels while he ate. Soon he watched Chevy Chase try to make the lights work on the front of his house.

Bored, he put the channel back to the last station viewed and turned off the TV. Adding his bowl to the dishwasher he stared out the kitchen window, fighting the urge to go outside. Colored lights strung along the eaves highlighted the snow in soft glows of green, blue, and red.

Restless, he headed for the coat rack. He guessed he had a couple of hours before anyone would be home. He didn't feel like going back upstairs for his sweatshirt, so he grabbed an old gray hoodie of Frank's and pulled it on over Luke's denim jacket.

A tangy whiff of Frank's cheap aftershave tickled the inside of Joey's nose. With a sneeze, he sat down to tie his boots. He grabbed Lorraine's keys with the dangling pink bear from the bowl on the table beside the back door and headed outside.

He locked the door and shoved the bulky keys into the front pocket of Frank's sweatshirt. He considered walking the tracks. The aloneness of empty miles suited his mood, but without a flashlight it was too dark. And he needed to be back before anyone noticed him gone. Without a phone, he'd have no idea of the time.

At the end of the driveway his feet once more developed a will of their own. He turned right when he reached the mailbox. It was a bad idea. Like so many things in his life lately, he did it anyway.

He only planned to walk past Detective Marek's house and turn around before he reached the single-wide mobile home where Greg Kelly and his brother Nate lived.

He didn't understand this sudden compulsion to walk toward the Marek house. Three months had passed since Luke went missing, two and a half since his body had been found. Over the past two days Joey could think of nothing but the murder and of Luke's father.

When Luke was alive Joey hadn't seen much of Detective Marek. He worked a lot. When he was home, Joey had found the man's penetrating blue-gray eyes unnerving. He never knew what the man thought, and the fact that he carried a loaded gun had Joey so nervous he constantly bumped into walls and furniture whenever Luke's dad was in the room.

Luke had said his dad liked him just fine. He was just a lot quieter, since Luke's mom had died. But Joey wasn't so sure. Luke's dad was probably like every other adult over the years who assumed Joey to be a bad influence on their kids.

Light shone from the living room and front porch. Their warm yellow glow invited him closer. Despite telling himself to continue along the road, his feet once again took him up the driveway.

Turn around, he told himself. *You have no business being here.*

A shadow moved near the bush at the corner of the garage.

He stopped. Every muscle tightened.

The blur of dark moved into the circle of light. Cody.

Joey's rigid spine sagged, as he released a long breath. The dog charged down the slope and slammed into him, forcing him to take a step back to keep from falling.

Cody's long golden tail wagged back and forth as he whined and wove around Joey's legs.

He bent forward and ran his gloved hands over the dog's shoulders and ribs. "How'd you get out of the yard?"

Suddenly, Cody took off toward the row of cedars along the property line, whirled around and charged straight toward Joey. At the last second the dog swerved, barely missing him, raced across the front yard, made two large circles, and ran back to Joey.

Bending down, Joey scooped up a handful of snow, packed it into a ball and hurled it toward the tree line. Cody raced after it and shoved his face into the hole where the snowball landed. A moment later, he lifted his snowy head, looking expectantly toward Joey who packed another and threw it in the opposite direction.

They played the game, until Cody quit chasing the elusive snowballs.

"Come on," Joey called and started around the side of the garage to the back gate.

Odd, he thought as he lifted the latch. Cody couldn't have gotten out this way. Locking the gate, he followed the snowy path to the back door of the garage and stopped.

The door was closed. How had Cody gotten loose? Reaching out, the knob turned easily in his hand. The hair on the back of his neck tickled. He expected the door to be locked. Cody pushed past him into the cave-like interior. Faint light spilled across the concrete floor from the light bulb above the landing at the door into the laundry room.

Detective Marek's vehicle was gone. Cody must have slipped into the garage and snuck outside while the automatic door was still open.

Luke used to keep an extra house and truck key in a magnetic box behind the seat of his pickup. Joey would just put Cody back in the house and be on his way before Detective Marek came home.

He stepped close to the truck and trailed his fingers along the width of the hood.

In his mind he heard Luke's carefree voice as clearly as if Luke were sitting behind the wheel. *Come on, Joey. Hop in.*

Moving to the driver's side, he lifted the handle and opened the door.

Cody leaped inside and hopped over the console, stealing Joey's usual shotgun seat.

Chuckling, Joey brushed the snow onto the floor and slid in behind the wheel. He wrapped his fingers around the steering wheel, pretending for a moment that he had his license.

In front of him, the darkness faded into a sunny day, an open road stretched before him. As if he were driving, he passed green trees and pastures dotted with cows. Fresh spring air blew through the open windows and filled the cab. Happiness swelled inside him, and he heard Luke laughing.

Let's go buy some new games.

When Luke had money, after his fighter in the most recent MMA fight won his match, he would buy a new video game or two for himself and one for Joey.

Don't sweat it, man. I got it covered.

If Luke's fighter lost, well, video games had a lot less value when you tried to resell them.

Joey shuddered with a sudden chill. He rubbed his hand across his forehead to ease the ache.

Cody whined.

Opening the door, Joey slipped out. After the dog jumped down, Joey reached behind the seat and groped through a coil of jumper cables. His fingers brushed the small magnetic box, and he pried it off the floor. The top slid to the right. Leaving the extra ignition key, he grabbed the one for the house, tossed the box on the seat, and closed the door.

Cody's nails ticked against the cement, as he followed Joey across the floor and up the wooden steps of the landing.

He slid the key in the lock and turned the knob. He pushed open the door and Cody scooted inside. The scent of fabric softener drifted through the area and clothes tumbled around in the dryer. He stepped inside for a better look at the timer. Forty minutes left. Detective Marek hadn't been gone long.

He shoved the key in his pocket. Maybe he should leave a note explaining how Cody got inside the house, but if Marek had known the dog was running loose he wouldn't have driven off.

Okay, he wouldn't leave a note. Maybe while he was here, he could return the denim jacket to the hall closet and reclaim his old winter coat. The switch would only take a minute.

Cody at his side, he moved through the kitchen, past the counter where he'd eaten soup and sandwiches just last night. At the table, where folders were stacked beside a closed laptop, he turned toward the foyer at the front of the house and the closet near the front door.

Joey rubbed at the ache in his head as he studied the floor, half expecting to see the image of a gun within the striations of the tile. Last night had just been a trick of the light. He wasn't crazy.

Shrugging off the uneasiness that tickled the back of his neck, he cautiously eased open the closet door. He wasn't sure what he imagined would happen, but his old coat was the only item inside the space. A sigh of relief eased the tension in his shoulders.

He yanked the coat off the hanger and tossed Lorraine's keys toward the padded bench. The keys hit the tile floor with a soft *chink*. As he slipped his arms into the sleeves of his old coat, the scent of Frank's aftershave wafted from the sweatshirt and he sneezed.

Before he could try pulling up the broken zipper, Cody grabbed the pink bear in his mouth, ran into the living room, and flopped down under the piano.

"Cody, come." Joey dashed after him.

He patted the side of his leg. "Bring it here, boy. Come on, bring me the toy."

Cody lay watching as Joey eased himself onto his hands and knees and crawled slowly forward. He reached out, his fingers a breath away from the dangling keys, when Cody jumped up, the pink bear still in his mouth. The dog brushed past him and thudded up the stairs.

Joey reared back and slammed the back of his head against the underside of the piano with a *thunk* and a discordant *twang*.

The pain in his temples now radiated to the back of his head. Rubbing the injury, he rolled to his feet. "Cody, come!"

Rounding the corner, he caught the glimpse of feathery tail at the top of the staircase. He moved quickly up each tread. His head pounded in time with each uneven footfall as his thigh protested the rush.

When he reached the second floor, he stopped. The dog was nowhere in sight. A wave of uneasiness washed over him. He shouldn't be up here.

"Cody," he whispered, searching for the dog. "Come here. Come on, boy."

All of the bedroom doors were closed, except for one. With each step he took, his breaths came faster. His chest tightened, as he inched closer to Luke's room.

* * * * *

CHAPTER 7

AT the threshold he stopped.

Night shadows shrouded the interior. All he could make out were the larger shapes of the bed, desk, and dresser.

He hated to turn on the light, but needed those keys. Without even a phone to act as a flashlight he had no choice but to flip up the light switch located just inside the door jamb.

He blinked against the sudden glare, though it was only the glow of a desk lamp. Everything looked the same as it had on that warm September day, right before they'd left to go walk the tracks. Even Cody had plopped himself in his usual place on the oval rug beside Luke's bed.

No keys in sight.

Crap.

"Cody, come mere." Joey patted his thigh and coaxed the dog to his feet. No keys.

Reluctantly, he lowered himself to his knees and lifted the bed skirt. Luke, much like his father, was an organized neat freak. There were only some books and a box labeled *Old PS Games.*

Joey crawled forward to look beneath the nightstand, though how the keys could have gotten there he had no idea.

A cold, wet nose shoved against his ear.

He pushed himself up, sat back on his heels, and looked Cody in the eyes. "Where'd you put the keys?"

As though the dog understood the question, he turned and trotted to the dresser that stood against the opposite wall. Dropping to his belly, Cody shoved his nose under the dresser.

Curious, Joey crawled up beside Cody and peered beneath. Way at the back against the wall was the pink bear. Ice water flooded his veins. He reared back.

What the hell?

He glanced over his shoulder expecting to see the ghostly image of Luke.

Nothing.

He shivered.

Get the keys and get out of here.

Dropping flat, he worked his arm under the low, wide space, but his upper arm was too thick and he couldn't quite reach the keys. He rolled to his knees, grabbed the back corner, and pulled the bulky piece of furniture forward.

As he did, the dresser tipped just enough to pitch a framed picture onto the floor. He picked it up.

Luke stood beside his dad outside PNC park. They both wore Pirates jerseys. Will Marek had his hand on Luke's shoulder.

Joey had seen the photo many times. As much as he liked it, he also hated it. Hated that Luke had a dad who would give him affectionate squeezes on his shoulder.

Now a crack split the glass between father and son.

Luke had never wanted his dad to find out what he was doing, never wanted to disappoint him.

"Come on, please? All you gotta do is tell my dad I'm with you if he calls."

"Where are you going, really?"

"You gotta swear you won't tell."

"I swear to God, Luke, I'll never throw you under the bus."

Betrayal. That's what it would be if he told Marek the truth. He was in Luke's room and wearing Luke's jacket. If lying was all Joey could give his best friend, then he would keep his word.

He'd find a way to protect him, just as he had on that day when Luke had shown him the gold watch he'd taken from his father's room.

"Luke, you can't pawn this. It's engraved from your mom to your dad."

"He doesn't care about her. If he cared, he'd wear it. Besides, I'm not selling it. I'm just going to pawn it. I'll buy it back as soon as my guy wins his next fight."

Moving the dresser those extra inches gave Joey enough room to reach the keys. He wedged his shoulder between the furniture and the wall. As he stretched for the keys, he spotted a blue thumb drive inside a plastic sandwich bag that was duct taped to the back of the dresser.

Curious, he peeled it free, pulling both the bag and the keys into the light. Joey's stomach tightened, as he parted the zipper seal. He had an idea what Luke had kept on the drive, but wanted to be sure. If it was nothing, he'd put it back for Marek to find. If it was something, well, he hoped it was nothing too bad.

The simplest thing would be to take the thumb drive back to Frank and Lorraine's. But Joey had sold his laptop along with his phone in order to get the watch back before Marek realized it was gone. His foster parents had their computer password protected, so he couldn't log on in the middle of the night to, as Lorraine had explained when he first moved in, *search for pornography.*

Luke's computer wasn't on top of his desk where he usually left it. Had Marek put it away somewhere? There were lots of photos and music, personal things Marek maybe hadn't gone through yet. Hopefully, he hadn't taken it to his room.

Joey pulled open the top drawer. Nothing but pens, pencils, and index cards. The extra flash drives Luke used to keep in this drawer were gone, as well.

He checked the next drawer. Nothing but magazines on mixed martial arts. In the bottom drawer he found Luke's power cord shoved down the side. Where was the laptop?

When was Marek coming back? Maybe Joey should just assume the flash drive he found was incriminating, take it home and throw it away. But what if there was some clue that could lead to Luke's killer?

He should take it and give it to Investigator Kraus. Detective Marek would never know. Joey pushed in the desk drawer, shoved the thumb drive in the side pocket of the denim jacket.

He pushed the dresser back against the wall, returned the picture to its place, and grabbing the keys, shoved them into the front pocket of Frank's sweatshirt.

A soft bang drifted up from downstairs. Cody's ears perked. His tail wagged, and he trotted from the room.

Shit. Marek was back.

How could he explain what he was doing here? He strained his ears, but heard nothing.

Then came the slow, measured steps of someone easing their way up the stairs. Not the way a man came up to change his clothes or grab something from his room. Would Marek come in here?

The back door into the garage was open, and the door from the garage into the laundry room was unlocked. Oh God, Marek probably thought there was an intruder. He probably had his gun out, ready to shoot.

Hide.

He glanced around. Under Luke's bed? No. Beds weren't safe. He made for the security of the closet.

The light. Had Marek noticed? Joey slapped his palm against the wall switch and slid open the bi-folding door. Luke's clothes were gone. With nothing to hide behind, he stepped inside and pulled the door shut.

His heart raced and each breath escaped in short gasps. Detective Marek was a better shot than Joey's dad. He wouldn't miss.

Joey's teeth chattered. His stomach trembled as though he stood in the snow wearing only a T-shirt. He drew his lower lip between his teeth to stop the noise, but the shaky breaths he blew in and out through his nose would surely be heard down the hall. He buried his face in the elbow of the blue coat.

He heard the slight squeak of a hinge. Was Detective Marek nudging the bedroom door wider?

Oh, God, this time I am gonna die.

His nose tickled. He grabbed the front of the sweatshirt and pulled it up over his nose, but the fabric smelled of Frank's aftershave.

Joey's nostrils flared, as he automatically drew in air. He reached up to pinch his nostrils tight before—*Ah-choo*!

The bi-folding door parted. Bright light replaced the dark.

He blinked against the painful glare. Unable to see, he raised his forearm against the light and found the barrel of a gun pointed straight at him.

Luke's voice screamed inside his head. *Run!*

Joey charged forward, lowering his head like a football player and ducking under Detective Marek's raised arms.

Spots danced before his eyes. He stumbled into the end of Luke's bed, slamming his shin on the bed frame.

His pulse thudded against his ear drums in counterpoint to the pounding of Luke's rapid heartbeat echoing in his head.

Run! Luke cried.

Joey reared back away from the bed. His arms windmilled, as he tried to regain his balance and locate the door.

"Joe! What the hell?"

Disoriented and still unable to see clearly, he ran into the hall and slid into the wooden rail which surrounded the stairwell, nearly pitching himself to the tile on the bottom floor of the house.

"Joe, stop!"

Run! Luke screamed. *He's going to kill me!*

Hand over hand, Joey fumbled along the length of the railing to the top of the stairs. Halfway down his foot slid out from under him, and he tumbled the rest of the way to the bottom.

"Damn it, Joe, will you stop?"

Run!

No longer sure if his own fear drove him forward or if it was Luke's, he scrambled to his feet and dove for the front door.

Please, don't be locked.

Pressing down, the handle offered no resistance. Joey pulled and the door swung inward.

He dashed outside and jumped off the porch.

"Joe!"

He's coming, Luke shrieked. *Faster!*

Joey raced down the driveway into the road.

Faster! God, he's really going to kill me! Don't look back! Run!

Despite Luke's warning, Joey glanced over his shoulder. In the shadows of the barren trees one shadow shifted. Like the striations in the floor tile, it altered its form into the silhouette of a male figure wearing a ball cap. At the center of the shadow, a left arm raised, a gun aimed in his direction.

There were no streetlights, no moon. Was this real or was he just going crazy?

Don't look. Don't look. Run, run!

Joey's feet skidded a few times, but he didn't fall. His thigh ached, and his heart and lungs felt as if they were about to explode. Sweat trailed down both sides of his face. His shin throbbed.

A car engine thrummed somewhere behind him.

Joey had never been so glad to see Frank and Lorraine's house in his life. He burst through the door of the enclosed porch and, hand shaking, pushed the key into the lock.

Inside, he turned the deadbolt and sagged against the door, waiting for his rapid huffs of breath to slow and grow quiet. The canned laughter of a sitcom drifted from the living room.

"Joey, is that you?" Frank called. "What were you doing out?"

Joey pushed away from the door. He pulled off the blue coat and the sweatshirt, and then hung both over the back of another coat.

"You're grounded."

Joey started for the stairs and cast a quick glance into the living room. Lorraine, curled on the corner of the couch, glanced up from her romance novel and frowned. Frank sat back in his recliner, his feet up. His gaze narrowed on Joey.

"I want to talk to you."

Ignoring him, Joey grabbed the banister and pulled himself up the stairs.

"Get back here, young man."

At the top he swung his leg over the baby gate. His hands were still shaking as he opened the door to his room. Head pounding worse than ever, he walked straight through into the small bathroom he and Benny shared and splashed cold water on his face.

A vehicle rolled up the driveway. Gravel and snow crunched beneath the tires.

Joey pressed the child lock above the mirror and grabbed a bottle of pain meds from the top shelf of the medicine cabinet. He twisted off the child-proof cap and swallowed two tablets dry.

A car door slammed.

Where were these headaches coming from? They didn't last long but they hurt. Maybe he had a brain tumor.

He rested the ball of his foot on the toilet and tugged up the leg of his jeans. Blood oozed from a cut about an inch wide at the bottom of his shin, the area around it red and swollen. He wiped it off with a wet washcloth.

The urgent pounding of knuckles against glass radiated up from the back door below him.

His hands shook as he swapped the pain medicine for a box of band aids. He flipped open the top, searching for one wide enough to cover the wound, but he dropped the box and the entire contents scattered across the counter and into the sink bowl.

"Damn it." He pressed the heels of his hands against his eyes and tried to calm his breathing, tried to stop the trembling in his hands.

Snatching up the nearest band aid, he struggled to separate the two halves of the wrapper. His hands shook too much to manage the task, so he tossed the bandage into the sink and shoved down his pant leg.

He wiped his hand across his face and walked back into his room. His gaze roamed over each shadowy corner. Nothing moved. No men with guns. In here, Luke's screams were silent.

A tense conversation floated up the stairwell. Lorraine's high-pitched voice was agitated. Frank's low rumbling drawl remained apathetic. Marek's raspy-edged deeper tones flowed with calm persistence.

Instead of pulling back the covers of his bed and diving in, Joey lifted the mattress and grabbed his knife. Once his fingers wrapped around the wood, the shaking in his fingers eased and his breathing slowed.

Snatching up one of his pillows, he crossed the room and slipped into the closet. Sliding to the floor, he pulled the door closed, enveloping himself in darkness. He rested the foam rectangle on his shoulder, wedging it between the wall and his head.

Clutching his knife, he wondered if he'd ever feel safe again.

The bathroom door squeaked.

Joey flinched and swiped a bead of sweat from his forehead.

A moment later, he recognized the soft scuffing of Benny's pajama feet against the hardwood floor. The closet door opened. Benny stood in silhouette, his blond hair spiky from sleep. Held against his chest was the shaggy blue, cartoon movie monster with which he slept.

As though he'd done it every night, Benny settled into Joey's lap.

Joey wrapped his free arm around the little boy's waist, holding him as securely as Benny held his stuffed toy.

"It okay, Joey," Benny said, reaching up to pat Joey's cheek with his warm small hand.

Benny lifted his toy. "Suddy keep monsters away."

Joey lay his cheek against Benny's silky head and inhaled the light scent of baby shampoo.

He closed his eyes. For a moment he was back home, hiding in the closet with his brother Kyle and their dog Charlie. Kyle wrapped his arms around Joey, while Joey wrapped his around Charlie's furry neck.

Down the hall in the kitchen, his father cried. The wrenching sobs had been more disturbing than the raised voices of his parents arguing.

"You'll find another job," his mother soothed. "As long as we're together, we'll be okay."

"Joey!"

From somewhere far away he heard his name being called. *Mom?*

"Joey, answer me!"

No. Not Mom, Lorraine. He sighed and squeezed his eyes against the sting.

For a half second, he'd been content. In that heartbeat of a moment his world had been right.

He lifted his head and shook off the disappointment.

"Joey!" Lorraine's voice snapped impatiently. "Detective Marek is here. He wants to talk to you."

How much time had passed?

"He never answers. Barely puts two words together."

Had it only been a few minutes?

"Joey!" Frank bellowed. "Come down here!"

"Frank, Allison is sleeping. I'll go up and send him down."

Knife clenched in his hand, Joey sighed and pushed to his knees, shoving his shirts along the clothes rod to give himself some headroom, holding Benny snug on his hip.

The bedroom door swung inward, spilling a beam of light from the hall across the hardwood. Lorraine stood just inside.

Joey nudged the closet door wider as he rolled to his feet.

Benny's stuffed monster fell to the floor. Joey stepped over it.

Lorraine gasped. "Oh, dear Lord! Fraaank!"

Benny started crying. He arched back, pushing against Joey's arm.

Instinctively, Joey brought his other arm up, across Benny's back, holding him tight to his chest, the knife still in his hand.

"Frank! He's going to kill Benny!"

*****

CHAPTER 8

STILL sobbing, Benny's attention swung between Lorraine screeching in the doorway and Joey. Turning into Joey, he twined both arms around Joey's neck and buried his face against the Metallica patch on the left shoulder of the denim jacket.

Joey tried to set the little boy on his feet, but Benny wrapped his legs tight around Joey's waist.

Allison peeked in from the safety of the hallway, wearing pink pajamas coveréd with white cats. Her eyes widened and her mouth fell open.

"Back to your room," Lorraine snapped. "Fraaank!"

Over Benny's wailing, the pounding of Frank's footfalls charged up the stairs, followed by a thud, a few choice swear words, and the clatter of a baby gate bouncing down the flight of stairs.

"What the hell is going on?" Frank demanded, his wide chest heaving.

"He's got a knife!" Lorraine cried. "He's as crazy as his father!"

Heavy boots double-timed up the stairs and down the hall. Seconds later, Detective Marek stood silhouetted in the doorway, head and shoulders above Frank and Lorraine.

Had Marek drawn his gun?

The same overwhelming panic, which sent him fleeing Marek's house, clawed against the inside of Joey's chest, urging him to run. Run and hide. He glanced over his shoulder at the open closet and then at the window across the room. He tightened his hold on Benny, swaying slightly, hoping the boy would stop crying.

Joey reached back and grasped Benny's arm to pull it from around his neck, but the kid held on like a spider monkey.

"No," Benny sobbed.

"I'm not hurting him." Joey tried to explain, but if they heard him they gave no sign.

Frank took a small step forward. He raised his hands waist high, palms out. "I know you've been upset about your father," he said in that smooth, condescending tone used by Doctor Mercer Don't-Worry-I-Understand. "Then you got into a fight at school. These things can be very stressful for someone your age."

"Why don't you two wait downstairs?" Marek suggested, though he kept his attention on Joey. "Let me talk to him a minute."

"But Benny." Lorraine raised her hand in a weak gesture directed toward Joey.

"The boy's fine," Marek replied, his voice low and reassuring.

He stepped between Frank and Lorraine. His pea coat hung open, revealing a glimpse of the gun at his hip held securely in its holster.

Joey's racing heart slowed. He pressed his chin against Benny's temple. "Shhh," he whispered.

Benny sniffled and hiccupped. He turned his face toward Detective Marek and rested his cheek on Joey's shoulder

Marek raised his hands, palms out, and took a small step forward. "Put down the knife, Joe. I'll give the kid to Lorraine. Then we can talk."

Joey wanted to let go, but his fingers wouldn't unclench. Like a hiker clinging to an outcropping of rock, fear of letting go prevented Joey from reaching out to grab the lifeline that dangled before him. The more afraid he grew, the tighter his fingers gripped the wooden handle.

This knife had protected him for six years. Now Marek was going to take it from him. How would he sleep? How would he ever feel safe?

Marek took another step. "I'm sorry I scared you. I meant what I said this morning. I won't hurt you. Ever."

Joey searched Marek's shadowy features. He couldn't make out his expression, but the sincerity of his promise was in the slight catch of his voice. And in that moment Joey wasn't looking at Detective Marek. He was looking at Luke's dad.

The tension in Joey's grip eased. His fingers went lax, and the knife thudded against the hardwood floor.

In two quick strides Marek was in front of him. His foot came down on the knife, and he kicked it across the floor toward the bed.

He reached out to lift Benny. Surprisingly, the little boy offered no resistance.

Lorraine came forward to take him, as Joey bent to get the stuffed blue monster. He rose and held it out. Lorraine flinched, even as Benny stretched both arms to grasp his toy.

Joey glanced away and caught a glimpse of a frown on Marek's brow before he walked to the bed and picked up the knife.

"I luff you, Joey," Benny called, looking over Lorraine's shoulder as she hurried from the room. At the door he waved goodbye.

Joey responded with a quick, finger-curled wave of his own.

Uncertain, he remained by the closet, watching as Marek turned on the bedside lamp and examined the old kitchen blade. A moment later, Marek dropped heavily onto the side of the bed and stared at the knife he held between his hands.

Joey didn't have to get close to see what Marek saw, because Joey knew exactly how every nick and scratch had come to be. He'd had the knife since he'd taken it from his house the day he'd been released from the hospital.

His social worker had taken him there to retrieve whatever possessions would fit inside the suitcase and two boxes she'd brought. She'd left him by the front door, shifting on his crutches while she went down the hall to the room.

The moment Mary Custer had moved from his sight, terror washed over him, pounding in his ears so loud, that if she asked him which shirt or toy he wanted, he wouldn't be able to hear a word. Did blood still soak his bed? Kyle's bed? Nausea churned his stomach. Acid burned its way up the back of his throat. He and Kyle would never talk again, never play video games or ride bikes. His brother was gone forever. Joey ached to throw himself into his mother's arms, but she was gone, too. He'd never feel her hugs or her lips on his forehead. Never hear her sing in the kitchen while she cooked, or while she played her favorite hymns on the battered upright in the corner of the room. Even his black lab, Charlie, had been shot.

Moving his crutches forward, he hopped to the kitchen. He opened the top drawer beside the sink and pulled out the knife his mom had used to chop vegetables. It was big and heavy in his nine-year-old hands. Now no one could get him. Now he'd be safe.

He'd gone out to the car, wrapped the knife inside the extra pair of jeans someone had given him, and then shoved them to the bottom of the plastic bag he'd brought with him from the hospital.

Mary Custer had come out a little while later, stowed everything in the trunk of her car and started the engine. *"Lord have mercy, child. You're shaking like a leaf in the wind."*

The first thing he'd done at his new foster home was take a nail and scratch the letters J-O-E-Y deep into the wood. Over time he'd added superhero stickers, until the handle and upper part of the blade were covered. Although the images had worn away through the years, he knew they were there, guarding him in the night.

Marek looked up. His eyes seemed unusually bright in the soft glow of the lamp. He pinched the bridge of his nose, squeezing his eyes tight as he sniffed. "Come." He cleared his throat. "Come mere."

Joey limped over and lowered himself onto the mattress beside Luke's dad.

Marek sighed. "I'm sorry I scared you. I went out for a pizza. When I got back, I heard someone in Luke's room. For half a second I thought he was—" He slid his hand around the back of his own neck and gave his head a slight shake. "We're a sorry-ass pair, you and me."

They sat in silence on the bed, side-by-side. Neither seemed to know what to say. Yet, the quiet was good, too. Maybe like him and Luke, Joey and Marek didn't have to say anything, either.

Marek tapped the tip of the blade against his palm. "I don't think Lorraine or Frank would understand this." He nodded toward the closet where the pillow lay on the floor. "That, either."

Turning his head, Marek looked at Joey for a minute and then switched his attention to the shaggy gold area rug beneath his feet. "I always knew what happened to you. Luke told me you were afraid of guns, afraid to sleep in a bed."

Joey shot him a sidelong glance.

Marek held out the knife. His thumb brushed over Batman. "You shouldn't have to be this afraid."

Joey rubbed his palm over his thigh. He didn't want to be scared all the time, but he didn't really know Frank, didn't really know any of his foster parents.

"Did you bring this when you slept over with Luke?"

Joey gave his shoulders a quick shrug.

"Where'd you sleep?"

"Luke gave me his sleeping bag."

Marek sighed. "Where did you sleep, Joe?"

Joey gnawed his lower lip. "Luke didn't care."

"And this?" He nodded toward the six-inch blade. "Did he know you slept with this?"

Joey shook his head.

Marek stared at the knife. "Do you feel safe at my house?"

Joey shrugged.

Rising, Marek glanced around the small room. "Do you think you could sleep if you came home with me for a few days? Just until things calm down around here?"

Joey stilled. He searched Marek's face. Did he mean it?

The thought of escaping Frank and Lorraine, their late-night whispers, and judgmental stares was almost euphoric.

See, they would tell Mary Custer, *he's crazy just like his father.*

Maybe they were right. Maybe he was crazy, seeing and hearing things he could never have known.

"Joe?"

"Okay."

"Then, how 'bout I keep this for now." He held open one side of his jacket and slipped the knife into an inner pocket. "I'll put it somewhere safe and if you need it, tell me."

At the last second Joey almost lunged for it, needing it like Benny needed his toy.

Luke had said once that he couldn't tell his father about his gambling debts, because he didn't want to disappoint him.

He hadn't said he was afraid of getting in trouble with the law or that his old man would kick his ass. He'd simply said he didn't want to disappoint his dad.

Marek believed Joey would never hurt Benny and understood why he needed his knife.

Now he knew what Luke meant. Joey didn't want to do anything to cause Marek to regret having trusted him even this little bit.

He watched his knife disappear, as the coat fell back into place.

"I'm going to talk to Frank and Lorraine. Pack up a few clothes and come down when you're ready."

Their eyes met. A moment later Marek walked from the room.

Joey didn't have a lot of clothes. By the time he'd stuffed his gym bag with socks, underwear, shirts, and jeans, he'd emptied the closet and dresser drawers.

From downstairs Lorraine's voice grew louder, shriller. "I want him gone. He's dangerous!"

"Look, can't you just wait until Monday before you call her?" Marek said something else, but his tone was too low to make out his words. "If you push this, he'll end up in juvey for Christmas."

Pulling open the bottom drawer of the dresser, Joey grabbed two thick photo albums and shoved them into his old backpack with the broken strap. He tossed his bag on the bed and then lay on the floor.

"It will be fine, Lori," Frank said. "He's slept there lots of times and Detective Marek is on the approved list."

"Fine, but I'm calling Mary Custer first thing Monday morning."

Great. Emergency placement. Another hearing. Another foster family.

Joey eased himself under the bed. He'd done this so many times, no light was necessary. By rote his hand found the tear in the fabric which covered the underside of the box spring. He reached into the hole and pulled a plastic freezer bag from its hiding place. Inside was Detective Marek's gold watch and the title to Luke's truck.

After wiggling out from under the bed, he took the flash drive from the inside pocket of the denim jacket, dropped it into the plastic bag, and zipped it closed.

The bag of secrets in hand, he shoved it inside his backpack and sealed it. He heaved the heavy bag over his shoulder by its single strap, grabbed his duffle, and headed downstairs.

"All set?" Lorraine asked in a too-bright voice as he stood outside the living room. A painted-on smile, like one of Allison's dolls, spread wide across her face.

Without a word, Joey went into the kitchen to put on his shoes.

Marek walked in as Joey stood pulled up the zipper of his jacket.

"Ready?" He grabbed the duffle bag.

The zipper separated at the bottom. Praying Marek wouldn't notice, he pulled the zipper down and back up again.

"Where's your new jacket?"

With a shrug he grabbed his backpack off the chair and slung it over his shoulder. He glanced down. The teeth had separated all the way to the bottom.

"Joe, I asked you a question."

He raised his gaze to the center button of Marek's pea coat. "I left it at school."

"You came all the way home without a coat in this weather, and the thought never crossed your mind to go back and get it?"

"Didn't want to miss the bus."

"Let's get one thing settled right now. Joe, look at me when I'm talking to you."

Joey's gaze eased upward, until he met the gray-blue eyes of Detective Marek. He didn't look mad, just determined. Maybe he wasn't going to change his mind.

"As long as you're under my roof, I ask you a question I expect a straight answer. I saw your face this morning when I gave you that jacket. You didn't forget it. Now where is it?"

"Someone stole it."

Marek's gaze narrowed. "Who?"

Joey shrugged. School was bad enough already. Throwing Greg Kelly under the bus wouldn't make it better.

"Does this stolen coat have something to do with the fresh bruises on your face?"

Lorraine walked into the kitchen, a gray plastic bag from the local discount store in her hand. "He was fighting in school today."

Marek switched his attention to Lorraine.

Joey focused on trying to wiggle the pull tab back to the bottom. Lying *and* fighting. He half expected Marek to decide Joey was too much trouble, walk out the door, and leave him behind.

"Fighting? With who?"

"That nice boy up the road. This one was trying to steal his coat."

Joey rezipped his jacket, but the plastic teeth pulled apart as usual. Why did she have to butt in?

He didn't have to look up to know Marek studied him. He could feel those penetrating eyes boring into his skull, waiting for an explanation.

Joey worked the zipper slider back to the bottom and started again. If he pulled it up slow enough through that one spot and kept the teeth together, maybe the two sides would stay locked. They came apart after a few inches. He worked the slide back to the bottom and started again.

"Forget that damn zipper," Marek said. "My car's warm enough."

Joey let go of his jacket with a sigh of relief. Marek still wanted him.

Lorraine stepped around the table and extended her hand toward Joey. The plastic bag hung from her fingers.

"Here's your Christmas presents. I didn't have time to wrap them."

He took the bag and peered inside. A pair of jeans filled the bottom, a flannel shirt lay on top with a pack of white socks, a DVD about a girl and a horse, and a country CD with the face of the same man who was on the cover of the DVD. Tucked in the side was the pair of black ski gloves he'd seen earlier in the box Marek had dropped off.

"Uh, thanks," he mumbled and picked up his backpack.

Marek headed for the door, pressing his key fob, and Joey followed. As he pulled the door closed, he glanced at Lorraine who stood watching, her arms crossed at her waist and her mouth compressed into a tight line.

The SUV stood at the end of the path, the engine running. Before he and Marek reached the car, someone flicked off the kitchen light.

* * * * *

CHAPTER 9

"STOW your gear in the back," Marek said, as he approached the rear of the vehicle. He raised the hatch, tossed in the duffle bag, and then waited for Joey to add his backpack and the plastic bag.

Marek slammed down the door and headed for the front.

Joey walked around and hopped into the passenger seat. Marek was right. The SUV was warm.

The temperature change sent a shiver up his arms and over his scalp. Frank and Lorraine's house was always cold.

Marek shot him a sidelong glance but said nothing. At the end of the driveway, he turned toward town instead of his house. They drove under the railroad tracks.

Was it just the other day that Marek had stopped here and given him a ride? It seemed so long ago.

They rode together in silence, but it was a companionable silence, not awkward, even though Joey wondered where they were going.

Just before the center of town Marek pulled up in front of a brightly lit convenience store. A shiny black sedan with a sunroof stood parked beside one of the gas pumps. Nate's multi-colored piece of junk sat alongside the building near the dumpster.

Joey slumped low in the seat.

Marek shifted his vehicle into park. "I don't eat at home much. You want to come in and pick out some stuff you like?"

Joey shrugged.

The front door of the store pushed open. A man wearing a black overcoat and hat stepped outside and started toward the pumps and the black sedan.

Joey slid lower.

"All right, Joe, what's the problem?"

"Nothing."

"What'd I tell you about being straight with me?"

"I ain't lying."

"You're not being straight either. Do you know that guy?"

"No."

The black car pulled onto the road.

Marek's mouth parted, as if he was about to say something. Instead, he gave a tired exhale. "You coming in?"

Joey shook his head.

"Is this about the fight? Is this because Nate Kelly works here?"

Joey kept his gaze focused on the glove box. He heard the click of the door latch. Cool air blew across the seats.

"I'm going to let this go. For now." He stepped out of the car and shut the door.

Joey rested his head against the edge of the window, just high enough so he could watch Marek enter the store. What could he say that wouldn't get him in more trouble with the Kelly brothers? More importantly, how would he be able to keep Luke's name out of it?

Inside the store between the window sign for breakfast sandwiches and the poster for potato chips, Nate stood at the counter.

Marek headed down one of the aisles. A minute or two later, he set his purchases on the counter. They talked, as Nate rang up the items and put them into bags.

Nate never once glanced through the windows toward the SUV.

Joey closed his eyes when Marek came out of the store. The back door opened and plastic rustled as he set the bags on the seat. The door thudded closed, and the driver's door opened. Cold air swirled inside for a moment, and then Marek got in the SUV and closed the door.

As Marek backed the car out of the parking space and onto the road, Joey wasn't sure if Marek believed the ruse or just accepted it.

They headed out of town. Joey visualized every stop and turn. East on the rolling two lane road. Around the bend. Under the railroad tracks. Past Frank and Lorraine's. And finally up the driveway at Marek's.

The engine idled loud in the confines of the garage, and Marek turned off the key. Behind them the automatic door rattled closed.

"Come on, Joe. Get your stuff."

Maybe Marek hadn't believed he was asleep.

Marek clicked the unlock button and climbed out of the vehicle. He lifted the back hatch, opened the door behind the driver, and reached for the groceries.

Joey slid out of the car and walked around to grab his backpack and duffle bag from the back. He considered leaving the plastic bag from Lorraine beside a coil of jumper cables and a bag of sand, telling himself he didn't have enough hands to carry it. At the last second, he changed his mind and grabbed it. Why leave his junk in Marek's car?

Catching sight of Luke's truck, he remembered he needed to return the house key.

He slammed the hatch closed and walked around to the truck. He set down his stuff, dug the house key out of his pocket and returned the key to the metal box. Grabbing his bags, he hurried after Marek.

"Damn it, Cody," Marek exclaimed. He set his groceries on the counter. A pizza box lay on the floor in scattered bits of white and red.

Joey his bags on the floor and bent to pick up the pieces of grease and tomato-stained cardboard. Though it had been a while, he recalled where the pull-out trash can was hidden beside the sink.

"Thanks," Marek said. "That was supposed to be my dinner. Damn dog." He dug through the plastic bags and pulled out a dozen eggs. "Guess I can scramble some eggs. You hungry?"

Joey shook his head, even as a low gurgling sound tumbled through his stomach.

Marek eyed him skeptically. "I'll call you when it's ready. Go ahead and take your gear up to the guest room."

Joey grabbed his backpack and bag of Christmas presents with one hand, his duffle bag with the other. He then headed to the foyer and the bottom of the staircase.

Cody trotted out from the living room greeting Joey with a happy wag and a nudge to the wrist with his wet nose, as though he had no idea a large pizza had just vanished off the kitchen counter.

Joey thumped him on the side and the golden retriever raced ahead of him up the stairs.

In the room across from Luke's, Joey took off his winter coat and tossed it on top of his duffle bag. There was no point in unpacking. Mary Custer would pick him up soon and take him to live someplace new. New family. New school. New therapist.

Why not? He hated that school, and Frank and Lorraine hated him. Luke was gone. There was no reason to want to stay, but he did.

He pulled off the hated blue jacket and sat on the bed staring at his backpack. His stomach churned as he tried to decide what to do with Luke's flash drive and Marek's gold watch.

Should he put back the watch? Marek already knew it was missing. It couldn't suddenly reappear. Nor did Joey have any idea where the title to Luke's truck had come from. If he got caught in Marek's room, he'd be spending the rest of the night in juvey.

He could just give them both to Marek along with the flash drive. But what would he say? Should he throw Luke under the bus? Would Marek believe him? Probably not. Joey would likely end up in juvey. The only other option would be to confess to something he didn't do. Again, that scenario led straight to juvey.

He shoved his hands inside the angled pockets of the denim jacket and hunched his shoulders, curling into himself.

I promised I wouldn't tell, but damn it, Luke, what do you want me to do?

Dizziness washed over him. The entire room pitched like a ship in a storm. He put his hand down to steady himself, but instead of touching the comforter his palm pressed against the hard surface of a table.

"Luke Marek. Sit down."

Instead of the guest room, Joey found himself in Ms. Angelica's art room. She stood a few feet away, her wiry gray hair pulled back in a bun, wearing the same paint-splattered smock she always wore.

"I know you'd rather be playing sports, but you chose this elective and I expect your best work. Now sit down and draw. A recent place you've been that stands out in your mind. Remember your vanishing point, and from which direction the light falls."

Joey scrunched his eyes tight. A knife-like pain slashed through his head from temple to temple. A soft whimper hummed in his throat as he clutched his head and fell sideways on the bed, curling into himself.

He rarely had headaches and had never suffered from hallucinations. Both were getting worse. What was wrong with him?

When the spinning stopped, he opened his eyes. The guest room had returned to normal.

Was Luke really speaking to him or was he just crazy? No. He couldn't let himself even think of the possibility.

Until Ms. Angelica yelled at Luke, Joey believed the images of the trestle bridge and gun to be his own memories. Suppressed, the same way his father couldn't remember what he'd done. But what about the man in the ball cap who'd been chasing him tonight?

Had a man actually been chasing him or had that shadowy figure been a hallucination? Were these visions suppressed memories? If Joey had been there, why hadn't he helped Luke? Why couldn't he remember?

No. He hadn't been with Luke that day. He was overthinking this.

Something else caused these headaches and visions. The gun. They'd recently found the gun. That had to be it. Or was it Luke's jacket? Because none of this happened unless he was wearing the jacket.

Shit! The jacket.

He rolled off the bed, yanking his arms free of the denim sleeves even as he came to his feet.

He tossed it on the bed beside his backpack. Now it was easier to believe Luke hadn't actually spoken to him. It had just been his imagination or maybe a brain tumor.

With Ms. Angelica's instructions in his head, he felt compelled to follow them. Maybe he had been there, seen something that could help him remember. Leaning over, he dug a pencil and a spiral notebook out of his backpack. He flipped open the notebook to a blank page.

In the first hallucination, he'd been looking down at the water from the top of the trestle bridge. He wasn't the best at sketching, but he could get through art class without embarrassing himself. He gnawed on his lip, ignoring the growing pressure in his head as he erased and redrew, trying to get the vanishing point in the center of the page so it appeared he was looking down at the water from the middle of the bridge. He erased again trying to create a perfect match to his vision.

What if these visions were the result of a guilty conscience? Had he killed Luke and didn't remember? Was Luke's spirit accusing him with every image he'd had seen over the past few days?

He tried not to think about why all of this was happening three months after Luke died. It was much easier to shove it all to the back of his mind and deny it, deny who he was and what he might have done.

The aroma of bacon drifted upstairs, and his mouth watered.

"Joe, food's up!"

Cody rolled to his feet waiting expectantly.

Moving his pencil quickly over the paper, he roughed in the rest of the bridge before he lost it. He could fill in the trees and all the trusses later. If he got it down on paper, maybe he'd know what happened that day.

Joey closed his notebook and stuffed it into his backpack, before changing into flannel bottoms and a long sleeve T-shirt.

Cody charged ahead as Joey padded barefoot down the stairs and walked past the vacant dining room, to the kitchen which stretched across the back of the house.

Marek switched off the exhaust fan above the stove and set two plates of scrambled eggs, bacon, and toast on the peninsula. He poured a glass of milk for Joey. Grabbing a bottle of beer from the fridge, he walked around the end of the counter to take up his seat near the wall.

Joey pulled out a stool and sat, hooking his feet around the tall legs of the chair. Now that his headache had faded, the pangs in his stomach made his hunger known.

"So," Marek said, as he munched on a piece of bacon, "how about you tell me why you were hiding from Pierson Mott?"

Who? Joey frowned at Marek.

Marek must have perceived the unasked question. "Pierson Mott, the accountant for Stiller Enterprises."

Still confused, Joey shook his head.

Marek continued. "Over in the valley? Stiller Enterprises owns North Creek Golf and Conference Center."

Joey studied the geometric pattern around the edge of his plate. So that's who the guy was. He packed quite a punch for an accountant. He hit almost as hard as Greg Kelly's foot. Resisting the urge to rub his stomach and draw more attention to himself, he watched Marek scoop some eggs onto a piece of toast and take a big bite.

"Hmmm," he mused around a mouthful of food. "You don't know who the man is, yet as soon as you see his car you hide before he can see you. Interesting. Care to tell me what's going on?"

"Nothing."

"Nothing? You were wearing Luke's jacket again. Is that why you broke into my house tonight?"

"I didn't." Joey poked at his eggs with a fork and moved them around on his plate.

"How'd you get inside?"

"Cody was loose. The back door of the garage was open, so I used the spare house key in Luke's truck to put him inside."

From the corner of his eye, he watched Marek tip the bottle to his lips and swallow. He set down the beer. "Eat."

Joey picked up a slice of bacon and took a bite. Normally the smoky saltiness made his mouth water, but at that moment the bacon was dry and wooden against his tongue.

"What were you doing in Luke's room?"

"I dropped Lorraine's house keys." He pushed the eggs onto a piece of toast. "Cody stole 'em and ran up there." Marek would never believe him if tried to explain their mysterious appearance behind the dresser. Joey didn't want to believe it himself.

He laid the bacon strips across the eggs and then topped it with the second piece of toast.

"What were you two fighting about that day?"

Joey stared at his sandwich and lowered his hands into his lap. Absently he rubbed his thigh.

"Joe?"

He shrugged. "Nothing."

"Damn it, Joe, it wasn't nothing. You and Luke were fighting."

Joey flinched. Maybe it wasn't a good idea to come here. Detective

Marek had shifted into cop mode, and Joey wasn't sure he wanted to talk about this. He stood.

He glanced around and spotted Marek's pea coat shouldered over a chair at the table in front of the French doors. Was his knife still in the pocket?

"Uh, thanks for the eggs, but—"

"Sit." Marek slid his hand around the back of his neck. "I'm sorry. Eat your supper. It's been a hell of a night and we're both tired."

Joey scooted himself onto the barstool and picked up the egg sandwich. He no longer felt like eating, but he didn't want to waste food Marek had made for him. He lifted it to his mouth and took a bite.

Marek carried his plate to the dishwasher and scrubbed up the pans he used to cook the bacon and eggs.

Joey finished his glass of milk as Marek wiped off the counter. He started toward the sink to rinse his dishes, but Marek reached out and took them from his hands.

"How's the eye?"

Joey shrugged. "Okay."

"Do you want an ice pack to take upstairs with you?"

"No."

"Okay. Goodnight then." Marek turned on the faucet and rinsed the glass.

Joey remained, shifting his weight off his right leg, aching from the strain of his earlier exertions. He ran his finger back and forth across the rounded edge of the granite counter.

Marek turned watching him expectantly.

Joey shifted and studied the various shades of black, gray, and silver in the granite. Hopefully, no more images would appear.

"Joe?"

Joey shot him a quick glance. Was this how Detective Marek got suspects to confess? Joey was tempted, and he wasn't even sure what he'd done.

"Luke's computer. I was wondering if I could borrow it?"

"Why?"

Maybe this was a bad idea. Could Marek tell he was hiding something? Is that why he'd fixed his narrowed glare on Joey?

"I, um, have some homework and I—I'm not tired."

"Homework." Some of the stiffness eased from Marek's shoulders, but he still eyed him skeptically.

Joey nodded. Most kids didn't start their homework this early over

Christmas vacation. Luke sure didn't and neither did Joey.

Marek pulled open the dishwasher. "The state police have Luke's computer, but if you can wait on your homework until tomorrow, I'll dig out my old laptop for you."

"Thanks."

Marek set the glasses and plates on the racks. "G'night, Joe."

Feeling as though he'd been dismissed, Joey headed upstairs, Cody right on his heels.

After brushing his teeth, he returned to the guest room. The soft mattress and clean white sheets beckoned, but he couldn't bring himself to slip between them.

The other night he'd slept on the couch in the basement. Maybe he could take a pillow and blanket down there after Detective Marek went to bed.

He yawned and scrubbed his hand over his face. Luke's jacket lay where he'd tossed it at the head of the bed. With nothing else to do Joey unzipped his backpack and withdrew his notebook.

Sitting on the bed, he added some detail to the trestle bridge. When he finished, he turned to a clean page and sketched out the barrel and grip of the gun he'd seen in the floor tiles. He wracked his brain, trying to remember what he'd seen without confusing it with other pictures of guns he had in his head.

He needed to get it perfect, exactly the way he remembered.

*****

CHAPTER 10

PIANO music drifted up from the first floor.

The barrel of the gun had been aimed to the right. There had been a hand holding it, the knuckles and thumb of a left hand. Joey scribbled out the drawing, flipped the page, and started again.

The lines blurred. He yawned and rubbed his hand over his aching eyes. He'd work on it later.

Leaving the notebook folded open, he shoved it into his backpack and left it on the bed beside Luke's jacket. Another yawn escaped, as he got to his feet.

Joey didn't recognize the song Marek played. Drawn to the haunting melody, he left the guest room and tiptoed down the stairs. Hugging the moulding around the room's archway entrance, he peeked inside.

Barefoot, wearing jeans and a green T-shirt, Marek sat on the bench with his back to the stairs. He seemed lost in the music, as his hands moved left and right across the keys. A brown bottle of beer sat on a coaster on the corner of the piano.

The white couch near the window tempted him with thick cushions, colorful pillows, and a fleecy throw blanket. Not wanting to intrude, Joey retreated to sit on the stairs.

Two steps below, Cody curled up on the floor.

Stifling a yawn, Joey leaned his head against the wainscoting and closed his eyes.

Luke's dad began to sing softly. The rough edge of his baritone voice offered Joey the same sense of contentment and security he felt when his mom's clear soprano used to fill the house with old hymns.

Joey relaxed and let his mind put on his blue suede shoes and wander through the lyrics of *Walking in Memphis*. Bon Jovi's *Always* came next, and then *The Sky is Falling* by Lifehouse.

"Joe?"

A deep voice spoke his name, the tone familiar and safe. The grip of a hand landed on his shoulder and gave him a quick shake. The weight remained for the briefest moment and then withdrew before Joey had a chance to savor its comfort.

"Come on. Wake up. You can't sleep here."

Joey opened his eyes. A dark shape loomed over him. He flinched, sucking in a breath on a gasp and tried to scoot backward away from the shadow, but his hand slipped off the edge of the stair tread and he whacked his elbow.

"Hey, it's okay. I keep telling you, I'm not going to hurt you." Luke's dad straightened, resting his arm on the banister and leaving one foot on the bottom step.

Joey scrubbed his hand over his face erasing the tension and blowing away the remnants with a sigh. He hoped Luke's dad didn't think him too big a fool.

"What are you doing down here?"

"Nothing."

"You're safe here, Joe. You can sleep in the bed."

He lifted his gaze to meet Marek's. Kindness, not judgment, looked back through gray-blue eyes.

"Jessica Bickman," Joey said.

"What?"

"The fight me and Luke had. He had a thing for her. But she didn't like him."

"Bickman. Isn't that the girl Luke took to his junior prom?"

Joey nodded. "But after, she kept blowing him off. Wouldn't get back with him or anything. I heard her in study hall tell her friends she just went to prom with him to make someone jealous."

"Who?"

"It don't matter. We were going to walk the tracks that day, but Luke was going on and on about her. I told him what she said, but he didn't believe me. Then I said she was a slut. He got mad and tore into me."

"Why didn't you tell me about this fight sooner?"

Joey shrugged, focusing on his hand as he pressed the heel of his hand deep into the muscle of his thigh.

"What were you afraid of?"

"If I hadn't said something about Jessica, me and Luke would've been together. He wouldn't of got mad and gone off."

Marek sighed. "God, Joe. Don't beat yourself up. It's not your fault."

Joey should have been elated to hear those words. That someone would have such faith in him, especially Luke's dad, should have had him floating on the proverbial cloud nine. In the back of his mind lurked the fear that what happened to Luke *was* his fault, and Luke was reminding him of it almost every day.

"If anyone's to blame, it would be me." With a gesture of his hand Marek urged Joey to head up the stairs. "I should have paid more attention to what was going on in his life. I just sort of lost track of the details after his mom died."

Joey moved up the stairs. Cody charged ahead of him, and Marek followed.

"Try to get some sleep," Marek said at the door to the guestroom.

Joey nodded.

"I don't blame you," Marek added, as Joey stepped inside.

Maybe you should, Joey thought as Marek moved down the hall, and Joey closed his door.

He stayed awake drawing the figure he'd seen in the shadow of the trees. When enough time had passed for Luke's dad to fall asleep, Joey shoved his notebook into his backpack. He grabbed the pillow from beneath the denim jacket and an extra blanket from the closet.

Silently, he moved past Marek's room and then downstairs to the kitchen.

His fingers itched to wrap themselves tight around the handle of his knife. It had to be here. He checked Marek's coat, but it was no longer in his pocket. He checked each drawer in the kitchen, hoping Marek hadn't hidden the knife in his bedroom closet. Instead, Joey found it stashed in the drawer next to the stove, shoved between a soup ladle and a rubber spatula.

He pulled it from the back of the drawer and held it in his hand, savoring its familiar weight, the curve of the handle beneath his fingers, and the faint gleam of the blade in the dark. But after a minute, he put it back. Marek promised he'd be safe here. To take his knife now would be a betrayal of that trust. He knew where it was and that knowing should have made it better.

Tonight, Joey had been an intruder in this house. The one person who promised never to hurt him had almost shot him. His leg ached. His chest hurt.

People had guns and bedrooms weren't safe. Someone had shot Luke. Nowhere was safe.

Joey retrieved his knife and some of his tension eased.

He tucked the blade into the folds of the blanket and headed for the basement. Cody followed and then curled up on the rug, while Joey got comfortable on the couch. He slipped his knife beneath the pillow and lay down. Pulling the blanket up over his shoulders, he heaved an exhausted sigh and closed his eyes.

* * *

"Joe!"

Marek's voice penetrated Joey's sleep-fogged brain. He lay on his stomach, his face burrowed into the corner of the basement couch. Opening his eyes, he pushed up on his elbows.

With the lights off it was hard to tell what time it was, but it was still dark outside the windows. Cody, who lay sprawled on the floor beside him, didn't even lift his head.

It seemed as if he'd just fallen asleep. How had Marek known Joey wasn't upstairs? Had he already checked the guest room, or had he assumed Joey would sleep in the basement?

The thought of someone in his room while he was unaware was what had driven him to the closet six years ago.

"Joe!" Marek called again.

"Yeah?"

"I have to go down to the station for a little while."

"'Kay."

"I'll be back. Two hours tops."

"Yup."

"The house is locked up, so you'll be fine. Don't go anywhere."

"'Kay."

"If you get hungry go ahead and eat what you find."

"Yup."

"Right. Well, see you."

Moments later the back door into the garage thudded closed.

Joey slid his hand beneath the pillow and wrapped his fingers around the handle of his knife. He waited, listening. Time passed with each beat of his heart. Silence. Joey released a long breath, snuggled into the pillow, and closed his eyes.

Cody's wet nose shoved under his arm and woke him some time later. He peered at the golden retriever who sat inches away, staring at him expectantly.

"You want to go out?" Joey rolled off the couch, grabbed his knife and followed Cody upstairs. At least there was daylight now. He pushed open one of the French doors. Cody trotted onto the deck and sniffed around the planters as Joey pulled the door closed.

He returned the knife to the drawer exactly the way he found it so Marek wouldn't notice it was missing. He opened the box of cereal Marek bought last night and poured himself a bowl. Standing in front of the glass doors he ate while Cody snuffed through the snow and sniffed each tree and bush in the yard. After rinsing his bowl and putting it in the dishwasher, he let Cody inside the house.

Nails clicking on the tile, the Golden Retriever followed him to the laundry room. Joey scooped food into the dog dish, the way Luke used to do, and set it on the floor.

With Cody fed he headed to the bathroom for a quick shower. He ran his fingers over his upper lip and checked his face in the mirror, making sure no stray hairs had sprouted overnight. After pulling on his jeans, and a clean flannel shirt, he wandered downstairs and found himself standing in front of the gleaming black, baby grand piano.

Luke had mentioned several times that his father didn't like anyone touching it, but Luke's grandma used to let Joey play if he asked.

The place he lived when he was twelve had a piano, but it had been out of tune and several of the keys had stuck.

Lifting the lid of the piano bench, Joey searched for some familiar sheet music. But Marek didn't have any of the old hymns Joey's mother had taught him to play. He pulled out the music for Bob Seger's *Turn the Page*. Maybe he could at least figure out the right hand.

His fingers felt stiff as he ran them over the keys. Warming up by playing scales helped, though he found himself wincing with each sour note.

By the time he finished his third run through the melody, he had the right hand down pretty good.

Cody woofed and trotted to the front window.

Joey stiffened. Was someone here? Carefully, he closed the lid over the keys.

Marek hadn't said anyone would be coming by. Maybe it was just Luke's grandma.

Joey moved to the front window. He peeked through the living room curtains the way Cody had the other night when Joey had hidden in the corner of the wide front porch and listened to Marek play.

A man, wearing a heavy canvas barn coat, reached into the cab of a dark blue pick-up truck. He straightened and turned toward the house. In one hand he held a small white bag and a cardboard holder with two cups bearing the logo of a popular coffee shop. His unzipped coat framed a cartoon reindeer in the center of a red sweatshirt. The festive shirt seemed at odds with the tough-guy image his high-and-tight hair cut presented, leaving Joey to wonder if this friend of Marek's was also a cop.

The man stepped onto the front porch and rang the bell.

Cody woofed and trotted into the foyer.

The doorbell rang again.

Should he let him in?

"Come on, Marek!" the man yelled, thumping the kick plate with the toe of his shoe. "You get me up at seven o'clock on a Saturday morning and tell me to meet you here. You could at least open the damn door."

The man leaned forward and peered through the narrow length of glass that framed one side of the door.

If this guy was expected, why hadn't Marek warned him?

"Come on, Will. The coffee's getting cold."

Answer the door, one part of his brain ordered.

Wait, the other part screamed.

Juggling the cup holder and bag he pulled a set of keys from the left pocket of his coat. He gave them a few shakes, trying to separate a single key, but dropped them on the concrete porch. He set the coffees and bag on the door mat and then picked up the keys. As he did, his open jacket caught on a black leather holster and gun positioned on his left side.

Joey went numb, as though a torrent of ice water suddenly sluiced over him. He wasn't even sure he was breathing. The guy was obviously a cop, but he was left-handed. That didn't mean anything. Lots of people were left-handed.

What if the guy assumed Joey was an intruder the way Marek had last night? At least Marek knew him. This guy didn't. What if he pulled his gun and shot him?

Joey had to hide.

Heart racing, he scanned the room. Built-in bookcases covered one wall. Think! There were cupboards along the bottom, but there wasn't time. Duck behind the couch. No. Moving it would make noise. Maybe the dining room on the other side of the foyer. No! Devoid of furniture there was no place to hide.

Upstairs. He dashed toward the staircase, but Cody cut in front of him. Joey slammed into the dog and pitched forward.

Cody yelped.

Joey reached out to catch himself on a small decorative table. His palm came down on the corner and the table tipped over, hitting the floor with a bang as the vase with the artificial flowers shattered against the tile.

The front door lock clicked, and the handle slowly eased down.

Joey whirled around. A soft moan escaped his lips.

The closet!

He darted forward, as the front door eased inward. Pulling the closet door closed, darkness surrounded him, yet all he could see in his mind was a gun now held in the man's hand.

Afraid his rapid breathing could be heard, he buried his nose and mouth in the crook of his elbow and prayed he wouldn't sneeze.

"Damn it, Marek," the man murmured, as he paused outside the closet where the broken vase lay scattered. "I hope your dog is just clumsy."

The soft click of Cody's nails on the tile echoed the man's footfalls as he and the dog moved toward the back of the house and the expansive kitchen.

Where was Marek? He'd promised Joey would be safe here.

He wanted to believe it, but he knew better. Nowhere was safe. Not when there was a gun.

What if this guy discovered him hiding in the house? What if Cody gave him away? Would the guy shoot him? Marek almost had.

He had to get out. Now. Before the guy came back. Joey inched open the door and peeked into the foyer. Empty. The front door stood ajar. Afraid to look toward the kitchen, he dashed for the door and slipped outside.

He stepped on the cardboard cup holder, knocking over the coffee cups. Moist heat soaked through the thick cotton of his socks. His lack of a coat didn't bother him as much as his lack of shoes. The shoveled concrete of the porch immediately cooled the coffee, chilling his feet.

He hopped off the edge into the bushes and snow, and ducked low.

Tires crunched over the icy road. Joey raised his head and peeked above the edge of the porch.

Marek's SUV eased up the driveway.

A huge sigh escaped him in a foggy cloud. He placed his palms on the snowy concrete surface, prepared to hop onto the porch, when the front door opened.

He dropped back into the bushes, terrified the man stepping onto the porch held his gun.

"Damn. What happened to my coffee?"

Joey pressed his side against the ridges of clapboard and hunched lower, praying he hadn't left wet footprints.

Silence. Joey braved another quick peek.

Marek sat in his SUV with the window down.

The stranger stood on the top step. "I thought you were in the house."

"I went to pick up the file on that gambling case at the high school and then had an errand to run. Saw Mott at the mini-mart late last night. I've got a couple scenarios I'd like to run by you."

"Let me guess, Kelly was working."

"You bet."

The garage door rattled as it raised. Marek pulled forward.

Marek's friend picked up the white bag and empty cups and carried them inside.

Now what? If Joey could sneak back into the house and down to the basement, Marek would never know he'd been hiding in the bushes like a terrified rabbit. He would never know Joey hadn't trusted his word that he'd be safe.

Joey climbed back onto the porch and tried the front door. Locked. He swung around, hurried down the steps and sprinted for the garage, ducking inside behind Marek's SUV before the door started to close.

He slunk alongside Luke's truck and hovered near the passenger door as Marek stepped out of his vehicle.

The other cop stood on the landing outside the laundry room. "Hurry up, I brought breakfast."

"I have food."

"Beer isn't food."

"Ass." Shaking his head, Marek reached inside his vehicle and grabbed something from the passenger seat. He closed the door and walked toward the bottom step. A messenger bag hung from his shoulder. Draped over his arm was a familiar black and green snowboarding jacket.

Joey dropped down and leaned against the front tire. Heat rushed over him chasing away the chill. Luke's dad had actually driven over to Nate Kelly's trailer, banged on the door and asked for the jacket.

It didn't matter what Greg would do to him, wearing it to school after vacation would show everyone he wasn't a thief. It would show them that Detective Will Marek believed in him, had gone out of his way to do something nice for him, Joey Kowalski.

He blinked against the sting that blurred his vision the way it had the first time he and Luke had gone to the mall and Luke had done something nice for him.

"You look good in those sneakers."

"No, they're too expensive."

"You're my best friend. I want you to have 'em. Nobody gets me like you do."

Joey rested the back of his head against the hard fender of Luke's truck. He missed Luke so much. First his mom and Kyle. Then Luke. What was wrong with him?

"Strangest thing," Marek's friend muttered, "I thought you were in the house. I swear to God I heard someone playing the piano when I got here."

"He loves to listen. I didn't know he played. Wait. Didn't he let you in?"

"Who? I let myself in."

"How?"

"You gave me a key."

"When?"

"Back when Aimee was sick, and you and Luke were always at the hospital. I used to come let your dog out. Remember?"

"But did you see Joe?"

"Joe? Hell, Marek. You call me up and tell me to come over. When I get here, you don't answer the damn door. I heard a crash and came in. That little table next to the stairs was tipped over, the vase broken on the floor. Your neighbor up the road likely knows we suspect him."

"Shit. Tell me you didn't draw your weapon."

Joey peered around the bumper.

Marek pushed past his friend and disappeared into the house. "Joe!"

* * * * *

CHAPTER 11

"WHAT the hell? Will!" The friend ran after him.

Joey rose and eased around the front of the vehicles, his wet socks silent on the garage floor and back steps.

He almost made it past the peninsula where the white bag and crushed coffee cups sat, when Marek came up from the basement.

Their gazes met across the room. Joey shivered. He shoved his hands in his pockets. Cody trotted over, circled Joey's legs, and sniffed his coffee scented socks. When Joey looked up, Marek still watched him, his blue-gray eyes assessing and perceptive.

Sadness darkened Marek's features, like a shadow cast by a fast-moving cloud on sunny day. "I'm sorry. I thought I'd be back in time."

Was he disappointed that, despite all he'd done, Joey still didn't trust him?

Marek started toward Joey, moving past the table as the other cop came up the stairs.

"This is my partner, Detective Lewis." Marek glanced at his partner. "Ted, this is Luke's friend, Joe Kowalski."

"Kowalski? Isn't he—"

Detective Lewis never finished his question. Something unspoken passed between the two men. It didn't matter. Joey knew what he was about to say. *Isn't he the kid they think killed your son?*

Marek ran his hand around the back of his neck. "Why don't you sit down? Have a—" He stepped up to the peninsula and peered into the bag. "Bagel." He nudged the white bag closer to where Joey stood.

Joey wiped his hands on the front of his jeans. "I'm not hungry."

"You have to eat something."

Joey watched Detective Lewis, who stood on the other side of Marek. Lewis' coat was now draped over the back of a chair. Beneath the hem of his reindeer sweatshirt, Joey could see the bulge of the man's gun.

When Marek removed his coat, Joey knew that pistol he hoped never to see again would be secured at the man's waist.

As long as he couldn't see the weapons in their hands, it was easier to concentrate on his breathing.

"There's plenty," Lewis said. His pleasant voice held the double-edged lure of a snake oil salesman, while narrowed eyes indicated suspicion. "I hope you like cream cheese."

Joey's stomach rumbled. Suppressing his urge to run, he took the bag and peered inside it.

"There's cinnamon, blueberry, and pretzel," Lewis said.

Joey withdrew the cinnamon raisin. Cream cheese oozed from between the two halves.

Marek hooked his foot around the leg of the closest stool and dragged it from beneath the overhang of the countertop. "Sit. Eat."

Joey eased around the bar stool and perched on the edge of the wooden seat, keeping both feet on the floor.

Marek turned to the table near the French doors, where he'd dropped his messenger bag along with the black and green snowboarding jacket. He removed his navy peacoat and hung it over the back of a chair. He picked up the green jacket and tossed it to Joey. "Here."

Joey dropped the bagel on the counter and caught the coat with both hands. He smoothed his hand over the nylon and then picked at a smear of cream cheese on the cuff.

"I'm sorry Greg's been bullying you at school."

Joey shrugged.

Detective Marek stepped around the peninsula and filled the coffee maker with water. "Luke watched out for you, didn't he?"

What was there to say? They both knew it was true. Without his best friend, the teasing and bullying in school since September had gotten worse. Whispered accusations and speculation about Luke's death hadn't helped.

Joey slid off the bar stool. "I'm going to go put this away."

"Hold up a minute."

Detective Marek disappeared into the laundry room and returned a moment later with an orange and white box bearing the logo of a local office supply store. "Here."

Stepping forward, Joey grabbed it with both hands.

"My old laptop. The power cord is in there. And a mouse, too."

"Thanks." After backing up a few steps, Joey whirled around, hurried to the front of the house, and then climbed the stairs.

In the guest room, he set the box and coat on the writing desk and changed into dry socks. Unsure where to put the wet ones, he hung them over a plastic hanger in the closet. Because he couldn't resist, he put on his new coat.

On the inside of the closet door hung a mirror. Joey stepped in front of the glass to see how he looked.

The black and neon green color combination was so cool he couldn't help smiling. Maybe he could learn to snowboard. After all it didn't seem much different from skateboarding.

Kyle had taught Joey the basics of skateboarding. He once dreamed of competing in the X-Games, but Luke had needed money so Joey sold his skateboards. He would never have been good enough for competition, anyway.

He pulled up the zipper and closed over the Velcro flap. Stale cigarette smoke lingered in the nylon fabric. His nose wrinkled. Maybe hanging it outside for a while would restore that new smell.

He smoothed his hands down the front and slipped them into the side pockets. The fingers of his left hand brushed what felt like a money clip filled with bills.

He pulled out a gold clip and flipped through a mixture of twenties, tens, and fives. A quick count revealed five hundred and fifty dollars.

Why would Greg bring this much money to school? Before the fight over the coat, Roger Wade had passed Greg something. Was this it? Was this part of the money Pierson Mott wanted from Nate? Yesterday was Friday. Why hadn't Greg given this to Nate? What had Mott said to Nate last night at the gas station?

He stuffed the money clip back in the pocket. As he did his fingers brushed the small and rectangular shape of a flash drive.

He pulled it out, curious as to what Greg had saved. He doubted the guy kept copies of history papers and English essays. He curled his fingers around the inch-long red plastic. More than likely it was just porn.

Walking over to the bed, he grabbed his backpack. He unzipped the inside pocket and felt around for the blue thumb drive he'd found taped behind Luke's dresser. Where did it go? Maybe when he'd dropped it in the plastic bag, it had missed the pocket and fallen to the bottom.

He dropped Greg's red thumb drive on the bed so he could get a better hold of the backpack. He tugged open the zipper as wide as possible. His hand groped around the bottom, sliding under his photo albums and the spiral notebook.

He paused and stared at his drawing of the gun, at the lines of the barrel and grip. Somehow the image seemed far more ominous today than it had last night.

Why was he seeing these things? What was happening to him? His fingers resumed their search and brushed over Luke's thumb drive.

Grabbing it, he stepped over to the desk, set the box on the floor, took out the laptop, and turned it on. While the computer warmed up, he unzipped the jacket.

Hopefully, there was something important on that thumb drive that Luke wanted him to find. The low murmurs of Marek and Lewis drifted up from downstairs, but Joey couldn't make out their words.

He pushed the drive into the USB port and clicked through to the first file. Names of MMA fighters were listed down the side of a spread sheet, with their ages, weights, dates, and injuries across the page. There were lists of fights, the favorite to win, their odds, who won the fight and how, whether by knockout, by submitting his opponent, or by decision.

Luke had tried to explain once how the wins and losses were calculated based on the little plus and minus numbers listed for each fighter's match and how to convert those numbers to percentages. Although it made some sense the way Luke explained it, Joey had never really understood.

The next file listed fights with the winners and losers and the amount of money Luke had bet on each match. Scrolling down, there were earlier entries from nearly two years before. The bets were small and infrequent. Gradually, they became more numerous, until last January when Joey moved in next door and Luke began betting larger amounts of money on several fights at a time.

While Luke had never come right out and said anything, Joey suspected that Luke and other kids at school gave a little extra juice to Nate Kelly to place their bets.

Was Pierson Mott, the man Nate and Greg met with at the underpass, a bookie or a loan shark?

Between that conversation and the money Nate had given Mott from recent football games, it was a good guess that Nate collected for Mott.

Greg might be a bully, but from the way Mott delivered a punch there was far more to the man whom Marek claimed was an accountant.

Luke had never told Joey who his bookie was or who he paid when he lost a bet. It hadn't been hard to figure out that Nate was involved. Luke had worked parttime at the same convenience store with Nate.

Had Luke owed Nate more money than he could pay? Had he stolen his father's gun and given it to Nate to pay what he owed? Had he pawned the gun along with the watch? No. Luke would never have done either one of those things. Not with a gun.

Joey was grasping at straws, struggling to make sense of things.

Was Marek's stolen gun the murder weapon? Would Nate kill someone who owed him money? Had Nate tried to scare Luke and gone too far?

No. Luke hadn't been scared or upset that day. At least not until he and Joey had gotten into it. And Luke had been shot in the back.

Mott had said something about the nosey neighbor cop. Did he think Luke had told his dad about the gambling? Had Mott killed Luke?

A shiver ran up Joey's spine, causing goosebumps to race up his arms. He shoved his hands in his pockets and hunched his shoulders inside the jacket.

Maybe Investigator Kraus should be looking at Pierson Mott.

Did Marek suspect the same thing? Is that why he questioned Joey last night about Mott?

Joey closed out of Luke's files and pulled out the flash drive. There was nothing on it that Joey hadn't already known. Why did Luke want him to find it? What was he trying to tell him?

Curious to see Greg's files, Joey walked over to the bed. He tossed Luke's flash drive into the backpack and grabbed the red flash drive off the comforter.

The first file to pop up on the computer screen showed a spreadsheet with a list of jumbled letters running down the far-left column. Moving to the right, additional columns listed dates and numbers with plus and minus symbols.

Scrolling down a few lines, he realized NWRB was just Brown spelled backward without the letter O. Some names he could guess. Others he couldn't. He thought he recognized what might have been the names of a few guys from school. He continued down the list and stopped.

KSLWK.

His heart skipped a beat, leaving a knot inside his chest.

What the hell? He had never placed a bet with Nate. He read through the dates and scrolled back to the top.

The data in this file only went back as far as the first of January, the week after Joey moved in with Frank and Lorraine. The earliest bet he supposedly made was placed on the fifth, right after he and Luke met. The bets continued until the week before Luke's body was found. It listed a MMA fighter, coded in the same backward, vowel-less way, placed to win by submission with two hundred dollars still owed on the loss.

He scrolled up and down the page. Nowhere did he see the letters KRM. There were even bets Joey had supposedly made on basketball and football games.

Staring at the screen Joey shook his head, his heart trying to deny what his eyes told him was true. No. He and Luke were best friends. Best friends didn't betray each other.

Pressure swelled behind his breastbone making it hard to breathe.

He'd only known Luke Marek for nine months before he died. Maybe Joey had been so desperate to belong that he'd only imagined they were best friends.

Tears burned his eyes. The whole time Joey had been selling off his stuff to protect Luke, Luke had been using Joey to protect himself.

Luke had never been his friend.

He smacked the lid of the laptop closed, yanked out the thumb drive and tossed it on the desk. It slid across the surface and fell off the back edge. Ignoring it, Joey shoved back the chair and stood. He paced to the window.

Large flakes of snow drifted down from the gray sky.

Was Marek also only using him? What did he expect in return for his generosity? A confession? Maybe the price tag Marek attached to this new jacket was just too high.

Heavy footsteps ascended the stairs. Down the hall, the door of Marek's room clicked open.

If life had taught Joey anything, it was that no one could be trusted.

The quick, double-tap of knuckles against the door frame sounded behind him.

"Joe?"

He swiped at his eyes with the heel of his hand and turned.

Marek stood in the doorway. From his right hand hung a flat, black plastic case, thicker and a little smaller than a laptop.

"Come on down for a minute. I want to show you something." He nodded toward the stairs.

Joey blinked hoping the stupid tears didn't show. He might as well go. Marek was like a dog with a bone when he wanted something.

"Cold?" he asked as Joey passed by.

Ignoring him, he shoved his hands back in the pockets of the jacket and headed down the stairs.

Lewis glanced up as Joey entered the kitchen. He searched Joey's face, his gaze perceptive but not as sharp as Marek's.

Joey moved up to the bar stool he'd sat on earlier and waited as Marek stepped around the peninsula and set the case on the granite countertop.

"You didn't finish your bagel. Come on. Join us."

"Not hungry."

"You need to eat, Joe. You're too thin."

For a moment, he wanted to believe Marek's concern was genuine. Guilt pricked at his conscience.

He shrugged and stepped closer to the counter, where the cinnamon raisin bagel waited for him.

Marek's cell phone buzzed, and he wandered into the laundry room to take the call.

"So how long are you staying here with Will?" Lewis asked from the stool next to the wall where Marek always sat. He raised a mug of coffee and took a sip.

Joey shrugged.

"I understand you and Luke were pretty good friends." His lips pressed together in a flat line. His gaze fixed on Joey, like a cat staring at a mouse, waiting for the precise moment to pounce. Better men than Detective Lewis had tried to get Joey to talk and failed. "It's good you cared about him. I know Will worried, especially after Aimee died."

Joey nipped off a small piece of the bagel, taking his time to chew the doughy bread.

Lewis set down his cup and leaned back, crossing his arms over his chest. "Yup, you and Luke were like partners. You had each other's backs. So how do you know Pierson Mott?"

Did all cops automatically fall into interrogation mode? Offer the suspect coffee and doughnuts, pretend to be a friend, and then transform from Doctor Jekyll to Mr. Hyde.

Lewis could ask questions all morning. Joey would ignore every single one. Over the years he'd gotten good at it. Selective mutism caused by survivor's guilt, one psychologist labeled it. Avoidance said another.

Joey didn't care. Say nothing at school. Eventually the other kids would leave him alone. Say nothing to Dr. Mercer Let's-Talk-About-Feelings. Eventually they'd send him to a new doctor, a new town, a new placement. Eventually, they'd all quit asking.

Marek returned and slid his phone into his pocket. As he adjusted the hem of his flannel shirt, a part of the black, textured grip of his service pistol was revealed.

Joey gulped. The memory of that barrel pointed straight at his chest remained vivid in his mind.

"That was the chief," Marek reported. "He said an Agent Martinez from the FBI office in Philadelphia wants us to turn all our evidence in the gambling case over to them."

"What?" Lewis looked confused. "What the hell for?"

"Don't know. Chief only said our case overlaps with something the state police and FBI are working on."

"In Philly? Wonder what that's about?"

Marek shrugged. "I only just started looking into who Mott might be connected to."

"Hmmm. What do you think? Mob? Money laundering?"

"Could be. I'd be curious to find out." Marek reached past Joey and pulled the black plastic case across the counter.

A tingling sensation raced through Joey's muscles, urging him to run. He crossed his arms over his stomach, hugging himself, his fingertips digging into the thickness of the coat.

The box looked newer than the one Luke had taken from his dad's closet and shown to Joey, but it didn't matter.

Marek slid his index finger into a niche in the front. A tiny green light activated. He lifted the side latches and flipped back the cover.

The contents were the same.

"Joe, I think the best way to get over your fear of guns is to learn how to use one."

* * * * *

CHAPTER 12

DETECTIVE Lewis leaned close. "Hmm. M11 A1."

"Yeah, I just got it."

"Pretty nice safe, too."

"Yeah. After the last one was stolen, I wanted something no one could break into. This one has biometric vein recognition."

Joey eased off the barstool, keeping the stool between himself and the counter where the box sat.

Lewis grinned and nodded. "Have you fired it?"

Joey eased back a step.

Marek shook his head and lifted out the gun. "Not yet."

"I wonder how it compares to the Glock."

Joey withdrew another step.

"I'm guessing accuracy is about the same." There was a soft click and the magazine dropped from the bottom of the grip.

"Yeah, but it's not a striker fire."

Marek shrugged. "You know I'm old school. Hammer fire. Full metal construction." He set the magazine on the counter. With another two clicks, he moved the slide back and forward to disassemble the weapon. Marek looked up. "Joe, c'mere."

"It's cool," Joey mumbled and slid his foot back another step.

A few clicks later the gun was reassembled. "And then you insert your loaded clip." Marek pushed the empty magazine up through the bottom of the grip with his open palm. "See, Joe. It's easy."

Detective Lewis nodded. "How easy is it for a lefty like me?"

Marek passed him the gun.

Lewis curled his fingers around the grip. Pointing the barrel at the floor, he tilted it left and right. With a grin, he raised the weapon with both hands and focused on something outside beyond the deck.

"Everything's on the right, but you can manipulate the slide with either hand." Marek looked up, locking his gaze with Joey's.

Joey froze mid-retreat.

A brief frown furrowed Marek's brow. Stepping around the end of the peninsula, he accepted the gun from Lewis.

"The way you reacted last night and this morning—" Marek paused. "I don't want to see that look on your face anymore." With the barrel pointed down, Marek held out the gun. "Here."

Joey leaned back and inched his foot toward the basement.

"Go on," Marek said. "Get a feel for it."

Joey shook his head, clenching his fingers into fists. "That's okay. I saw how it worked."

"It's not loaded. Although you always want to treat a gun as if it is."

Pulse thudding against the back of his jaw, Joey forced his hand to open. He tried to swallow as he reached for the gun's grip, but all the moisture in his mouth vanished, as if he'd ingested a spoonful of sand.

With his fingertips a few inches from Marek's hand, Joey jerked back, pressing his elbows against his sides, squeezing his fingers together at his waist.

"I know you're scared, Joe, but it's okay."

Red and blue lights bounced off the walls of their bedroom. Someone pounded on the front door. Where was Charlie? He should be barking. Joey wanted to get up and see what was going on, but he couldn't make his body move. All he could do was stare.

Across the space between their beds, Kyle looked like he was sleeping, his face turned toward Joey, his eyes closed, his arm tucked under his pillow.

Except for the blood.

It looked like old motor oil in the dark, but smelled warm and coppery. It spread from beneath Kyle's chest over the edge of the mattress onto the carpet. Joey could feel his own blood doing the same, seeping from his body, warming him as he shivered with cold.

"Come on," Marek urged. "I won't let you get hurt. But you need to get past this."

Did the man ever quit? Joey blew out a long breath. He reached out again, his fingers trembling as they stretched toward the weapon.

Marek stepped closer. "Trust me."

Joey yanked his hand back. For a moment, he almost believed Marek was sincere in his desire to help him get over his fear of guns. Now, doubt overshadowed his foolish desire to believe.

Marek was a cop. He was good at luring suspects into his web of friendship, getting them to trust him, tripping them up so they'd give out information.

Is that what was going on? Did Marek think Joey's fear was a ruse? Was he pushing him to reveal some hidden proficiency?

Well, Joey didn't have to pretend. Acid already churned inside his stomach.

"It's okay, Joe. Take it."

He swallowed. Hand trembling, he reached out. His fingers wrapped around the textured grip as Marek let go.

And there it was. Solid and heavy in his hand. His nostrils flared. The scent of steel and oil blended with the smell of his own fear, wafting through his senses with each reluctant intake of breath.

Marek's penetrating gaze searched every nuance of Joey's expression, as though seeking an explanation for a fear Joey didn't understand.

Except for the day Luke had made him hold his father's gun, Joey had never held a pistol. Or had he? He shifted uncomfortably.

No. The only reason this gun's weight and textured grip felt familiar against his palm was because he'd held Marek's other gun which was similar to this one.

"Come on. My dad won't care if I show it to you."

They'd gone into Marek's bedroom, into the closet. Luke pulled the black case down from the top shelf, punched in a code, and lifted out the handgun.

"It's a Sig Sauer P220. Here take it."

Joey had refused at first, but Luke had been as insistent as his father was now. However, the sight of bullets in the magazine that day had triggered a flash of pain through his leg and intense pressure in his chest that had squeezed all the air from his lungs. His stomach had pitched violently. He'd tossed the gun and magazine onto the bed and bolted from the room.

Two weeks later Marek reported the weapon stolen.

"...Planning to shoot."

Shoot? Joey's attention snapped back to the present. How long had Marek been talking to him?

"I said, never, I mean never, point it at anyone unless you're planning to shoot."

The blood drained from Joey's face, leaving him cold and clammy. *No!* He'd never shot a gun and had no intention to shoot one now. Unless. *No. Don't think about it. It's not true.* Exhaling a shaky breath, he tried to pass the weapon to Marek.

Marek shook his head. "Hold it for a minute. Two hands."

Shoulders slumped, he did as Marek asked, keeping the barrel pointed down. The doughy bite of bagel he'd eaten bounced around in his stomach like a super ball. His head pounded. He shifted his weight from one foot to the other. His back hurt.

"That's right. Keep your thumbs up and your finger alongside the barrel. Always treat your gun as if it were loaded and keep your finger off the trigger until you're ready to pull it."

He gestured toward the French doors by the kitchen table. "Come over here. You can dry fire on a target outside."

"After you insert the magazine, pull back the slide to load the first round in the chamber. This gun is a double action, single action, which means with the first shot the hammer is set, and then you can fire." He pointed outside. "Try aiming on that bird feeder by the fence."

Joey shivered and stepped up beside Marek. Taking a deep breath, he raised the gun.

"Good. Extend your arms a little more."

Joey tried again. How long was Marek going to make him raise, site, and lower the weapon?

"That's pretty good, Joe. Maybe this week we can go out to the gun range, and you can actually shoot it."

Shoot it?

Saliva pooled around his tongue. Bile swelled and pitched against the walls of his stomach. His balance wavered as if he'd just stepped off one of those carnival rides that spin around and upside down.

"Can I be excused?" Joey shoved the gun at Marek.

Whirling around, he dashed past Lewis and headed for the half-bath off the laundry room. There wasn't much in his stomach to come up, but he dry-heaved several more times. Drained and shaky, he flushed the toilet and slid to the floor, waiting for his racing heart to slow.

"Are you okay in there?" Marek gave the partially closed door a cursory knock and then nudged it inward.

Joey pushed to his feet, ignoring Marek's outstretched hand. He turned on the cold water and scooped up a handful to rinse his mouth.

Raising his gaze to the mirror, he caught Marek watching him, his expression pensive. Joey turned to leave the room, wiping his hand on his jeans as he waited for Marek to step back.

"You, okay?"

"Yeah," Joey answered. "Just don't like guns."

"Seems to me, you're more afraid of yourself than you are of the gun."

Marek's words slammed into his sore stomach with the accuracy of a well-placed punch, knocking Joey's breath from his lungs.

He eased around Marek and dashed through the kitchen past Detective Lewis who leaned against the counter. He headed up the stairs and into refuge of the guest room.

He paced to the window. Thick snowflakes fell from the sky nearly obscuring the trees across the road. Rubbing his hands over his coat sleeves couldn't erase the chill that shivered deep inside him, any more than it could erase the feel of that grip against his palms.

Swinging around, the closet beckoned. Unable to stop himself, he headed into its sanctuary. He slid to the floor and pulled the door closed, enveloping himself in darkness.

His good leg drawn up close to his body, he wrapped his arms around his shivering stomach. His trembling fingers ached to grip the hilt of his knife, even as he wished he could stop being scared all the time.

Trust me, Marek had said. More than anything Joey longed to tell Marek of this terror that chilled him to the marrow of his bones, to cling to the solace of Luke's father with the same urgency that compelled him to cling to his knife.

He resisted. If he didn't think about what frightened him, he could pretend it wasn't true. Saying it out loud would make it real. If Marek learned of it, whatever faith he did have in Joey might shrivel into hate.

Joey shoved his demon back into the deepest recesses of his soul and tried to pretend it didn't exist.

The low timbre of male voices drifted up the stairs. The rapid, shorter sentences exchanged between the men sounded like an argument. Though they had tempered the volume of their voices, making it hard to understand their words, the rough tone of Marek's hushed tones was easy to discern. Lewis grew insistent, as Marek turned abrupt and defensive.

Pressing his forehead against his up-drawn knee, Joey wrapped his arms around his shin and squeezed his wrists tight.

For a moment he felt his brother Kyle's arm around his shoulder, hugging him close as they huddled together in the closet of their bedroom. Down the hall, their parents argued.

* * *

"I can't do this anymore," his mother cried.

"I'll get another job."

"When? In the spring when people start spending again? Or the summer when the seasonal jobs open up? Or this fall when businesses start hiring for the holidays?"

"You make it sound like I'm not trying. It's hard. No one wants to hire someone my age."

"I'm tired, Paul. With what I make I can barely keep up with the utilities and putting food on the table. We're six months behind on the mortgage, and we haven't paid our taxes in two years."

"It's not my fault unemployment ran out."

"I know that, but we can't live like this anymore. We have to sell the house. Until

then, I'm taking the boys and going to my sister's."

"You can't do that. You promised we'd stay together. Things will work out as long as we're together."

"God, Paul. It was almost a year ago when I said that. It's not realistic. The boys deserve more. I deserve more."

"No, I won't let you. We stay together no matter what. I'll find a way. You'll see."

* * *

"Joe? Where are you?"

The closet hinge creaked. Daylight filled the space.

Joey lifted his head.

Marek stood looking down at him, his blue eyes wide, his face pale. He opened his mouth as if to say something, but instead rubbed his hand around the back of his neck.

He shook his head. "I'm—" His voice cracked. He cleared his throat. "I'm sorry. I didn't think."

Cody shoved his way into the space, his nose cold and wet as he pushed against Joey's face and neck.

Joey rolled to his feet as Marek stepped back, leaving room for Joey to move into the room.

He headed straight to the window. A snowplow rumbled past the house. Its yellow light flashed through the cloud of white kicked up from the wing plow.

Footsteps ascended the stairs. A moment later someone entered the room.

"The kid okay?" Lewis asked.

A palpable silence descended. Snow continued to fall, adding inches to the piles of white that coated skeletal tree branches and bowed the pines across the road.

Joey envisioned Marek and Lewis standing on the other side of the room, communicating through nods and shrugs about the crazy kid who hid in closets and freaked when he saw a gun.

Marek came up behind him.

Drawing a deep breath, Joey turned.

Marek's attention was on the bed, on Joey's open backpack and the notebook open to the drawing of the gun he'd made from his vision in the tile floor.

Dread hung on Joey, heavy and weighted, as if he carried his backpack stuffed with every book from his locker. His neck stiffened. His back hurt.

Marek stepped closer to the bed and with his forefinger lifted the flap of the backpack wider, making the drawing visible. He faced Joey. "What's this?" His closed off, cop expression masked any emotion in his face.

Joey dropped his gaze to the blue and cream Oriental rug beneath his feet, hoping somehow one of circles would open up and swallow him, suck him into a swirling vortex of fog, and transport him into another time, another place.

"Hey, Will, what do you got there?" Lewis moved closer to the bed, closer to the drawing. "That sort of looks like your old Sig." His eyes widened. His intense gaze locked with Marek's.

Marek slowly nodded. He turned his attention to Joey. "Do you want to explain this?"

A lump rose up the back of Joey's throat. He shouldn't be ashamed. He wasn't guilty of anything. Was he?

He glanced toward the open door and the hallway beyond. Escape taunted him.

Marek patiently waited as though he knew silence and time would be enough persuasion.

Joey rubbed his hands down the sides of his jeans and swallowed.

Waiting out Marek wasn't as easy as waiting out Investigator Kraus or Doctor Mercer Tell-Me-How-You-Feel-About-This.

It sucks.

Marek had fixed those forceful blue eyes on Joey and wasn't backing down.

"You won't believe me."

"Try me."

"It's weird."

"So?"

"I mean really out there, but nothing else makes sense."

"Just say it."

Joey drew a deep breath. "Luke told me what to draw."

From the corner of the bed, Lewis choked on a laugh.

Marek said nothing but went still and pale. He stepped closer to Joey. "I thought there was enough between us that you could trust me. I want the truth."

"It is." Joey's pulse pounded against the back of his jaw. He shouldn't have said anything. The tenuous relationship between them was now in jeopardy. "It's like Luke gets in my head. I hear his voice. I see what he saw."

Marek drew closer, stopping right in front of Joey. "Tell. Me. The. Truth. Not some sci-fi, paranormal bullshit."

Each word filled Joey's ear with a huff of breath that sent a shiver through his body.

"Were you there? Did you see him die?" His arms crossed, his face expressionless, Marek was as intimidating as any bad ass cop in the movies, except for the flicker of pain in his overly bright eyes.

"I'm not lying," Joey persisted. "Luke gets in my head. I see things he saw. I hear his voice, but it doesn't happen all the time. Just sometimes. Just whenever I wear the jacket."

The realization slammed into him at that moment. He could no longer avoid the truth. It *did* only happen when he wore the jacket. Marek's old denim jacket with the band patches, the jacket Luke loved to wear, the jacket that appeared mysteriously and compelled Joey to slide his arms into the sleeves and savor its warmth.

Joey dropped his gaze to the carpet, to Marek's sock-clad feet. Those feet turned and moved from sight. He should have kept his mouth shut. Why had he dared to hope Marek would believe him?

"Is that my watch?" Marek's voice choked out, his words low and raspy.

Joey's head jerked up.

Marek stood beside the bed, staring into the open backpack. All color had drained from his face. With wide eyes he ran his hand over his face and then around the back of his neck. In silence he shook his head.

Betrayal.

The emotion twisting Marek's expression was too raw for Joey to deny it as genuine. And Joey didn't know how to deny it because it was true.

Lewis stepped up beside Marek. He stared at the notebook, visible in the open bag. "Shit. This don't look good."

When Marek said nothing, Lewis continued. "We got to call that trooper investigating Luke's—This is evidence."

Marek and Joey stared at each other. The silent question in Marek's eyes hung ominous in the air between them. *Why?*

Joey's heart rate accelerated. His pulse beat wildly against the back of his jaw. Unable to maintain eye contact he dropped his gaze to Cody who lay on the floor ripping the green fuzz off a tennis ball.

"You were a guest in our house," Marek whispered. "You went into my room, rifled through my personal things, and took something very special to me."

Cody released the ball. It rolled from between his paws across the rug and stopped at Joey's feet.

"Did you take my gun, too?"

Joey rested his foot on top of the neon green orb and rolled it back and forth on the carpet.

Cody whined.

Joey's stomach slowly twisted into a painful knot.

What good would it do to deny any of it, or tell Marek that Luke had stolen the watch? Joey could have returned it months ago, just sucked it up, knocked on Marek's front door and let him believe Joey was a thief.

He should have told Marek last night about the blue thumb drive, told Kraus about Luke's gambling, but he'd stupidly been trying to protect Luke.

Now there was no hiding it, for all Luke's secrets lay spilled beside his jacket.

* * * * *

CHAPTER 13

JOEY continued to roll the ball back and forth. He wasn't sure what he waited for. For Marek to blame him for everything that had gone wrong in the world, gone wrong with Luke?

Maybe Marek would just wash his hands of Joey Kowalski forever.

Maybe, just maybe if he explained that Luke was the one who had stolen his father's things, after the shock wore off Marek would realize Joey was telling the truth and would still believe in him.

"Have you been gambling?" Marek demanded.

Joey flinched but couldn't bring himself to look up and see the condemnation in Marek's eyes.

"Is that where all your bruises came from? Can't pay up? So, you've been stealing? Do you know Lewis and I've been investigating a complaint of underage gambling at the high school for the past few days? Is that why you're suddenly hanging around my place? Spying on me for Nate Kelly? And why were you hiding from Pierson Mott last night?"

Joey's foot rolled off the ball and Cody snatched up the toy.

"Look at me, damn it!"

Joey swallowed. His heart pounded.

"Here I make an ass of myself going over there this morning, demanding Greg give me that coat when you probably gave it to Kelly for payment on money you owed him. Now tell me the truth."

Three angry strides brought Marek back to Joey's side.

Please believe me, he silently prayed. He took a breath.

"It was Luke," Joey whispered to the carpet.

"Bullshit!" A puff of coffee scented breath drove the angry word straight into Joey's ear, fluttering the hair at his temple.

Joey's gaze shot to Marek's face in time to see tears fill his eyes just before he turned away.

I'm sorry, he wanted to say, but the words stuck fast. He blinked against the burn in his own eyes.

The bedroom door stood wide open, beckoning him toward the hallway and the stairs beyond. Of their own volition, his feet eased his body in the direction of the opening.

From the periphery of his vision, a figure moved toward him.

"Hold up, kid," Lewis called. "We need to talk to you."

Talk and take him to jail. No way. He'd been stupid to cling to the hope that Marek might believe him. Joey bolted.

Lewis lunged toward him. Cody, racing to get ahead of Joey, charged right into Lewis' path.

Cody yelped. From the corner of his eye, Joey saw Lewis go down with a thud. A string of curses flew from his mouth.

"Joe!" Marek called.

Joey rounded the banister at the top of the stairs.

Cody charged past with the green ball in his mouth, reaching the bottom moments before Joey.

"Stop!"

Joey whirled around to see Lewis on his way down. Joey grabbed the ball from Cody's mouth and threw it toward the top of the stairs. Without waiting to see what happened next, he dashed for the laundry room.

"What the—" echoed from the foyer behind him. It was followed by a loud thud accompanied by a single, loudly expressed curse word. Lewis must have fallen, either on the tennis ball or over the dog.

"Damn it, Joe," Marek yelled. "I want to talk to you!"

Joey shoved his feet into his lace boots without bothering to tie them. He yanked open the door to the garage. On the landing, he hit the button for the automatic opener and made his escape before the door had clattered all the way to the top.

He ran down the driveway, expecting Marek or Detective Lewis to come through the front door and chase him down like cops on TV.

Instead, except for the pounding of his heart, the world was quiet. Heavy snow fell from a steel gray sky. A pick-up truck passed, as Joey turned onto the road. He zipped the coat all the way to his chin and shoved his hands in his pockets.

Halfway back to Frank and Lorraine's, he jumped across the ditch and ducked through the sagging barb wire fence of the empty cow pasture. Keeping out of sight, he skirted the edge of the pasture where most of the bushes grew and snow lay the deepest.

A cardinal, perched on the thin branch of a boney tree, took off. It darted low, a streak of red just above the surface of white, and was quickly lost in the swirling snow.

Though he kept his ears tuned for the sounds of pursuit, he only heard the hollow crunch of his own footfalls punching through a layer of ice-encrusted snow.

When he reached the place where the train tracks bordered the back of the pasture, he stopped and tied up his boots. Removing his coat, he hung it on a fence post. He ducked through the fence, pushing down on the tighter strand of wire. One of the barbs snagged on his shirt. He rolled his shoulders. When that didn't work, he reached back and tugged the wire from the flannel.

He winced as the top of the barb cut the meaty part of his thumb. He pressed the wound to his mouth and sucked on it for a moment. When the bleeding slowed, he put on his coat. With his opposite hand he pushed through a leafless tangle of brush before climbing the steep gravel bank to the railroad tracks.

He paused to catch his breath and check his thumb. It stung, but the bleeding had almost stopped. Shoving it into the coat pocket he brushed flakes of snow from his wet hair. He should have brought a hat.

For a moment he considered heading east. There was an old railroad maintenance shack on the State Game Lands where some kids went to drink, make-out, or get high. He could hold up there and figure out what to do next.

No. The shack was too close to the trestle bridge.

He walked west instead, away from the possibility of being haunted by more images of Luke's death. However, he wasn't wearing Luke's jacket. If he was right, that meant no visions.

Part of him wished he had the jacket. For some reason it always kept him warm.

He matched his stride to the spacing of the railroad ties. When he reached the place where the tracks crossed over the creek, where he and Luke used to fish, he stepped quickly. If he paused to look down, that falling sensation might return.

He kept walking. Marek hated him now.

Why had Luke been gambling under Joey's name? Everything Joey had done had been to protect Luke. Had Luke just been using him? He had used Luke, doing whatever it took to buy his friendship?

A thick squall of snow engulfed him and obscured the overpass where Nate Kelly and Pierson Mott had grabbed him the other day. He stuck to the main rail line that bypassed town, instead of following the spur toward the feed mill and the grain elevators rising in the distance.

Go back a tiny voice whispered in his ear like a cartoon angel hovering over his shoulder.

Giant snowflakes swirled around him like a shroud. If he kept walking maybe he would disappear into nothingness.

Nobody wants you, the devil on his opposite shoulder reminded.

The wind picked up, and he shivered. Snow stung his face. His nose and cheekbones felt numb. He kept his head down to block the wind. Falling snow blurred the edges of the railroad ties. After stumbling a few times and nearly falling once, he slowed his pace and forged on through the sludge.

Vibration radiated up his legs through the heavy soles of his shoes. Jarred from his daze, he stopped and blinked. A circle of light backlit the heavy curtain of snow. The accompanying rumble grew louder as the bright circle widened.

He glanced around for the easiest place to scramble down the steep bank, but no place looked easier than the other. He hopped off the edge of the railroad tie. The thick heels of his boots dug deep through the snow into the gravel, slowing him as he half-jumped, half-skidded down the short slope.

"What about Luke?" the angel persisted. *"You have to help his dad figure out who killed him*."

The engine roar grew louder. Discarded railroad ties piled near a scrawny tree lured him with a chance to sit and rest. He brushed snow from one of the weathered timbers. As he sat, he shoved icy hands deep into the corners of his coat pockets.

"Why?" the devil argued.

Three massive blue and yellow locomotives charged past, the heavy wheels clicking a rapid tempo over the iron rails.

Cold seeped into Joey's tailbone sometime after the seventy-eighth car. Lightheaded, he looked away as the steel boxes clattered monotonously down the tracks.

"Why do you think Luke is haunting you?" the devil continued. *"What did you really do that day?"*

Shivering, he sniffed his runny nose, drawing the numbing air down the back of his dry throat. The last car faded into the eastern horizon.

Joey rose and hauled himself up the steep bank, his cold fingers digging into snow and loose rock as he climbed.

He checked his thumb, manipulating the skin to see how deep the three-corner cut actually was. He probably should have a large band aid, but the cold seemed to keep it from bleeding.

His stomach rumbled a demand for food, but he ignored it just as he ignored the sting in his hand, his wet shivering head, and the growing pain in his leg as he mindlessly put one foot in front of the other, stepping from one oblong railroad tie to the next.

The wind picked up as daylight faded.

Joey's shadow stretched long across the snowy ground to tangle with those cast by barren tree branches.

He no longer knew where he was and didn't care. He shoved his hands deep into his pockets and kept walking.

He limped past a white metal sign with black letters and numbers. Luke used to walk the tracks a lot. Though he had once explained what the numbers meant, all Joey cared about was the chance of a sidetrack ahead. Uneasy with the thought of spending the night swallowed by the pitch black of night, he hoped the sidetrack would lead to a town. He had Greg's money in his pocket. He could find someplace warm and maybe get something to eat.

What would have taken minutes for the train to reach took Joey until past dark. Teeth chattering, he left the main tracks behind. He swiped his nose and stumbled along. Dark woods shrouded the tracks on either side, so that the slate gray snow became the only illumination. The sidetrack branched off into even more tracks, stretching five wide as the loud discordant pounding of several machines echoed through the night air.

Ahead loomed the boxy silhouettes of four massive buildings. Yellow light spilled from transom windows along the snowy ridgelines of the brick and metal structures.

Near the end of one building were piled massive iron bars, their ends jutting from beneath a thick snowy blanket. Teeth chattering, he left the tracks behind. He limped around the snowy pile, bluish gray under the brilliant glare of a security light which hung from the corner of the nearest building.

Pick-up trucks and cars lined up in six rows across a large open lot lit with streetlights as bright as day. A tall chain link fence, with barbed wire strung across its angled top, enclosed the perimeter.

Hoping to find a quiet place to at least get warm and think, he followed the length of a long gray corrugated metal building hoping for a way inside. His wet hair and jeans, damp from the knees down, had leached his body heat so slowly he hadn't realized his toes had gone numb until now.

"Hey, you!"

Joey whirled toward the voice and blinked, raising the back of his hand to his eyes against the glare of a brilliant white orb.

"Who are you? What are you doing here?"

The circle of light widened, growing brighter as the man moved closer.

For just an instant it crossed Joey's mind to run, but his body couldn't summon the energy.

"You got some ID?"

Joey kept his gaze focus down, away from the painful glare of the guard's flashlight. "I asked you what you're doing here. This is private property."

He stared at the tops of the man's black combat style boots and his black pants which had been bloused in neat military fashion. From the ankles down, his feet were buried in fresh snow.

"You want to turn around?"

Joey turned, grateful to escape the glare of the flashlight. A gust of wind blew through the area, cutting through his wet hair. He shivered. A wall of white momentarily shrouded the nearby building.

"Hands on head."

He raised his elbows but could seem to summon the energy to lift his hands any higher. Maybe he should say something.

Big hands patted him under the arms around his waist and down his legs.

He could say he'd gotten lost and needed to use the phone. But who was there to call?

The security guard's radio clicked. "I got a trespasser. Some kid. Looks like he walked in on the tracks. Could be one of them that vandalized the place on Sunday night."

Static distorted the response of the garbled voice on the other end.

"Yeah, guess they forgot to close that gate again."

More static.

"Sure. Headin' to you now." Using the beam of the flashlight he pointed the way. "Go ahead, kid," he said.

As Joey moved forward the security guard fell into step behind him.

"You hurt yourself? You got a black eye and you're limping."

Joey wanted to rub his thigh, but his fingers were too numb and once they'd reclaimed the warmth of his pockets, they refused to leave.

"You live around here? Those tracks are a dangerous place to be, train comes through doing sixty mile an hour. All that weight. Engineer can't stop even if he could see you in this storm."

The beam of his flashlight rose from the ground in front of them to illuminate the corner of a small structure of corrugated metal and blue wood trim. "See, next to the gate, that little building with all the windows? That's where we're going."

Joey angled his direction toward the building and the chain-link gate with a stop sign in the middle, like a military checkpoint to Area 51 or the border crossing of an eastern-blocked country.

Inside the brightly lit building another security guard rose and moved to the door. Tufts of gray hair stuck out around his ears like the feathers of hair on the backs of Cody's legs. He pulled the door open when they reached the snow-covered step.

Joey moved inside first. A blast of warmth washed over his face. He shivered and sniffed, bringing his wrist up to swipe at the bottom of his nose. Beside a gray desk chair sat an electric space heater and he eased a few steps closer to its warmth.

The younger guard who'd brought him here, closed the door and stomped off his boots. "Getting bad out there."

"Wonder how the roads are?" The other guard asked, looking through one of the big windows.

"At least it will be getting light by the time we punch out." He set his flashlight on the closest desk. "You got a name, kid?"

When Joey said nothing, the man gestured to the black phone beside a logbook. "You got someone we can call?"

Frank and Lorraine would have to come get him, but they wouldn't want to. After last night he had no desire to speak to them. Likewise, Marek would hardly want to help someone suspected of stealing his watch and murdering his son. He didn't know Marek's number anyway. He'd always called Luke's cell phone.

"You don't answer, I'm going to have to call the cops."

Sure. Why not?

The older guard gestured toward a coffee maker on top of a small refrigerator. "You cold? Want a cup?"

Joey shrugged.

The guard lifted the glass pot from the burner and with his opposite hand picked up a white ceramic mug. He tilted the mug, peered inside, and then filled it with black coffee. "Milk? Sugar?"

Joey inclined his head.

"Yeah, my grandkids don't like it unless it's good and sweet." He poured in a generous amount of powdered creamer and then set down the cup to add four packets of sugar.

Like a mini bucket brigade, he passed the cup to the other guard who passed it on to Joey.

The heat radiating from the mug into his frozen hands was almost better than the anticipation of having that warmth spread through his stomach. He raised the mug close to his face, letting his cheeks absorb the steam as the bittersweet aroma filled his nose.

The first guard dropped his hat on the desk. The top of his shaved head gleamed beneath the overhead florescent light. He unzipped his jacket, which fell open on either side of his belly as he lowered himself into his chair. The fabric of his blue shirt pulled tight against the buttons. He lifted the receiver slowly, keeping his eye on Joey as though waiting for him to speak so he wouldn't have to call.

Finally, he pushed one of the clear buttons along the bottom of the phone and then tapped several numbers on the keypad.

Joey glanced around the cluttered interior of the tiny building. Notices about workman's compensation and employee injury were pinned to the only window-less wall. To the left of them hung a calendar with the photo of a red monster truck, detailed with orange and yellow flames, parked beside a Christmas tree. Below the picture was the name of an auto parts store in Thatcher, a town on the western side of the county.

Had he really walked that far?

"I don't know," the guard said into the receiver.

The older guard pointed to a chair patched with gray duct tape. "You look dead on your feet. Go ahead and sit down."

Joey didn't have to be told twice. Grateful, he swiveled the chair and sat, stretching his aching leg beneath the desk. The coffee was sweeter than he would have liked, but he downed the whole cup and then leaned over the desk and rested his forehead on his crossed arms.

"Could be one of the ones did the vandalism or could just be a runaway. Don't know. He won't talk."

The guard on the phone droned on to someone, but the words that floated through Joey's consciousness sounded like the distorted *wha-wha-wha* of an adult in a kid's cartoon.

Would the cops call Frank? Would Frank call Mary Custer?

Something jostled his shoulder. "Wake up, kid."

He raised his head and blinked.

"Your ride's here."

Joey straightened and turned.

A woman in a State Police uniform stood watching him, her thumbs hooked in her wide utility belt. The black grip of her gun all that was visible of the weapon secured in her holster. The top of her winter hat with its fuzzy ear flaps and turned-up brim was level with the top of the guard's bald head. How long had she been here?

"Can you tell me your name?" Her soft, modulated tones seemed at odds with her stance and the unapproachable authority of her uniform. Gifford, according to her name tag, seemed young. He wondered if she was some kid's mom.

"He don't talk," the gray-haired guard spoke from the other side of the room.

She glanced over her shoulder but kept her attention on Joey.

"Could you stand up please?"

Joey pushed to his feet and massaged his leg, mostly out of habit. It didn't ache any more than the rest of his body.

"Turn around and put your hands on the desk."

Hands splayed on the fake wood surface, he counted overlapping coffee rings beside the keyboard.

Four, no five.

"Are you carrying any weapons I should be aware of? Any drugs?"

He shook his head.

She methodically patted his pockets. She pulled out the money clip with the wad of bills. "Where'd you get this cash?"

What was he supposed to say? My jacket was stolen and when I got it back the money was in the pocket? She probably thought he was selling drugs.

When he said nothing, she continued patting him down: chest, arms, waist, legs, and ankles.

Had she ever shot anyone with her gun?

It was weird to think of a mom who could do that and then go home and hug her kids.

Maybe it was no different for Marek to go home and hug his wife, go home and hug Luke.

After returning the money to his pocket, she moved around behind him. "If you're not going to talk to me, then put your hands behind your back. I'm arresting you for trespassing."

* * * * *

CHAPTER 14

THE fabric of Joey's coat swished, as he shifted his hands to the back of his hips.

Though he knew what was coming next, he flinched when the weight of the first handcuff closed around his wrist. He stared at the floor and the puddle of melted snow under the desk where he'd been sitting.

The second cuff clicked in place.

Now what? *You have the right to remain silent?* Sure. No problem.

Juvenile detention? He should care, but maybe he was just too tired. His brain felt disconnected, as if he were watching it happen to someone else. At least Frank and Lorraine would be happy to be rid of him.

"Have a seat."

He lowered himself back on the chair.

She studied him with a direct assessing gaze. "Are you going to tell me your name and what you're doing here?"

Beyond the window behind her, thick flakes of snow fell, illuminating the security lamps like stars across a back-lit sky.

Heaving a sigh, she pulled out her pad and jotted down the guards' names, the company, a contact name, and a number.

"All right, son, let's go." She gripped his arm above his elbow. The pressure of each finger pressed firmly against his muscle through the thickness of his coat.

"You gentlemen have a good night." She guided Joey to the door and down the step.

The older man chuckled. "No problem. You livened up a boring shift and gave us something to type in the computer log."

"Take care of yourself, kid." The bald guard closed the door behind them.

Trooper Gifford opened the rear door of her SUV cruiser and rested her hand on Joey's head as he slid into the seat. She clicked the seatbelt into place, closed the door, and a moment later slid in behind the wheel. Picking up her radio mic, she called into the station that she was coming in with a juvenile trespasser.

She looped the car around. The gate rolled open to let them pass.

He was riding in a police car for the second time in as many days.

At least the car was warm. He stared through divider, past the computer mounted on the dash, and through the windshield. There wasn't much to see, just the hypnotizing vision of snow flying into the headlight beams and the steady swish-thump of the wipers. Outside his window was nothing more than the monotony of barren trees, and scattered houses glowing with holiday color.

He closed his eyes and dozed, losing track of time until they turned into the parking lot of the state police barracks.

Trooper Gifford guided him from her car to the building, staying right behind him through the side door. They walked down a short hall through another locked door into a brightly lit room. "Hang on. Let me get those cuffs off."

She turned the key and released first one side and then the other. He rolled his shoulders to relieve the stiffness and rubbed his wrists.

She stepped around him and gestured toward a long counter with a few desks on the other side. "Come on over here and empty your pockets."

He dropped Greg's money clip in the plastic bin she set out.

Another officer rose from one of the desks. He tugged up his pants and moved to the corner of the long counter beside a miniature Christmas tree. "Who you got here?"

Her gaze flicked back to Joey. "He hasn't said." Her eyes narrowed with the same disproving glare his mom fixed on him when he and Kyle played video games instead of cleaning their room.

"The security guards at Cooper Industries over in Thatcher found him. A couple of nice guys. They didn't want to press charges, but they've had some recent vandalism and some stolen tools."

Deaver waved Joey close. "C'mere, kid. Time for prints and a photo." The trooper gave his short hair a quick finger comb.

Officer Gifford sat at a nearby desk draped in swags of silver garland and began typing on the computer.

Joey shoved his hands in his pockets. Shouldn't he have a lawyer or something? Be able to make a phone call? He'd seen on TV shows where people refused DNA swabs. Could he refuse to have his fingerprints taken?

"I'll take your coat, too."

Joey remained where he was. Ignoring Trooper Deaver was no harder than ignoring Investigator Kraus.

Deaver frowned, his mouth compressed in a tight line.

"Come on, kid. Might as well get it over with. Tell us your name."

He shrugged out of the coat and passed it over, missing its warmth immediately. "Joey. Joseph Kowalski."

The trooper gestured for Joey to move ahead of him into the room he'd indicated. "Now was that so hard?" Deaver followed close behind and had him stop at a mark on the floor for his photo. "Might as well give me your address and phone number, too."

Joey sighed. He might as well. What did it matter anyway? "It's 1326 Cabbage Hill Road, Easton at 555-5621."

The trooper typed the information into the computer and then told him to look forward.

It was like going to the school office for his student ID, except instead of a generic blue background this one was white and had black lines to indicate his height.

When he finished turning to the side, Deaver gestured him over to the counter, before a small box-shaped machine in front of a computer. He took Joey's hand and pressed his fingers against the back-lit plate of the scanner. Simultaneously, his prints appeared on the monitor.

"Okay," Deaver said when they finished. "Take a seat out there for a minute."

He pointed through the open door to a row of blue molded chairs along the wall, hooked together like a bench, reminding Joey of the seats in the waiting room of Dr. Mercer Wait-'Til-Lorraine-Tells-Him-About-This.

Joey limped over, releasing a long sigh as he sat. He crossed his arms and let his head fall back against the cinderblock wall.

What would happen now? Juvenile detention? One step away from jail. Two steps away from prison. Like father, like son.

Across the room a black and white wall clock read twenty minutes until eight. He stared at it, watching the thin red secondhand tick past each bold, black number. Funny, he'd thought it must have been at least two in the morning.

He ached to find some dark corner, curl up with his knife, and go to sleep.

The lights dimmed for a moment and then blackness engulfed the room. The low hum of the florescent lights fell silent.

For an instant he wondered if he'd conjured the sudden darkness, if Luke was communicating through another vision. Joey stilled, listening.

"Oh, crap." Trooper Gifford muttered.

"Power's out," said an unfamiliar voice.

"No shit, Sherlock," Deaver replied.

"Shut up."

From the area of Gifford's desk, chair rollers grated against the tile floor. "Great," she grumbled. "I probably just lost everything I typed. Where's the back-up generator?"

As if on cue, white fluorescence illuminated the building once more.

The third trooper, his salt and pepper hair cut high and tight, leaned against the counter, a pair of reading glasses slid halfway down his nose. "I knew that would happen tonight."

Deaver snorted. "What? That the power would go out or that it would come back on?" With a shake of his head, he returned to his desk.

"Your psychic abilities are astounding." Trooper Gifford laughed, the sound light and mischievous.

A twinge of pain pricked at Joey's heart. He could no longer remember how his mom sounded when she was happy, when they'd all been happy, before his dad had lost his job.

Gifford chuckled. "Since it happens every time there's a bad storm, we all know a power outage is inevitable."

Maybe that's all his life had been the last six years, a postponement of the inevitable.

*****

CHAPTER 15

"ALL right, boys and girls, back to work." A fourth trooper stood in the doorway of an office. A string of colored lights outlined the windows that divided his space from the larger room.

"My computer is down," Gifford complained.

"Mine, too." Deaver thumped the top of his monitor and gave his mouse a bang.

"Hang on, people," said the man in the doorway. "Do the best you can. I'll see what I can do to get us up and running."

Joey shifted on the hard plastic chair and closed his eyes. Voices hummed around him as people came and went. Deaver said something about calling tech support. Trooper Gifford headed back into the storm. Doors opened and closed. The footfalls of various people thumped and clicked back and forth across the tile floor.

"Kowalski."

Joey jerked upright.

Deaver stood over him. "Your foster parents are here."

He passed over the black and green snowboarding jacket and had Joey sign the receipt for his meager belongings.

Frank stood on the other side of the thick bullet-proof glass. Snow covered his hat and shoulders. The trooper with the graying hair slid some papers under the glass and spoke to Frank in low tones.

Joey rose and followed Deaver, who buzzed him through the door to Frank's side of the room.

"You're being released to your foster parents. You'll get a notice in the mail with the date for your appearance before the juvenile master. Don't miss it and don't be late."

Joey nodded and sidled along the counter, inching closer to Frank.

Frank glanced up. His eyes narrowed as their gazes met. The vein in the center of his forehead bulged, anger oozing from every pore.

Joey looked around the lobby area, half-expecting to see Marek. It was stupid to be disappointed.

He stared at Frank's boots, whose snowy coating melted and vanished into the nylon fibers of the charcoal-gray rug.

Marek probably hated him now anyway.

"So, do you have any questions?" the trooper asked Frank.

"No." Frank turned to Joey. "Get over here and sign what you need to sign. The roads aren't getting any better."

Movement in the front entry caught Joey's attention. Detective Marek filled the space between the two sets of glass doors. He stepped into the small lobby area. The aura of self-confidence which surrounded him drew the attention of both Frank and Trooper Webster.

Marek's gaze shot straight to Joey. "Are you alright?"

Joey glanced down, focusing on the pale gray lines between the twelve-by-twelve white floor tiles.

"Damn it, Joe. Where have you been? I've been looking for you all day." He stepped up to the counter, blocking Frank's boots from Joey's view. "Why didn't you call me?"

The edges of the rug blurred. Joey blinked to bring them back into focus. He shifted his stare and fixated on the snow dropping off the bottom of Marek's jeans.

Marek seemed more than willing to endure Joey's prolonged silence and wait.

Looking up, Joey watched Marek watch him. He shrugged. "I didn't think you'd come."

Marek exhaled a disbelieving huff of breath and rubbed his hand around the back of his neck. "Joe, if you'd called me, I'd have been here sooner."

Joey wanted to believe. He wanted to believe Marek didn't have an ulterior motive. That Marek had come here now because he wanted to help. That Joey wasn't all alone in this slow unraveling of his life.

"Come on," Frank whined with impatience and stepped toward the door. "I'd like to get home before the roads get any worse."

Marek gestured for Joey to follow Frank, as he brought up the rear.

Outside, thick snow had turned all of the vehicles in the parking lot into mounds of white, except for Marek's. His black SUV, backed into a space between two pick-up trucks, had only a thin layer of white across the hood and windshield.

Frank climbed into the front passenger seat. "Appreciate the ride. I didn't think our mini-van could've handled these roads."

"No problem." Marek leaned in and started the engine. He grabbed a snow brush from the floor of the back seat. Turning to Joey, he held open the door like a chauffeur. "Get in. We'll talk about this when we get home."

Joey slid in and Marek shut the door. Home? What did that mean? It almost sounded like they belonged together. Didn't Marek hate him, think him a thief and a murderer? What had changed?

A few minutes later, they were headed east on the highway.

"You warm enough back there?" Marek asked.

Joey nodded, forgetting for a moment that Marek couldn't see his response. Before he could say anything, Marek turned the heat on high.

Even at the State Police Barracks Joey hadn't felt warm. He'd been warmer than when he was walking, but the chill deep in his bones had remained. He closed his eyes, relaxing against the seat.

He half-listened while Frank droned on like an annoying insect, heaping Joey-complaints on Marek's captive ears. "I just couldn't handle another problem with this kid by myself."

Marek snorted. "Trespassing? Seriously? Give him a break."

"You're a cop and you couldn't handle him. You had him one night and he ran away."

"He ran off. He didn't run away."

Joey smiled, feeling warm for the first time all day.

* * *

"Come on, Joe, wake up."

Joey groaned, straightening from his awkward position against the car door. He rolled his aching shoulders and looked out the window.

Thick snowflakes swirled around Frank, who strode head down past the blow-up snow globe and polar bear toward the house. The once shoveled path had nearly filled in with accumulating snow.

Marek twisted around in his seat, facing Joey. "I know you don't want to stay here, but you were released to Frank. You can't stay with me."

Joey nodded and unbuckled his seatbelt.

The dome light flicked off making it hard to read Marek's expression. "I'll be back in a few minutes with your duffle bag. Investigator Kraus was here while you were gone. He checked your backpack and took your notebook and the flash drive that was on your bed."

Popping the door latch, Joey left the heat of the SUV and stepped into the cold.

The ice around the driver's window crackled, as the glass lowered. Marek leaned out. "This whole thing is damn awkward. You're involved in my gambling case. You were either there, or you know who killed Luke. I don't know who or what you're so afraid of, but you can't keep running. There must be someone you can trust. Talk to them. You just can't talk to me."

When Marek said nothing else, Joey started for the house.

"I'm sorry," Marek called and then drove forward, passing behind Joey as he followed the driveway out to the road.

* * *

Joey stomped off his boots on the back porch. Once inside, he set them on the newspaper under the coat rack.

He would have hung up his coat, but his stomach was trembling, either from the cold or from fear. Would Kraus arrest him after he saw the sketches of the trestle bridge and gun?

Frank and Lorraine stood in the corner of the kitchen whispering, their tones harsh and abrupt.

Lorraine's hand clutched the top of her pink robe. She watched him from the corner of her eye, as he passed by on his way upstairs.

He flipped on the light in his room and sat on the bed. As tempting as the pillow and blankets looked, Joey couldn't make himself curl up in that bed and fall asleep.

The closet wasn't safe, either. Nowhere was safe without his knife.

His stomach rumbled. He hadn't eaten since breakfast, and he'd thrown all that up when Marek brought out his gun. Maybe if he had a bowl of cereal he'd feel better.

He laid the coat Marek had given him on the bed and then headed to the bathroom. When he finished washing his hands, he opened the door to Benny's room and tiptoed over to his bed. The boy lay on his stomach, the blankets kicked to his feet.

Joey pulled up the covers and watched him sleep.

Thumb in his mouth, Benny's other hand gripped the foot of his stuffed, blue monster.

The poor kid didn't have many toys, just a bucket of snap-together blocks, a few trucks, and that stained monster. He should get the little guy a present, maybe a new stuffed toy or a puzzle or some books.

If Joey had good grades, he could have sold his homework services for extra cash like Luke used to do. The only thing of value Joey had left to sell was his new snowboarding jacket.

He would really miss this little guy. Hopefully, Frank and Lorraine had gotten Benny nicer stuff for Christmas than what they'd given Joey.

He wandered back to his room, anticipating the wet heat of a nice hot shower pelting down on his aching shoulders and back. Frank and Lorraine would be asleep soon. There would be no one to yell at him if he used all the hot water.

Someone had set his duffle bag on the floor just inside his bedroom door. He grabbed the black nylon bag and tossed it on the bed. He tugged open the zipper and reached within for a pair of clean boxers.

Instead of cotton, his fingers brushed denim.

He peered inside. Somehow he knew what he'd find. He no longer thought to question how it got in his bag. He knew. Luke.

He pulled out the denim jacket, running his fingers down the front, over patches with logos for Metallica and Nine Inch Nails. Compelled to put on the jacket, he slid his arms inside the sleeves and shrugged it over his shoulders.

He sighed and leaned against the wall. He shoved his hands inside the pockets. Warmth settled into his muscles.

Luke's presence filled the room.

Suddenly, Joey knew. He felt it deep inside. Luke hadn't made those bets in Joey's name. He didn't know how he knew. He just felt it. It had been Nate, not Luke. Luke had not betrayed him.

He thought about the notebook and the sketch Marek had seen. In his head, Joey visualized the trestle bridge and gun. His breath caught. A heavy weight settled inside his chest.

Maybe he was the one who had betrayed Luke.

He pushed away from the wall and yanked off the jacket. He didn't deserve to be warm. He tossed it on the bed beside the snowboarding jacket Marek had given him, leaving the denim sleeves wrong-side-out. He didn't deserve either one.

Gathering his clothes for a shower, he headed into the bathroom. He stood in the tub, his hand braced against the wall, he rested his forehead on his arm while hot water sluiced down over his hair and shoulders.

Eventually, he wrapped his fingers around the bar of soap. His fingers tingled with the memory of that money clip. There was five hundred and fifty dollars in that coat.

He could get Benny something nice, maybe for his turtle, and a nice doll for Allison instead of the cheap knock-offs Lorraine bought. Carrie might like a stuffed animal or some blocks.

He could even get a gift for Marek. Maybe sheet music. *Nirvana* or some other old band. Maybe newer. *Disturbed.*

Did Greg know he'd left the money and flash drive in the jacket?

Joey lathered the soap and scrubbed his arms. Maybe he could just spend part of it, and when Greg asked for it back, Joey could give him what was left and pretend that's all there was.

Nah, Greg would never believe it.

When the water cooled, he turned off the faucet. He toweled dry and pulled on flannel bottoms and a T-shirt.

What could Greg do about it? He wouldn't complain to the cops. He could send Nate to collect the money, or worse, tell Pierson Mott.

He wiped the steamy mirror and peered close at his upper lip. Those dark hairs were starting to show again. Joey stepped from the steamy bathroom. Goose bumps raced up his arms. He grabbed his razor from his duffle and returned to stand in front of the sink.

He might as well spend the money. Make someone happy. Who knew where he'd end up Monday after Mary Custer came to get him? Emergency placement? Juvenile detention? Either way Greg would have to come up with the missing money on his own. He'd be screwed.

Too bad. So sad. A smile tugged one corner of Joey's mouth as he scraped the lathered hand soap from his upper lip.

He rinsed his face and hung up the towel. He checked his face in the mirror one more time. Satisfied no hairs had been missed, he flicked off the light and closed the door.

He glanced at the denim jacket he'd tossed it on the bed. The promised warmth called to him. Resisting the temptation, he pulled a pair of socks from his duffle bag along with the flannel shirt Lorraine had given him.

He tossed the jacket to the end of the bed and tried to sleep but ended up staring at the ceiling. After what seemed like hours, he sat up. The shadowy form of the denim jacket drew his attention. Was that where he'd left it or had it moved closer? He shivered.

"Damn it, Luke." He rolled off the bed. Crossing his arms, he stared at the mound of denim. "What do you want from me?"

He moved to the closet, pulled the door closed, sank to the floor, and rested his forehead on his knee. He dozed, but without his knife he startled awake with each creak and groan of the old farmhouse. He missed Cody. He missed knowing Marek was close by. And he hated that he couldn't forget the denim jacket laying at the end of the bed.

Shoving to his feet, he pushed open the door and snatched the jacket off the comforter.

"All right." He turned the sleeves right side out. "I'll wear it."

He padded down to the kitchen for a bowl of cereal. As he stepped into the room the interior suddenly blurred and twisted. He stopped and blinked, trying to bring things back into focus. His vision cleared but he was in Marek's house, moving from the garage into the laundry room.

* * *

"Mom, I'm home."

The back door slammed behind him. Cody charged ahead into the kitchen. Steam wafted from a pot on the stove. Onions sizzled in a pan. Chocolate chip cookies cooled on wire racks.

A woman turned toward him from the stove. Her smile beamed as she met his gaze, making her even prettier than in the many photos scattered throughout the house, despite the penciled brows and the blue scarf around her head.

"Hello, sweetie, how was your game?"

"I pitched three whole innings without a hit."

"That's wonderful, Luke. Come here so I can give you a big hug."

* * *

The vision blurred. Joey blinked and the kitchen with the birch cabinets and Formica table was back to normal.

He rubbed his temple, hoping to ease the throb that began pounding inside his skull.

In those moments Luke had been so content, so joyful, so at peace. Was he with his mom now?

Jealousy pricked Joey's heart. It wasn't fair. He missed his own mom. He missed his brother Kyle. And Luke had been so happy.

The words to a Christmas song bounced through his head. *You better watch out. You better not cry. You better not pout.*

What right did Joey have to complain? Luke was dead. If anything wasn't fair, that was it. Sometimes life just sucked.

Nauseated from his headache he changed his mind about the cereal and instead lay on the couch. He picked up the remote and clicked on the TV. Content to watch *A Christmas Story* in the dark, he kept the volume a whisper above mute.

* * * * *

CHAPTER 16

A door banged upstairs.

Joey raised his head from the arm of the couch. He rubbed his eyes. A faint pinkish glow backlit the curtains. *A Christmas Story* still played on TV, but now Ralphie's mom tended his black eye while the Bumpus hounds gobbled up the turkey.

The last thing he remembered was Ralphie abandoning his friend outside the school with his tongue stuck to the flagpole. The movie must have been playing on repeat all night.

After clicking off the TV, he went upstairs and traded his flannel bottoms for a pair of jeans. He considered hanging the jacket in the closet, but the house was so cold. With his hands in the pockets of the jacket, he headed down the hall toward the stairs.

Frank and Lorraine moved around in their room, talking softly as Joey passed. Today was Sunday. Maybe they'd let him miss church without too much fuss.

* * *

"No," Frank declared, glaring at Joey from across the island.

Behind him, Lorraine came in from the porch, set the newspaper on the table, and hung up her coat.

Frank poured a cup of coffee and passed it to Lorraine, as she took a seat at the table.

"If anyone needs to spend time in church, it's you." Frank blew a quick breath across the steaming liquid in his own cup. "Going out when you were grounded, talking back, fighting, stealing, threatening Benny with a knife."

Was Frank planning to go to confession in his place?

"Running away. Trespassing. Vandalism."

How many sins could Frank list in one breath? Even Allison stopped munching on a banana and shot Joey a look of pity.

Joey reached across the island and snapped a banana from the bunch nestled in the basket. He peeled it halfway, broke off the top and passed it down to Benny, who hovered near Joey's elbow.

Lorraine made a short *tsking* sound from beside the coffee maker. "Don't give him that. He's wearing his good clothes."

Joey ignored her and took a bite from what remained.

"Belligerent and defiant," Lorraine added to Frank's growing list.

Regardless, they couldn't force him to go to mass.

Lorraine sipped her coffee. "I was just getting the paper and those nice Kelly boys from up the road were driving by and stopped to say hello."

"Which one?" Frank asked, reaching for the bottle of creamer.

"They were both in the car, but the younger one was driving."

"Greg."

"Yes, Greg. He was giving his brother a ride home from work. He saw me and wanted to thank us for the video games and to apologize for his part in the fight the other day."

Joey popped the last bite of banana into his mouth and folded the peel in half. Yeah, Greg was an angel, and Lorraine couldn't even bring herself to speak Joey's name.

He walked to the end of the island and tossed the peel in the garbage.

Frank blew on his coffee again and took a sip. "Yeah, he's a nice kid."

"Those boys have had such a hard time." Lorraine set down her coffee with a sad shake of her head. "First their mother walked out on them. Then their father."

Joey grabbed a dish rag and wet it in the sink.

"You can't help but admire the oldest one for taking the responsibility of raising his younger brother."

Frank glanced at this watch and compared it to the time on the stove. "He's a hard worker, too. I see him every time I get gas."

"He's always so cheerful." Lorraine drained the last of her coffee, rose, and set the mug in the sink.

Joey gave Benny's hands and face a quick wipe. Why was Greg kissing up to Lorraine?

Tossing the rag in the sink, Joey headed to the living room. He grabbed the remote from the coffee table and clicked on the TV. Dora chatted happily about her latest adventure. He flopped face-down on the couch, sprawling across the cushions.

Frank and Lorraine herded the other kids upstairs to dress.

Lorraine brought Benny down first, wearing a different shirt, his face pink from a recent scrubbing. He sat beside the couch with a pile of colorful snap-together blocks.

Reaching down, Joey popped together a few of the over-sized plastic squares.

Benny watched him for a minute and then pulled his turtle action figure from under the couch. "Make house for him."

"He doesn't live in a house. He lives in the sewer."

Benny cocked his head and frowned.

Joey grinned. "A sewer is way cooler than a house."

The little boy nodded and pushed some of the plastic blocks closer to Joey. "Make sewer."

Benny watched the construction process fascinated, holding his turtle in one hand while he passed Joey more blocks with the other.

Maybe he could get Benny a train or racecar set. They had them for little kids. Or he could get him a new stuffed toy. Something cute, that he could sleep with and remember Joey.

He snapped together some more blocks. When he finished, the sewer looked like a cross between a three-sided box with an extra-tall, extra-wide chimney, and a small, multi-colored hamster condo.

Benny didn't care. He grinned from ear to ear, dropping his turtle down through the sewer opening over and over.

Frank trotted down the stairs wearing his coat. He held Benny's jacket and hat in one hand. "Hurry up, Lori," he called over his shoulder. "I'm going out to warm up the van."

He stepped into the living room and tossed the small jacket in Joey's direction. "Can you at least get Benny ready to go out?"

When Joey made no move to pick up the coat, Frank swore under his breath and stomped from the room.

Once the back door slammed shut, Joey rolled from the couch and picked up Benny's hat and coat. Red mittens dangled from the sleeves, and it took Joey some twisting and turning to get the little boy's thumbs into the thumb holes so that the bunny faces were on top of his hands rather than his palms.

Lorraine came down a few moments later, Carrie on her hip. Allison followed a few steps behind. Benny ran from the room to greet them.

The back door opened. "Lorraine, we're going to be late!"

Joey threw himself back on the couch and raised his head enough to peek over the arm of the couch.

Lorraine passed Allison a pair of gloves. "We're right here. Can you grab Benny?"

Frank strode in from the kitchen and scooped the little boy into his arms as Lorraine and Allison headed for the van. He shot Joey a poisonous scowl. "Selfish, rude, inconsiderate, and lazy, too," he mumbled under his breath.

"Bye-bye," Benny called over Frank's shoulder, as Frank stomped through the kitchen and slammed the back door.

Joey sat up. "Later," he replied to the empty house.

He guessed he had about an hour and a half before they burst through the door in a flurry of hats and coats and talk of Sunday brunch.

Chuckling, he headed upstairs and pulled the snowboarding coat over Luke's denim jacket. He peeled a hundred dollars from the bills in the money clip, returned it to the coat pocket and shoved the loose bills into the front pocket of his jeans.

Returning to the kitchen, he quickly tied up his boots, grabbed some gloves and a knit hat, and headed out the back door. The muscle aches from yesterday's strenuous exercise had faded. Humming, he limped down the driveway, his stride back to normal.

In his head, Bruce Springsteen sang *Santa Claus is Coming to Town.*

Not a single cloud floated through the brilliant blue sky. Gusts of wind kicked up the loose powder, whipped it through the open areas, and across the road in random triangular drifts.

At the end of the driveway, the jacket—no, Luke—pulled at Joey and urged him to turn away from town and walk up the road toward Marek's house.

Struggling against the compulsion, Joey pushed onward. He kept his head down to lessen the glare of the sun bouncing off the snow. Maybe he'd buy himself a good pair of sunglasses, nicer than his old ones.

A steady pain throbbed inside his skull. He tried to tell himself it was because of the sun, but who was he kidding? He should have left Luke's jacket on his bed. He felt like Frodo fighting the power of the ring.

Behind him, a car approached, rumbling like a stock car at Daytona. Joey didn't have to turn around. He knew who it was. He veered into a thick ridge of plowed snow along the edge of the road.

Instead of passing by, the car slowed.

He glanced over his shoulder and watched that wide maroon hood draw closer. The left headlight was cracked. Funny he would notice that.

Run!

He wasn't sure if the desperation came from his own inner voice or from Luke's.

The car rolled up beside him. The driver's window was down.

"I was just coming to visit you, Gimp," Greg said from behind the wheel. "And here I see you up ahead, walking down the road like a gift from God."

Joey kept walking.

"I left a couple of things in the pocket of that coat you're wearing. Hand 'em over."

"I don't have nothing."

Greg's left arm stretched out. His fingers grasped for Joey's arm, while he managed to steer his car through the deeper snow along the side of the road.

"You sure as hell do. Now where is it?"

Joey leaned away from Greg's hand and moved closer to the snowbank along the shoulder.

"I spent it."

"Don't play me, Gimp." Greg eased the car closer. "Hand it over and I'll let you keep your teeth." Latching on to the sleeve of the snowboarding jacket, he twisted his fingers in the nylon and tugged Joey toward the car door.

Joey's foot caught on a chunk of snow, frozen to rock hard with sand and salt. He stumbled. The forward momentum yanked the jacket from Greg's grip.

Joey landed on his hands and knees, his little finger less than an inch from the front tire. Heart pumping, he scrambled to his feet as the car rolled toward the snowbank, cornering Joey in a kind of funnel.

He whirled and dashed back the way he came.

Run!

Greg shifted into reverse. The rear tires spun, giving Joey a few extra moments to escape.

The tires stopped spinning, and the car sped backward past Joey. The rear end swung into Frank and Lorraine's driveway and blocked Joey's escape.

Run! Luke screamed again.

For Luke, safety lay beyond Frank and Lorraine's old farmhouse. Luke's sanctuary was up the road and around the bend within the walls of the Marek house.

The driver's door swung open.

Joey could never outrun Greg. He needed time.

He reached into his pocket and pulled out the money clip. As he passed the nose of the car, he threw it toward the other side of the road.

Expecting Greg to go fetch, Joey poured on a burst of speed. He ran parallel to the barbed wire fence which traced the length of the heifer pasture all the way to the row of pine trees at the property line and Marek's house on the other side.

His feet slipped and slid in the soft churned powder. He'd reached the halfway point along the fence line when Greg's car roared past. The brake lights flashed red and the rear end fishtailed.

Joey ran, taking a chance that he'd make it beyond the car before Greg had the vehicle under control.

If he was more agile, he would have scrambled over the top of the snowbank, ducked through the wire, and angled through the pasture to Marek's garage. But there was a snow-covered ditch on the other side. The last thing he needed was to get trapped in waist high snow.

Greg turned the nose of his car into Marek's driveway.

Joey dashed for the opposite side of the road, skidding through the slush and salt. He charged forward up the road, praying Greg would follow and the rear-wheel-drive muscle car would get stuck. Then Joey would double back to Marek's. If he could manage to hug the side of the road without falling under the car, maybe he could lure Greg close enough to one of the drifts.

The back tires spun for a moment, and then the car shot across the road. Greg angled close.

"Give me that flash drive!" he yelled through the open window.

Flash drive? Dread clawed its way up the back of Joey's throat. His breath escaped in short panicking gasps. "I don't have it."

"You damn well do have it, and Nate's gonna kill you!"

Run!

Joey swung on his heels and bolted toward the rear of the car.

Greg slammed the vehicle into reverse and sent the rear fender straight toward him.

This time there was no room to maneuver. The only escape route was over the snowbank. His feet sank deep, and he floundered through thick snow.

The driver's door opened, but the corner of the bumper had knifed into the icy wall of the snowbank. Turning sideways, Greg climbed from the driver's seat.

Joey pulled his knees high and held his arms wide. He struggled to keep his balance through the snowbank past the length of the car. He eased around the trunk and slid into the road.

He almost reached the sandy middle, when fingertips raked the back of his head, pulling off his hat. A moment later he was jerked backward by the collar of the snowboarding jacket.

Greg flung him around and with his hands on Joey's shoulders he pushed him toward the car.

Trying to resist, Joey dug his heels in the snow, but Greg was too strong. Joey's boots gouged two narrow furrows in the slush, as he was dragged across the road.

Oof! Joey slammed into the front fender of the car. Unable to breathe, he lost the ability to fight the weight of Greg's arm across his back.

Keeping Joey pressed tight against the cold metal, Greg shoved his free hand into each of Joey's pockets.

"Where is it, Gimp?"

The trees along the roadside shifted and grew dark. Joey closed his eyes against the dizziness, against the intense pounding in his head. The banana he'd eaten earlier tumbled around in his stomach. He tried to keep it down by taking deep breaths. God only knew what Greg would do if Joey puked on his car.

He opened his eyes.

* * *

Board and batten walls surrounded him. The only light in the shadowy building spilled from the open door behind him and the knot holes in the wood.

A figure stood in the shadows, radiating cold menace.

Luke recognized the figure, although he couldn't see his face.

"What are you doing?" Luke cried. Disbelief warred with cold dread.

The figure stepped toward him, a gun in his left hand.

Luke tried to laugh, but fear had squeezed his chest so tight it was hard to breathe. All he could manage was a short squawk. "No."

The figure moved forward, dark and ominous, like the ghost of Christmas Future. The gun was like a ghostly skeletal finger pointing straight at Luke's chest.

Time slowed. Thoughts tumbled through Luke's head, one on top of another. Get out of here. Run. He's not playing. Hide!

He whirled and rushed toward the light, toward the tangle of brush and trees near the trestle bridge. The fear that drove him to run loomed greater than the fear that compelled him to avoid the bridge.

The crack of a gunshot echoed through the ravine like the boom of a cannon.

Brush and twigs scratched at his arms and face. Another gunshot exploded behind him. He hurtled over a rotting log. The toe of his sneaker caught on the pulpy wood and pitched him forward.

Face down, the musky scent of dried leaves filled his nose. He tried to push up to his knees, but his right arm was numb. Searing pain lanced through his back into his chest. He tried to breathe, but the coppery taste of blood filled his mouth.

A stick snapped somewhere behind him. The rustle and crunch of leaves moved closer.

Run! His brain screamed.

The footsteps stopped beside him.

Moments passed, or maybe minutes. Luke didn't know. He felt himself being lifted, carried.

It will be all right. It was an accident. He didn't mean it. Help is coming.

Wait. This is wrong. We're on the tracks. Where are we going?

Then he was falling. Or was he floating? Trees flashed by. The crisscrossed timbers of the trestle bridge went by like descending floors through a glass elevator.

His left arm flailed. He rotated around. The deep olive green of the river grew closer. Sunlight glinted off the water. Its brilliance grew brighter, engulfing him in a shroud of white light.

"Daddy!"

* * * * *

CHAPTER 17

JOEY gasped and struggled to breathe. Tears filled his eyes.

Oh, God, Luke!

He'd been alive when he went off the trestle bridge.

Saliva pooled in Joey's mouth. His stomach roiled. He swallowed and swallowed again. Rearing back, he struggled against the weight that bore down across his shoulders, fighting the terror that clawed at his chest, the knife-like pain that tore through his back.

Greg pushed down on the back of Joey's head. "Where is it, Gimp?"

"I don't have it!" Joey cried, the side of his mouth pressed tight against the hood.

"You stupid little shit. You sure as hell do. I left it in the pocket of this jacket."

"I don't have it. I swear."

"You damn well better find it. My brother needs it, and he has friends. Important friends!"

Greg released the pressure on Joey's head.

Joey straightened as much as he could under the force of Greg's arm. Then Greg's hand slammed against the back of Joey's head. His face hit the hood of the car like a basketball slam dunk.

Tiny white fissures of light flashed through the darkness behind his closed eye lids. His temple and cheek bone throbbed. The hood likely now had a big dent.

"I left it at Detective Marek's house. Ask him to give it back."

Maybe he shouldn't have thrown Marek under the bus, but he just wanted Greg to leave him alone. If Greg got in trouble with Nate and Pierson Mott, oh well.

Greg shoved Joey's face one more time against the cold metal. "Now," he whispered. "I don't care how you do it, but you're gonna get me that flash drive before my brother wakes up."

The whisk of car tires through slush grew closer.

Greg stepped back, and the pressure on Joey's head vanished.

Grateful to the driver of the approaching car, Joey straightened and turned.

Marek's SUV slowed and came to a stop in the middle of the road. The engine idled as the driver's door opened and Marek stepped out. A cloud of wind-tossed snow blew across the road.

Wearing only a heavy cotton sweater over a flannel shirt, Marek should have been cold. "What's going on here?"

Greg withdrew a couple of steps. "I was heading into town. Kowalski here was walking down the middle of the road. I didn't see him. Maybe I was going just a little bit too fast." He shrugged, his dimples flashing. "I swerved and hit the snowbank. I was just checking to see he was okay."

"By bouncing his head off the hood of your car?"

"That was an accident. I slipped and fell into him."

Marek nodded. "Get over here and stand by the trunk."

Greg glanced back, shooting Joey that narrow-eyed *keep your mouth shut or else* threat.

Marek walked to the center of the road, picked up the knit hat and returned to the car. Placing himself where he could watch Greg who leaned against the back fender, he passed the hat to Joey. "You want to tell me what's really going on?"

Joey studied the toes of his boots. His day officially sucked. "Nothing."

"Nothing? What I saw didn't look like nothing."

"My bad leg slipped. Greg just tried to help, and we both slipped."

"Into the car with his arm across your back?"

Joey shrugged. He squashed a lump of slush with the toe of his boot and studied the imprint of his boot tread.

"Fine. Go sit in my car and wait for me." He gave Joey a long look, that promised the discussion wasn't over.

Grateful Marek hadn't pursued the issue in front of Greg, Joey headed for the car.

Marek's pea coat lay on the passenger seat. Joey tossed it in the back and hopped into the front. He pulled off his gloves and held out his hands, his numb fingers grateful for the heat which blasted from the vents.

Run!

"Stop it!" Joey rubbed at the growing headache behind his temples.

Greg ducked into his car.

Marek started toward his SUV.

Through the windshield the winter landscape blurred and shifted.

"No!" Joey frantically unzipped the snowboarding jacket and popped free the buttons of the denim jacket. A dull ache throbbed behind his temples. The inside of the vehicle grew dark.

Desperate, he reached back between his shoulder blades and yanked both jackets over his head. He wadded them into a ball and threw them on the floor, well away from any chance even his feet might touch them.

"Leave me alone!"

There was a soft click, and a cold draft blew across the seats. Joey shivered and shot a quick glance toward the driver's door.

Marek stood watching him, deep furrows tugged at his brow. "Are you alright?"

Joey crossed his arms, shoved his hands into the warmth of his armpits, and slumped down in the seat.

From the corner of his eye, he watched Marek lift the jackets from where they lay by the gas pedal. He brushed away the snow and salt, and then draped the denim jacket over the console.

Joey inched closer to the door, keeping his elbow well away from the denim. Unwilling to risk contact with the denim jacket, he ignored the snowboarding jacket Marek held out.

Shrugging, Marek tossed the jacket in the back. "Are you even going to answer me if I ask who you were yelling at just now? Or how you keep getting my old denim jacket?"

Joey turned away and stared through the side window as he got in and shut the door. Luke. Marek wouldn't believe him anymore today than he did yesterday.

Marek heaved a sigh and shifted the SUV into gear. He executed a quick K-turn and headed down the road to Frank and Lorraine's.

Near the back porch, a black sedan idled in the driveway. Joey's gut twisted. Had Pierson Mott come for the thumb drive?

Snow crunched beneath the tires of the SUV, as Marek looped in behind the sedan and shifted into park.

Run! Joey's mind screamed, but this time it wasn't Luke's voice.

The outer door of the porch opened. Two men stepped outside and down the steps. Dressed in hats and coats, Joey couldn't tell who they were. They walked along the shoveled path with purpose, past the polar bear and snow globe, along the passenger side of the sedan, straight toward the SUV where he sat.

Neither man was Mott, but Joey's relief at not seeing the finely dressed, sucker-punching bookie stride toward him was short lived.

Investigator Kraus from the State Police and his partner Rogers or Robbins or Roberts strode down the snowy path, their jaws set with determination.

If Joey had thought his day sucked before, it had just gone right past the double-dog suck to a triple-dog suck of a day.

He slid lower in the seat.

Marek stepped from the SUV. He moved around the hood between the vehicles, positioning himself at the bumper with arms crossed and casually blocking the pair.

The tiny hairs at the back of Joey's neck prickled. Maybe Kraus and Roberts just wanted to ask him again about the fight he and Luke had had. Maybe they'd found something on Luke's computer about the gambling and needed to ask Joey about it.

But Marek must have recognized something in the expressions of both men, some mutual silent cop-speak for Joey-is-in-big-trouble-now. He nodded.

Dread, like a punch to the gut, left Joey pressing shaky hands against his churning stomach.

Marek opened the passenger door. "Let's go."

Joey bit down on the inside of his mouth and glanced up.

All expression erased from Marek's face, except for his eyes. In his gray blue depths lurked something Joey couldn't quite define. Was it anger? Disappointment? Betrayal?

Joey shivered and eased from the car.

The edge of the open door brushed against the snowbank, forming a barrier between him and Marek, and behind Marek, the two investigators. The wall of snow cut by the snow blower when Frank cleared the driveway this morning, narrowed the space alongside the vehicles.

"Morning, Joey." Kraus called from just beyond Marek. He sounded friendly enough, but his tone was flat, as though his greeting was given by rote and his thoughts were focused elsewhere. "Are your foster parents returning soon?"

Whatever was going on, it wasn't good. Joey should have listened to Luke and run. Run far away and never looked back. What the hell. He whirled and ran.

*****

CHAPTER 18

"DAMN it, Joe!" Marek yelled.

Behind him the car door slammed. The heavy footfalls of three cops pounded after him.

If he could make it to the empty cow barn, he could hide. He knew the old building like the back of his hand. After Luke died, he'd spent a lot of time out there.

Frank kept a path cleared from the driveway to the door of the old milk room. Joey poured on an extra burst of speed and slid around the turn onto the narrow path, ignoring their calls to stop.

They wouldn't shoot, would they?

Without wasting time to see how close they were, he jerked open the aluminum storm door and shoved the thick wooden door inward. The heavy-duty spring groaned as it stretched. Joey let go of the door. It slammed back in place with a sharp bang that echoed through the empty cinderblock room.

Joey grabbed the snow blower and dragged it in front of the door. Then he jammed the end of one handle under the wooden door latch.

The aluminum outer door opened, and someone shoved against the inner door.

"Damn it, Joe," Marek yelled. "Open this door."

"You keep trying." Kraus called. "We'll go around to the side."

Joey spun and charged past the place where the bulk tank once stood. He pulled open a second heavy door, gaining entry into the main cow barn.

Kraus and his partner would have to wade through deep snow to reach the drifted-in side door of the barn, and that door opened outward.

From the milk room came a loud crash. Marek was stronger than Joey had thought.

He had known this day would come, had resigned himself to it. At least he thought he had. Now that prison loomed before him, he was scared. Terrified. He didn't want to go.

He raced toward the silo room and ducked inside.

Hopefully, Marek hadn't seen him.

A large grain bin and two concrete stave silos had at one time emptied feed into power carts for the cows who once produced milk here. The first silo stood empty. The second one was half-full. After Luke had been killed, Joey had carried a sleeping bag up the discharge chute, spread a tarp across the old corn silage, and spent his nights out here.

From the main barn, the cadence of boots against concrete moved his way. With a sharp bang and a rattle of glass, the side door was flung open. The low voices of Kraus and his partner carried through the long empty barn.

Joey grabbed onto the steel rungs that ran up the side of the silo and climbed. Several feet up, the rungs were enclosed by the cylindrical silo chute. Hand over hand he moved upward into the darkness.

He'd nearly disappeared from sight when a hand wrapped around his ankle, just above the top of his boot.

The grip tightened and pulled.

"Get down here!" Marek demanded. "Where in the hell do you think you're going?"

Desperate, Joey tried to kick free. The toe of his boot connected with what felt like Marek's face.

Marek grunted but didn't release his hold. Instead, the fingers of his other hand twisted into the loose denim behind Joey's knee.

Joey gripped the flat metal rungs tight, but the cold steel bit into his palms. Ignoring the pain, he held on, his left hand on a rung level with his cheek, his right-hand clinging just above his head.

Marek pulled hard.

Joey lost his grip on the higher rung. As he dropped, his lower hand squeezed tight around cold steel, stretching out his arm.

His free hand groped for another rung as Marek dragged him down. Joey's other hand slipped. His fingertips held momentarily, but Marek was determined. Joey dropped.

Marek caught him before he fell, but as soon as Joey's feet hit the floor, he shoved at Marek's chest and swung away.

The dark shapes of Kraus and his partner filled the doorway, backlit by the sunlight which streamed into the barn through the many windows along the outside walls.

Joey started toward the two men, thinking to duck low and charge through the narrow space between them, but Marek grabbed Joey by the arms and swung him face-first against the corrugated metal wall.

"Stop!" Marek yelled.

Joey's breath heaved in and out, fluttering the thick gray cobwebs which clung to the wall and hung from the heavy black wire which drooped between the breaker panel and silo like the moss draped trees he'd seen in a picture of a southern plantation.

"Enough!" Marek's fingertips pressed deep into the backs of Joey's biceps. "I've tried to be patient with you, but I can't do it anymore. I know you know something, but you won't talk. What are you so afraid of?"

"Detective," Kraus warned.

Joey's pounding heart seemed to vibrate through his chest into the icy metal wall.

Slowly, Marek's grip eased. He stepped back.

Joey turned. Hugging himself, he pressed his spine tight against the wall as if by pushing hard enough, he could somehow slide through the cold steel barrier and vanish.

"These men are here to take you in for questioning. They wouldn't do that unless they had new evidence. Damning evidence. Do you understand that?"

Kraus stepped forward. "Detective, calm down. We got this. Show me your hands, son." A sliver of sunlight slipped between a space where the metal wall met the curve of the silo, glinting off the silver handcuffs Kraus held.

Behind Kraus his partner stood, his gun raised. The dark hole in the center of the barrel trained on Joey.

Joey's blood seemed to drain from his body, leaving him cold and shaking. He raised his hands and dropped his gaze to the pockmarked concrete floor. Anything to keep from looking at that gun. Anything to keep from seeing the accusation in Kraus' eyes, the betrayal in Marek's.

"Did you kill my son?" Marek asked.

Joey clenched his teeth and said nothing.

"Is that why you ran?"

Kraus took a step forward. "Detective!"

"No! I need to know. Did you kill Luke?"

The pressure behind Joey's chest grew. The words he'd been holding inside for so long jammed in his throat. He focused on Marek's hands, clenched into fists, slightly raised at his side.

"Damn it, Joe!" he yelled. "Did. You. Kill. My. Son?"

Joey flinched under the impact of each word. He shivered. His stomach hurt. His eyes burned. Pressure built inside his chest.

"I don't know!"

The air stilled. The silence so complete, Joey wondered if he or any of them even breathed.

"What?" Though softly spoken, Marek's question ripped through the quiet like a gun shot on a frosty morning. His rigid stance relaxed. His fists loosened. "Talk to me, Joe."

Not sure how to express the jumble of feelings and doubts churning inside him, he said nothing. His gaze focused on the gold wedding band at the base of Marek's fourth finger.

"I think—" Pain closed off the base of his throat. He gulped past the knot of words and fought for air, his insides fracturing like ice under the pressure of a footstep. "Maybe I shot Luke and can't remember. Like *him.* That I'm crazy like *him.*"

The air between them went heavy and still like a summer evening in the moments before thunder cracked and rain pelted the earth.

Marek shifted closer. A hint of spice wafted through the space between them. "Is that what you think?"

Joey gave a slight nod.

Marek heaved a weighted sigh. "Then I must be nine kinds of crazy for believing you're not."

Joey's gaze snapped up, locking on Marek's intense blue eyes. Could someone in this world, could this man actually believe in him? He ached to latch on to that lifeline and never let go. But what if it was a trick?

He searched Marek's face, afraid to hope. His fingers curled into fists, squeezing tighter and tighter until they ached.

"Don't lie to me," Joey choked out. "Not you."

Two vertical creases tugged together at the bridge of Marek's nose. "I would never."

Joey's lungs swelled with the pain of a held breath, terrified to grab onto the hope Marek offered. For maybe it was better to let himself drown than to discover hope was a lie.

Marek stepped forward and put a heavy hand on Joey's shoulder. "You are not your father, Joe."

Those fingers tightened into a squeeze.

The inside of Joey's nose burned. He blinked trying to hold back the tears that welled in his eyes, but his throat closed off and they spilled onto his cheeks. His breath gushed out on a sob that expelled like a cough.

The grip of that hand vanished and slid around his shoulders.

Joey stumbled forward into a bear hug. His arms slid around Marek's back, clenching fistfuls of cotton, his face buried against Marek's shoulder.

Great wrenching sobs ratcheted from his lungs like hiccups into Marek's sweater. Joey felt as if he were three, wailing like Benny, unable to stop, caught in a pathetic mess of snot and tears.

"Why'd he do it?" The question tumbled out, uncensored, muffled against the solace of cotton and strength. "Why'd he shoot us like that? I hate him." The words spilled out like a mantra. "I hate him. I hate him. I hate him."

The weight of Marek's hand ran up and down Joey's back.

"It's okay, son," Marek murmured. "It wasn't your fault. Something went wrong inside him. I don't know. You have every right to hate what he did. It was gruesome. It was horrific. But you are not him. And it was not your fault."

Adrift for so long, Joey surrendered to the solace Marek offered, desperate to trust someone, aching to trust this man.

Marek eased back, withdrawing his embrace, leaving Joey off balance, like a sailor trying to find his land legs after months at sea.

He looked up and met Marek's gaze, reassured by the steady calm he found there. "It'll be okay, Joe."

As the truth of Marek's words penetrated that dark place inside him, the agonizing dread of who he might be and what he might have done was vanquished like a moonless night with the golden streaks of dawn.

His father's destiny was not his.

He had not killed his best friend.

"We can get through this," Marek said. "But you have to tell these detectives what you know."

Drawing a deep breath, Joey gave a slow exhale and nodded.

*****

CHAPTER 19

AN hour later, Joey sat behind a table at the State Police barracks in what looked like every interrogation room he'd ever seen on TV.

A camera, mounted high in the corner below the dropdown ceiling, kept a steady watch.

Marek seemed to believe Joey knew what had happened to Luke. But if Joey hadn't killed him, who had?

Luke knew. He'd been trying to tell Joey through the visions, but Joey must have missed some little clue, some vital piece of information that would make it all fall into place.

He leaned over the table and rested his forehead on his crossed his arms. He thought back to the first image. He'd been so focused on looking down from the trestle bridge that he hadn't paid attention to what might have been lurking at the edges of the vision. He closed his eyes and tried to remember. He should have kept on the jacket. He should have listened to Luke.

"Joey?"

His eyes popped open, and he straightened.

Investigator Kraus gazed down at him from the end of the table.

Joey hadn't heard him come in. He rubbed a hand over his face.

Kraus held out a Styrofoam cup.

Whirls of chocolate-scented steam filled Joey's nose. His mouth watered.

"You look tired. Me, too. It's been a tough morning." Since Joey agreed to talk, the lines of tension which had earlier furrowed Kraus's brow had vanished.

While the trooper's offer appeared sincere, Joey suspected Kraus was nothing more than *a Greek bearing gifts*, as his mother used to say.

When Joey didn't take the cup, Kraus set it on the table. "We've got chips and candy in the snack machine. You want something?"

Joey shifted, and the blue molded chair moved. The scrape of metal legs against the tile floor echoed loud and hollow in the cubicle.

"Okay. Then I'll be right back. I've got to go grab a couple of things." Kraus smiled. A flash of dimples and white teeth appeared. His easy grin was like those Joey remembered from his first meeting with the state trooper.

He stared at the open door, wondering if Kraus had forgotten to close it or if it was a test to see if Joey would try to run again. Neither Kraus nor the other detective had said one word about being under arrest. Maybe he really was just here for questioning.

Kraus returned with a thick, brown file folder and notebook in one hand, a bag of nacho chips and a pack of cookies in the other. He put down his pile and set the snacks beside the cup of hot chocolate and lowered himself into the empty chair on the opposite side of the table.

"Here you go. I figure you're hungry."

Kraus was certainly one of those gift-bearing Greeks.

Joey's stomach rumbled as his tongue imagined absorbing the flavors of cheese and taco seasoning, but he left the chips, as well as the cookies, untouched.

Kraus leaned back and rested his ankle on his knee.

On the table, beneath the file folder and yellow legal pad, lay the spiral notebook Joey had used to sketch the visions.

Then again, maybe he was under arrest. Nerves twisted his stomach tighter and tighter, until the center of his body felt as solid as a rock.

Marek had said: *"It'll be okay, Joe."* He believed Joey was innocent, but did Kraus?

"I'm not such a bad guy, you know. You don't have to starve yourself to prove you don't trust me."

Joey glanced away, reluctant now to even try the hot chocolate, as though drinking it would give Kraus the advantage in whatever cat and mouse game was being played between them.

He had seen enough movies to know the routine. Pretend to be the suspect's friend. Load him up with fluids, until he asked to use the bathroom. Then not let him relieve himself, until he said whatever the detective wanted to hear.

Roberts-Robbins appeared in the doorway. "The kid's father is here."

He's not my father! Joey crossed his arms over his chest and dropped his gaze to the floor. Why did Frank have to be here? He could handle things just fine by himself.

Kraus's chair legs slid back, and he stood.

Rogers' khaki clad legs and black laced boots stepped away from the entrance. "I'll be next door."

Frank's brown hiking boots moved into the small space.

Kraus's military style footwear side-stepped to the end of the table.

"Mr. Denys. Thank you for coming."

"Detective," Frank replied.

The chrome legs of the third chair slid to the end of the table where Frank stood.

"Here you go," Kraus said. "If you could take a seat, this shouldn't take too long. I just have a few questions for Joey."

Joey raised his chin a few notches. He jerked his thumb toward Frank. "Does he have to be here?"

Frank gave an indignant huff.

Why should Frank get to learn personal stuff about Luke that Marek didn't even know?

"It's not his business."

"You're a minor. It's for your own protection that a parent or guardian be present when we question you."

Kraus pulled the yellow pad from the bottom of his pile and clicked the end of his pen. "When I talked to you the other day, I told you we have a witness who saw you and Luke fighting. Are you ready to tell me what that fight was about?"

Joey dropped his gaze to the floor again.

Kraus nudged the pack of cookies closer. "Relax. Have a snack and pretend he isn't here."

Joey said nothing. Would Kraus believe him?

"I have a brother," Kraus began. "Boys fight, even best friends. I get it. But I need you to answer the question."

"It was nothing." Joey shrugged. "Just about a girl."

"What girl?"

"Jessica Bickman."

"Did you both like her?"

Joey shook his head. "Just Luke. He really liked her, but I heard her in study hall talking to her friends. She only went out with him to make someone else jealous. I tried to tell him, but he wouldn't believe me. I called her a slut. Luke slugged me and took off."

Pain clogged his throat. The edges of the gray striations in the white tiles blurred.

Could he have prevented Luke's death, if he had gone after him? A sensation of dark, spindly fingers crawled over him. He shuddered. A new kind of nightmare before Christmas.

Tap, tap, tap.

Kraus flipped his pen against the pad of paper.

Tap, tap, tap.

"I talked to a lot of kids at the high school, even Jessica and her friends, but no one mentioned any of this. Why do you think that is?"

Joey's gaze shot up.

Kraus narrowed a fixed stare on Joey.

What had the other kids said? Why bother talking if Kraus wasn't going to believe him? Joey glanced at the upside-down handwriting scrawled in tiny blue letters across the page.

"Come on, kid, don't shut down on me now."

"I guess no one said nothing, 'cause he's a jerk."

"Who?"

"Greg Kelly."

Detective Kraus jotted a quick note on his pad.

"Greg is Nate's younger brother." Frank supplied. "I've known them both for years. They are good, hardworking boys. I don't know why this one is saying these things."

Kraus nodded. "Hmmmm." He met Joey's gaze.

A question hung in the air between them. Did Kraus think he was lying? Did he believe Frank?

Joey heaved a sigh. "Greg's a big guy. He's a bully. No one wants to get on his bad side."

"Have you ever been on his bad side?"

Joey shrugged.

"Your face has some old scratches and bruising. Did Greg do that to you?"

Frank leaned forward. "He got them fighting at school, when he tried stealing Greg's new jacket."

Kraus glanced toward Frank and frowned. Opening the file folder in front of him, Kraus withdrew a plastic evidence bag. He pulled out a blue thumb drive and set it on the table. "We obtained a warrant to search your backpack and found this. Have you ever seen it before?"

Joey gave another quick shrug.

Kraus sighed. "We have Luke's computer. Our tech guy accessed the temporary files. Several of those files match the files on this." He placed his finger on the bag and pushed it closer. "You and Luke were friends. Did you use his laptop? Is this yours?"

Averting his gaze, Joey stared at the cookies until the letters on the bright blue package swam together. What was Kraus doing, playing both good cop and bad cop?

"Who are you protecting? Luke or yourself?" Kraus reached into the side pocket of his sports coat and pulled out another plastic bag with

Marek's watch inside. He set it on the table. His thumb brushed across the face beneath the plastic. "We also found this in your bag. I know it's not yours. Where did you get it?"

They both knew to whom it belonged. Joey had read the inscription many times. *Will: Love you always, Aimee.*

"Did you take it from Detective Marek's house?"

Frank jerked back in his chair. "You stole his watch?"

"Please, Mr. Denys." Kraus sent Frank an intimidating scowl.

"Sorry," Frank grumbled crossing his arms.

"Now, Joey," Kraus began, his tone friendly again. "Can you tell me how the watch got in your backpack?"

Joey rubbed the heel of his hand over his thigh, pressing deep into the muscle. His other leg began to bounce.

Kraus opened the file folder and set another evidence bag on the table. This one held a single piece of paper.

Joey didn't need to read it. He knew what it was, the title for Luke's truck.

Kraus reached under the file folder and slapped Joey's spiral notebook on the table. With a rustle of paper, he flipped the pages until he reached the drawing of the trestle bridge.

"Interesting drawing. Can you tell me why you drew it?" He swished the page to the drawing of the gun.

"Explain this. A picture of a gun that looks a lot like this one."

He opened the folder and slapped down a photo of a gun.

Joey laced his fingers together, squeezing so tight his bones hurt. His tongue flicked out to moisten his dry lips.

He glanced at the photo. Dried mud smeared the barrel and grip. Bits of grass were tangled in the trigger guard. It was the gun he'd envisioned in the floor tile, the one he'd tried to draw the other night, except in that image there was a hand wrapped around the grip and the barrel was pointed the opposite way.

"I have a little problem here. See, when the trooper took your prints yesterday, the system matched you to a print we lifted off this gun magazine." He reached inside his folder and pushed a new picture closer to Joey. "That magazine belongs to this gun." Kraus used his pen to tap the picture of the muddy gun. "Did you know this weapon belongs to Detective Marek? That he reported it stolen in September? Would you know anything about that?"

And there it was. All the evidence lined up like ducks in a row. Kraus moved his finger down the line, tapping each one in succession. The thumb drive, the watch, the title, the sketch, the first photograph, the second.

Tap, tap, tap, tap, tap, tap. Like a hammer driving nails. Driving nails into Joey's coffin.

Using his index finger, Kraus nudged the picture of Marek's Sig Sauer closer to the edge of the table, closer to Joey. "Because this gun is the murder weapon."

"Do you have any idea how your print got there?" Kraus persisted.

Was Kraus going to charge him for Luke's murder? Why didn't Frank say something? At least ask for a lawyer?

Joey crossed his arms, hugging himself tight.

Kraus was lying about the fingerprint, trying to trick him into saying something incriminating.

"See how all the evidence falls into place?"

Frank shoved back his chair. "My God. You killed that poor boy."

* * * * *

CHAPTER 20

MAREK had told Joey it would be okay if he got in the car with Kraus and his partner. This didn't feel okay.

Kraus pulled out another photo and slapped it down, right in front of Joey.

His stomach lurched. His throat closed off and pressed up against the back of his mouth. He leaped to his feet, shoving his chair back. Saliva pooled around his tongue, and he gagged. He whirled away from the image of Luke lying dead, swollen and gray, on a cold, stainless-steel table.

With nowhere to hide, he turned into the corner. He leaned forward, pressing his forehead against the painted cinderblock wall. He wrapped one arm around his stomach and cupped his opposite hand over his mouth. Breathing slowly through his nose, he tried not to puke.

Christmas trees. Skateboards. Baby grand pianos. He struggled to conjure any image that would erase that horrible picture of Luke from his mind.

How had Marek done it? How had he gone down to the morgue and had the strength to look at Luke that way?

Marek had seen the watch in Joey's backpack, seen the sketch of the trestle bridge. He knew about the fight. He believed Joey wasn't like his father. After all that had happened Marek still trusted in Joey's innocence. Trusted that he hadn't killed Luke, trusted that he would tell the truth.

Joey turned from the shadows of the corner and met Kraus's gaze across the brightly lit room. "Detective Marek believes me."

"I know he does," Kraus replied softly. "And you promised him you'd talk to me. Come sit down. I put away the pictures." Kraus gestured to the empty chair. "We can't find Luke's killer if you don't tell me everything you know."

Joey took a cautious step. After the first, the second one was easier and he returned to the table.

Kraus's keen investigator gaze zeroed in on Joey like a hawk spotting a rabbit. "Start with how your print got on the magazine."

"Luke." Joey whispered. He drew a shaky breath and crossed his arms, cupping each elbow in his palms. "Luke showed me the gun."

"When was that?"

Joey shrugged. "Back in the summer."

Kraus leaned forward and set out the photo of the murder weapon. "And is this the gun Luke showed you?"

"I think."

"You were questioned when Detective Marek's gun was reported missing. Correct?"

Joey rubbed his thigh, watching his hand slide up and down over the denim, the heel of his palm pushing deep into the muscle.

"Correct?"

"Yeah, so?" he mumbled. "I didn't take it."

"Tell me what happened the last time you saw it."

And the story gushed out, like water released from an unkinked hose twisted up tight for too long. He told Kraus about the afternoon in Marek's bedroom, when Luke tried to help Joey get over his fear of guns by showing him the Sig and how, sickened, Joey had tossed the gun and magazine on the bed.

"Did you see the gun again after that day?"

Seeing it in the floor tiles probably didn't count. Joey shook his head. "No."

"Did Luke take it?"

Joey shook his head. Luke wouldn't have been that stupid.

"See, now that we know this is the murder weapon, we know the person who killed Luke was someone who had access to the house and knew where the gun was kept."

Joey crossed his arms, hugging himself tight. He studied the white line of salt stains on his boots.

"Without any sign of break in, can you understand how this might point to you? If it wasn't you that leaves Luke, Detective Lewis, Detective Marek, and Marek's mother."

No. Marek believed him. He didn't kill Luke. But what if Marek was wrong? What if Joey had been so mad that day, he'd gone to Marek's house, gotten Luke's spare key from the truck, taken the gun, and gone to the trestle bridge all without remembering what he'd done? Just like his father claimed happened to him after he'd shot his entire family.

Wait, the gun went missing before Luke was killed. Joey rubbed his churning stomach and looked up, meeting Kraus's gaze.

"The key."

"Key?"

"Yeah, Luke's spare house key. He had an extra truck key and a house key in a magnetic box behind the seat under his jumper cables."

"A spare house key? Why am I just hearing about this?"

Joey shrugged.

"Who else knows about this key?"

"Maybe Jessica or Nate Kelly. Luke worked at the same place as him. Or some of his friends maybe."

Kraus heaved a deep sigh and scribbled something on his note pad. He pulled out the bag with the blue thumb drive and set it on the table.

"It's Luke's," Joey said.

"And how did it get in your bag?"

"I found it in his room the other night, taped to the back of his dresser."

"Do you know what's on it?"

"MMA stats. Luke used to bet on fights."

"He was underage. Do you know who his bookie was?"

Joey shrugged "Nate? Maybe that Mott guy?"

Kraus leaned forward and nudged the pack of cookies closer to Joey. "Eat. Did you ever make any bets?"

Maybe Kraus wasn't going to arrest him.

"No." Joey replied as he accepted the package and pulled apart the cellophane. "Luke tried to get me to. Told me who to bet on. But I never had any money." He popped a cookie in his mouth and chewed.

"Did Luke win a lot?"

"Sometimes. When he won, we'd go to the mall and he'd buy me stuff. But if he lost, I sold the stuff at school and gave Luke the money to pay off Nate."

"Did Greg do any collecting?"

"Only from the kids at school, but everyone knew he gave the money to Nate, and Nate'd come after them if they didn't pay."

Surprised by how hungry he suddenly felt, he ate another cookie.

Kraus nodded. He pulled out the title for Luke's truck and set it beside the flash drive. "And this?"

"Luke gave it to me."

"Why?"

"He owed me money. He couldn't sell his truck, 'cause he wouldn't have been able to get to work. His dad would've noticed if it was gone, so he gave me the title to hold 'til he could pay me back. I told him he didn't have to, but he wanted to."

He picked up the cup of once-hot chocolate and downed the lukewarm liquid in a few gulps.

"And the watch? How'd it end up in your backpack?"

"Luke took it. He said his dad wouldn't notice it was gone, 'cause he never wore it. He pawned it, but planned to get it out of hock soon as he could get enough money. I figured his dad would notice, and Luke would get in trouble. So I sold my cell phone and my game system, and next time Lorraine went to the city I went with her and bought it back."

"When was that?"

Joey set the pack of unfinished cookies on the table. "End of August sometime. I think." He rubbed chocolate crumbs off his fingers onto his jeans. "I wanted to put it back in Detective Marek's closet, so he wouldn't know Luke took it. But I never got the chance."

"Do you know if Luke was paid up, or did he owe Kelly money?"

Joey shrugged one shoulder. Was the file he had seen on Greg's flash drive was right? "Two hundred?"

Kraus flipped his notepad to a clean sheet. "Do you remember where he took the watch?"

"Kind of. We sold some video games at an exchange place near the mall. Then drove downtown. It was a couple streets over from the one with all the bars and clubs."

"Can you describe the shop?"

"There was a guitar in the window and like an iron gate thing across the front of the glass. The guy who bought the watch was bald on top, but the rest of his hair was in a ponytail, like some kind of old hippie."

"And you think Luke might have given the gun to Nate as payment on his debts?"

Joey shook his head. "He never would have taken that gun or given it to anyone."

Kraus jotted a few notes on his pad and then pulled out Joey's notebook. He turned to the page with his sketch of the gun. "Did Luke draw these pictures? Or you?"

Would admitting that he had, make him look even more guilty? He could say it was Luke. Kraus would never know Luke couldn't draw a straight line with a ruler.

Joey gnawed on his lower lip and then nodded. "Yeah, me."

"Why these?"

If Marek didn't even believe him when he'd tried to explain that Luke had told him what to draw, what chance did he have with Kraus?

"Were you there at the trestle bridge?"

"No. And Luke wouldn't have been either. Not on purpose. He was really scared of heights."

Kraus added a few more hasty scribbles to his pad.

There was a quick two-beat knock and the door opened. Roberts-Robbins stepped in. Kraus rose to meet him, notepad in hand. He held it up and pointed toward something with his pen.

"Our pool of suspects on the stolen gun just widened," Kraus said in a low voice.

Rollins-Robbins whispered something, handed Kraus a photograph and a sheet of paper, and then backed out of the room closing the door behind him.

Kraus returned to his seat and slid the paper across the table to Joey. "Do you recognize the name of the pawn shop?"

Joey picked up the paper. He scrolled through the list of business names and shook his head.

"You sure? Anything else you remember?"

"We ate at a burger shop around the corner."

"Good. That helps." He swapped the list for a photograph of Pierson Mott. "How about this guy? Do you know him?"

"Saw him talking to Nate and Greg a couple days ago at the underpass on Cabbage Hill Road."

Kraus ran his hand over his shaved head. "Do you remember what they were talking about?"

"Money." He reached for the nacho chips and pulled open the bag. "Nate gave the guy some money, but the guy said it wasn't enough. He was mad, 'cause Nate let some people slide for Christmas. He told Nate no more bets from kids and to get him the rest of the money by Friday. They caught me listening." Joey paused. He didn't want Kraus know that he'd allowed himself to be beaten.

Roberts pushed open the door. "I got hold of that agent from the FBI. You want to talk to her?"

"Yeah." Kraus's brow furrowed. He jotted a few more notes and then got to his feet. "Sit tight. I'll be right back."

He gathered his pile of evidence and left the room.

Frank shifted in his chair and glared at Joey. "Those Kelly boys are so nice and polite, why would you accuse them like this?"

Ignoring Frank, Joey stuffed two chips at a time into his mouth and crunched as loud as he could with each mouthful, which didn't seem to annoy Frank as much as he'd hoped. He crumpled the wrapper and dropped it into the Styrofoam cup.

The door opened. Kraus stepped in. "You folks can go now. You've been a big help, Joey. I'll let you know if I have any more questions."

Frank slipped between Kraus and the door. Joey stood. He should leave right now before Kraus remembered to ask him why he'd drawn the pictures of the trestle bridge and gun.

He traced his finger back and forth over the edge of the table and then looked up.

Kraus raised his brow in silent question.

Joey met the trooper's gaze. "There's another flash drive."

"What? Luke had two?"

"Greg."

"Explain." Kraus moved into the room.

"I think it's really Nate's." Joey shifted his weight from one leg to the other. "Greg stole my coat. When I got it back, I found a bunch of money and a flash drive in the pocket. I looked at it. It's got gambling stuff on it. Who owes what and stuff."

"Okay. Where is it now?"

"I left it in the guest room at Detective Marek's house."

Kraus frowned, as if his mental wheels were spinning on high. "Thanks for your help. But, Joey, please keep this conversation to yourself."

He reached into the pocket of his jacket and withdrew a business card. He jotted something on the back and then passed it to Joey. Beside the State Police emblem it read *Investigator Mathew Kraus, Pennsylvania State Police* with a number beneath.

Joey flipped it over and glanced at the handwritten number.

"That's my cell phone number," Kraus said. "If you think of anything else, call me. Please."

Joey met Kraus' gaze and nodded, as he shoved the card in the back pocket of his jeans.

Frank leaned in through the open door. "Hurry up. Get your coat. Let's go."

Since he'd left his coat in Marek's SUV, Joey stepped past Frank without a word and headed to the front of the station.

* * * * *

CHAPTER 21

THE smoky aroma of bacon filled the kitchen. Joey's stomach rumbled in response as he closed the back door.

Lorraine cracked eggs into a bowl, while Allison set a cookie sheet of cinnamon buns on the counter. Their casual chatter ceased. Inside the playpen, even Carrie's baby talk stopped. Her wide-eyed gaze zeroed in on Frank as he draped his coat over the back of another on the crowded row of hooks.

"What happened?" Lorraine asked, a wire whisk in hand.

"Nothing," Frank said. He picked up the Sunday paper.

Joey sidled past on his way to the living room.

"For a few minutes I thought they were going to arrest him for killing the Marek boy."

"What?"

"They just questioned him about some gambling Luke did with the Kelly boys."

"Gambling? Those two? I don't believe it."

Frank nodded. "Yeah. And Pierson Mott from over at the country club. Luke Marek owed him money."

Joey slipped unnoticed into the other room. He didn't want to hear anymore. He was out of it now, and it felt good. Lighter somehow.

He'd seen a picture of Atlas once, struggling to hold the world on his shoulders. Until now, he hadn't realized that's how he'd felt under the weight of his lies and secrets. Now he was free. He wasn't like his father. He hadn't killed Luke.

But who had?

"Joey!" Benny jumped up from beside the couch and ran straight for him.

He scooped the little guy up in his arms. "Hey, Ben-jam-in. What are you up to?"

Benny held up his plastic turtle. "He lives in a sewer."

"I know." Joey carried Benny over to the couch, stepping over the colorful pile of snap-together blocks he'd assembled that morning.

Benny squirmed to get down, and after lowering him to the floor, Joey flopped onto the couch. Maybe Benny would like another turtle for Christmas. He seemed to do okay with this one.

Maybe after the late brunch Lorraine was cooking, he'd walk over and get his jacket from Marek's car. He still had that hundred in his pocket. He could go shopping and maybe Greg had been so focused on the flash drive he'd forgotten about the money clip Joey had tossed into the road. Might as well look to see if it was still there.

He probably should give it all to Marek, but he didn't want Benny and Allison to have a crappy Christmas.

He rolled onto his back and stared at the ceiling. The tiny white bumps did kind of look like exploded popcorn. Or snow.

At least there was snow for Christmas this year. Joey didn't care much about the holiday, but Allison and Benny did.

Tomorrow would be Christmas Eve. The realization dropped heavily against his chest. Six years. Six years ago tonight.

Kyle would have been a senior, like Luke. Would Kyle have made plans for college or joined the Marines like their Uncle Mike? The weight of loss swelled up into his throat. Uncle Mike. His mother. Kyle. His dog Charlie. Now Luke. Kyle would have been a good Marine.

Did their father feel any remorse for what he'd done? Did he regret the future he'd stolen from Kyle, from their mom? Did it bother him to know one son had survived?

Maybe. He knew Joey was alive, wanted to write. Pain pricked at the back of his eyes. No. *I hate him.*

He rolled off the couch. He needed to keep busy. Not think about his father. Not now. Not ever.

Returning to the kitchen, he pulled five plates from the cupboard. Lorraine, Frank, and Allison watched him as though he were an elephant who'd just entered the kitchen and decided to set the table. A reluctant smile tugged at the corner of his mouth. It was fun having the power to shock them into silence.

Brunch was eaten without a word. The only sounds were the clinking of silverware against China, until Benny threw peaches on the floor.

Lorraine made that annoying *tsking* noise under her breath. It meant she was pissed but too polite to swear. She wiped up the mess.

When Joey finished his meal, he rinsed his plate in the sink and then placed it in the dishwasher. Instead of going upstairs, he veered toward the coat rack and rooted through the jackets, looking for something warm.

"Oh, no," Frank declared. "You're not going anywhere."

Lifting Frank's heavy gray sweatshirt off the hook, Joey slid his arms into the sleeves. The frayed cuffs were stretched out around the wrist and hung to his fingertips. Grease and coffee stains splotched the front, but the thicker lining was probably warm enough for the walk.

Lorraine made that *tsking* sound again.

Frank sighed, as though he knew further argument was useless, but he somehow still felt the need to assert his authority. "Where are you going?"

Joey stuffed his feet into his insulated work boots. "Out."

"Haven't you gotten into enough trouble lately?"

The metal zipper on the sweatshirt whizzed as he pulled up the tab.

Lorraine huffed. "Insolent and rude." More sins added to the list she and Frank had begun earlier that morning.

Grabbing some gloves, Joey left the house.

His nose was cold before he reached the end of the driveway. Though sunlight reflected off the pristine white around him, the temperature had to be in the teens. He turned onto the road and headed toward Marek's house. His nose ran, and he sniffed. Catching a whiff of Frank's aftershave, he sneezed.

He flipped the hood over his head, but the strings were gone and unable to tighten them, the wind seeped in to sting his ears.

He scanned the center and edges of the road. Blowing snow had filled in the tire tracks from Nate's car, though the places where the bumper had gouged the snowbank were still visible. Joey shivered, whether from the cold or the memory, he didn't know. He really wanted to get back that snowboarding jacket, even if Greg had picked up the money.

To be sure, he angled into the middle of the road searching for a bit of green or a glimmer of the gold money clip.

He kicked at every suspicious lump of slush.

Hopefully, Marek was home. He should have called first, but he didn't have his cell number and Joey would be damned if he'd ask Frank.

He followed the line of tire tracks up the driveway and climbed the steps of the front porch.

Stomping the snow from his boots, he thumbed the bell. Nothing but silence radiated from inside the house. He pressed the bell again. Maybe Marek was sleeping. He knocked. When Luke was alive, he and his dad ate Sunday dinner at his grandmother's. Joey had even joined them a few times.

He peeked through the narrow glass along one side of the door.

Odd. Where was Cody?

He stepped off the front porch, crossed the driveway, and walked to the corner of the garage. Lifting the latch on the gate, he moved into the back yard, and closed the gate behind him. Stepping between a rose bush and the first of two garage windows he peered inside. Noonday sun made it difficult to make out anything beyond Luke's truck. Was the SUV here? Was the snowboarding jacket still on the back seat?

Joey tromped through the snow to the back door of the garage and turned the knob. Locked. He hiked over to the deck and checked the French doors. He pressed down on the lever. Locked. Cupping his hands around his eyes, he peered through the glass at the kitchen table. Marek's laptop sat on the table strewn with papers, some of which had scattered onto the floor. Strange.

He knocked. There was no sign of Cody.

Had something happened to the dog? Maybe Marek had taken Cody with him. Should he wait? He shivered. As much as he hated returning to Frank and Lorraine's, it was too cold to hang around.

Head down, he followed his own footprints back the way he came. As he approached the rose bushes alongside the garage, he noticed an extra set of prints in the new snow. Someone had entered the yard and stopped by the rose bushes.

Joey leaned closer. Back here the impressions had been protected from the blowing snow. The distinctive lug-sole treads looked similar to his own boot prints but were a couple of sizes larger.

Maybe they were Marek's prints, but why had they come in through the gate and stopped here? Weird that they hadn't continued into the yard or gone back through the gate.

Whoever made the footprints had moved between the rose bushes and the side of the garage, right up to the window farthest from the gate. He stared at the window. Then it dawned on him. The bottom half of the glass remained black while the upper portion reflected the sunlight in the same way the first window had. In fact, the entire bottom half of the double-paned glass was missing.

Avoiding the worst of the thorns, Joey stepped close to the window. He braced his hands on the sill and leaned in. Shattered glass covered the floor between the wall and Luke's truck.

He boosted himself up and over, sliding headfirst into the garage, grateful for his gloves as glass crunched between his palms and the concrete.

While he told himself there was probably a logical explanation for both the footprints and the broken window, a heavy, uneasy feeling churned in the pit of his stomach.

He moved around Luke's truck. The black SUV was gone. He needed to stop imagining things. Marek went out. No big deal. He crossed the garage and limped up the steps to the back door. He brushed off the gloves, but tiny shards of glass glistened in the black fabric. He pulled them off and dropped them on the floor of the landing.

Taking a breath, he pressed down the door lever. It offered no resistance.

As he stepped into the laundry room, the absolute stillness raised tiny hairs at the back of his neck.

"Hello? Mr. Marek?"

He stared past the washing machine, beyond the peninsula, and across the table to the opposite wall.

Papers lay scattered on the dark hardwood floor. Normally, not so much as a paper clip would have been out of place.

Marek had probably just gone somewhere and forgotten to lock the back door. But where was Cody?

Maybe he'd taken Cody with him. But that didn't explain the window. The glass hadn't been on the floor yesterday morning when he'd hidden there beside Luke's truck.

His mind spun like a wobbling top. He needed to get a grip.

Footprints outside led to the window and stopped. Greg wanted that flash drive. Had he told his brother that he'd lost it? The last time Joey had seen it, he'd tossed it on the writing desk.

Kraus hadn't mentioned having it when Joey told him about it. Had Marek found the flash drive? Had Nate come here looking for it while Marek was gone?

How would the thief have gotten into the house? Luke's key. What about Pierson Mott? Maybe he'd come to get it back. Maybe he knew how to pick a lock. If so, why break the garage window?

He eased forward into the kitchen.

The countertops were wiped clean. Nothing was out of place, except for three unpacked bags of groceries.

* * * * *

CHAPTER 22

JOEY glanced inside the closest bag. Bread, cheese, and eggs.

He shivered. His fingers itched to wrap around the wooden hilt of his knife, to feel the security its familiar weight offered. He pulled open the drawer beside the stove. His hand bypassed the horizontal rows of kitchen knives organized in their appropriate slots and reached to the very back, hoping his knife was right where he'd last put it.

The sticker coated handle was easy to spot between a soup ladle and a rubber spatula. Wrapping his fingers around the well-worn grip he heaved a sigh of relief, braver now than he'd been a moment ago.

Holding the knife at his side, he eased the drawer shut and sidled along the counter to the refrigerator.

He peered around the corner, down the hall to the foyer. Aside from the open closet door, the padded bench seat and the little table were undisturbed.

He darted to the open basement door and peered down the darkened stairway.

Holding his breath, he listened. He flipped on the light. Quiet.

Heart pounding, knife at the ready, he eased down the stairs. Cupboard doors hung open. Video games and DVDs lay scattered across the floor. On the other side of the wall, the drawers of Marek's toolboxes had been pulled open. Several plastic bins had been pulled off of their shelves and dumped out, spilling Christmas lights, decorations, and ornaments across the work bench.

Should he call 911? Or had Marek come home from shopping, found the mess, and gone to the station to file a report?

Joey headed back to the kitchen. Was someone still in the house?

Maybe he'd better check upstairs before he called. Make sure Marek wasn't there.

Would the police even believe that he wasn't the one who'd broken in and done all this? Would Kraus think Joey had come looking for the second flash drive?

Easing toward the front of the house, he peeked into the dining room. Empty. Across the foyer in the living room where the piano stood, there was deafening silence. Again, the contents of cupboards and shelves had been spilled haphazardly onto the carpet.

Joey gazed up the darkened staircase. One leaden foot at a time, he ascended the treads to the second floor.

He gulped his breaths, telling himself to relax, but his chest hurt almost as bad it had that night exactly six years ago this day.

Was it an omen, a portent that history would repeat itself?

No. What happened to him had not happened to Marek. Luke's dad was not lying in the warmth of his own blood struggling to draw each breath.

Marek had probably gone to his mother's house for Sunday dinner and taken Cody. All this mess had happened afterward. He'd just forgotten to put away his groceries.

Yeah, sure.

He paused mid-step. His foot hovered above the tread. Was that a moan?

Straining his ears to capture every nuance of sound, he heard nothing but the escalation of his own pulse pounding against his ear drums.

Slowly, he continued upward. He froze again. He definitely had heard something this time. A soft cry, like Benny made when he fell and wasn't sure if he was actually hurt.

Ears tuned to nothing else, he waited. There it was again. Not a cry. A whine? Cody?

Joey turned when he reached the top, staring at Marek's door. Not quite closed.

Stepping forward, Joey clenched the knife and reached with trembling fingers to push against the door. It swung inward without a sound.

Daylight spilled through the windows, crossing the room in two broad stripes. One shaft of light stretched across the beige carpet. The other band highlighted the center of the four-poster bed's blue comforter.

He crouched down and looked under the bed. All he saw was the wall on the other side.

Standing, he tiptoed into the room. Just to be sure, he checked the space between the wall and the other side of the bed. Empty. The drawers on the bedside tables were pulled open, but there wasn't a sock on the floor or a wrinkle on the comforter.

He took several steps back and bumped against something solid. The wall. He drew a deep breath and released it. The invisible vise that squeezed his chest, breath by breath, loosened. One part of his brain lectured that he was overreacting. The other part told him he was correct.

Something had happened to Marek.

A soft whimper came from the closet.

Knife gripped tight in front of him, he marshaled his courage and moved forward.

A soft scratching came from the bottom of the closet door.

Joey pressed down on the handle and pushed.

Weight from inside shoved the edge of the door into Joey's shoulder. He stumbled back, as a low flash of golden fur streaked into the center of the room. Cody ran in a circle and then bounded up to Joey, barking.

"How did you get in there?"

None of it made sense. Marek never would have locked Cody in the closet. Added to that were the unlocked door, the broken window, and the groceries.

Did it have something to do with the missing flash drive or Marek's investigation?

Had Mott come here with Nate and done something to Marek? Had the same thing happened to Luke? Had Nate been putting extra pressure on Luke to pay up? Had Luke threatened to tell his dad?

Nose to the carpet, Cody snuffed around the bed and dressers. He then left the room and headed down the hall to the guest room.

Joey followed.

Head down, Cody zigzagged through the room.

Everything was as empty as it had been when Joey left yesterday. Except his backpack was gone. That had been taken to the State Police. Kraus had the contents. He'd shown Joey Luke's blue thumb drive.

Had Kraus already found Nate's flash drive? On TV, cops held back showing all their evidence. As soon as Joey told Kraus he'd never placed a single bet, wouldn't Kraus have at least challenged him by showing him the flash drive? Most likely he would, especially since Joey's name was on the list.

So where was it? He'd had it yesterday. Looked at it on Marek's old laptop. Now that was gone too. Whether Kraus had taken it or Marek had put it away, the desk was clear.

Joey'd had that red flash drive yesterday. When he'd seen his name on the list, he'd yanked it out and tossed it on the desk. Had it fallen on the floor? He bent and looked underneath. All he found was Cody's tennis ball rolled up against the back leg of the desk near the wall.

Beside him, Cody whined.

Joey glanced at the dog, who stared at the ball with his head lowered and his ears perked.

He set his knife on the desk, reached under, and grabbed the ball. As he did, he spotted the thin, red rectangle lying on the carpet between the baseboard and the back leg of the desk.

He tossed the ball over his shoulder, reached back, and snatched up the flash drive.

With it clenched tight in his palm, he straightened. The State Police didn't have it. Had Nate broken in to look for it? That would explain why Cody had been locked in the closet.

Had Greg mentioned to Nate that Marek had been going somewhere earlier this morning? But how did either of them know when Marek would be back? Or had Marek come home from shopping and caught someone searching his house?

Where was the SUV? Again, why was Cody in the closet?

Joey dropped onto the end of the bed. Cody trotted over with the ball and released it. The fuzzy green orb rolled toward Joey's foot and bumped against his arch.

If Nate had broken in to hunt for the flash drive that would explain the window, but how had he gotten inside the house? Did he know about the spare keys under the jumper cables in Luke's truck?

No matter how Joey looked at it, things didn't add up.

"Cody, c'mere."

Joey patted his thigh and the dog trotted over. He leaned down and gave the dog a quick hug. Dogs followed their instincts and that's what Joey would do. He rose, shoved the flash drive into the front pocket of his jeans, and grabbed his knife.

With Cody trailing behind, he hurried down the stairs.

He picked up the cordless phone from a table in the corner near the French doors, intent on calling Marek's cellphone. He stopped short. He didn't know the number, and he was not calling Frank.

Instead, he searched through Marek's papers on the kitchen table. Maybe he had a business card with his number like Investigator Kraus. Unable to find anything, he checked the pockets of the navy peacoat draped around the back of one of the chairs.

Peacoat? Joey stared at the garment. People had more than one coat. Just because the peacoat was here didn't prove anything. This morning Marek had worn just a flannel shirt and a sweater.

This was crazy. He was overreacting. He'd just call the station.

He set his knife on the counter and pulled open the drawer beneath the phone. He shoved aside pens, batteries, tape, and a screwdriver to reach the battered phone book at the back.

Even as he dropped it on the counter, the little voice taunted him, calling his worry absurd, ridiculous, unreasonable. He flipped through the pages anyway.

His heart raced as he dialed. He took a breath, silently counting each ring. One. Two. Three.

"Easton Police Department," a woman said. "Can I help you?"

"Um, is Detective Marek there?"

"No, he isn't. Let me transfer you to the detective on duty."

Restless, he paced to the laundry room and back.

"Detective Crosby, can I help you?"

"Um, I wanted to talk to Detective Marek."

"He's not here. Can I help you?"

"I need to talk to him. I just need his number."

"No can do."

"But we're, um, neighbors."

"I can take your number and leave him a message to call you. Or you can call back tomorrow."

"Uh, I need to talk to him today."

"Look, is there something I can help you with?"

"Is Detective—" What was that guy's name? His partner with the reindeer sweatshirt. Little? Layton?

What should he do? Should he tell this guy about the broken window and the groceries?

Should he tell him that Cody had been in the closet and his gut was telling him that something had happened to Marek?

"Hello? You still there?"

Maybe this was all nothing. Marek was a grown man. He was a cop. He could take care of himself.

"Hello?"

He probably went to the grocery store, wearing a different jacket. Nate broke in looking for the flash drive and locked Cody in the closet. Marek came home and what? Would this Detective Crosby believe him?

The connection went silent.

Deflated, Joey stared at the handset. He should just grab his new jacket as he had planned and head back to Frank and Lorraine's. He'd suck it up and ask Frank for Marek's number. A quick call would probably reveal a logical explanation.

Cody whined and Joey let him out through the French doors. The dog trotted down the steps of the deck and nosed around the bushes and trees. A dozen chickadees pecked through the loose seed that littered the snow beneath the maple tree. Above, a blue jay screeched from the roof of a bird feeder, as though yelling at Joey to hurry, to do something.

The broken window in the garage nagged him. Something or someone had broken through there, but who? And where was Detective Marek?

Cody bounded through the snow toward the feeder, scattering the chickadees into the branches.

What he needed was a crystal ball.

The jacket.

He'd tossed both the denim jacket and the snowboarding coat into the backseat of the SUV. Would Marek have left them there or taken them out? He was always careful with Luke's jacket. Maybe he grabbed it and hung it up.

Dashing to the front foyer, he shoved wide the closet door. The snowboarding jacket hung beside his old blue one with the broken zipper. Where was the denim jacket?

Luke's room. He charged up the stairs as best he could. He half-ran, half-hopped, following the railing around to Luke's bedroom above the living room. The closet door had been slid open. Empty.

Every drawer of the dresser was also empty. He checked under the bed and even the drawers of Luke's desk. Nothing.

Whirling, Joey dashed across the hall. He checked the closet and every nook and cranny of the guestroom, but found nothing.

Where could it have gone?

Once more he found himself standing outside Marek's bedroom door. Heart pounding, he stepped inside. The wing chairs near the window were empty. Nothing lay on the bed, under the TV, or in the blanket trunk.

His shoes silent on the carpet, he pushed open the closet door.

The denim jacket was draped over the shoulders of a valet stand.

Slanted red eyes and the toothy evil grin of the band logo for *Disturbed* laughed at him from a green circle of cloth sewn just below the left front pocket of Luke's jacket.

He jumped back. Had that patch always been there? He shook his head. It must have been. He'd just forgotten.

Shrugging off the ratty sweatshirt, he hung it from a hook on the side of the shelving unit. He reached out and yanked the jacket off the hanger so hard the stand teetered.

As soon as he slipped his arms into the sleeves, warmth enveloped him. He shoved his hands into the pockets and waited for an image.

He stood there in the absolute quiet, listening to the whispers of his own slightly winded breathing.

Closing his eyes, he pictured Marek and concentrated. Minutes passed. Nothing.

Come on. This has to work.

Maybe he needed to hold something personal that belonged to Marek. That's what the psychics did on TV. He pulled a white button-down shirt from its hanger and squeezed it with both hands. Closing his eyes, he tried to picture Marek as he last saw him this morning, wearing a cream color sweater and blue flannel shirt. Nothing.

"Come on, Luke. Talk to me."

The silence closed in on him. His skin crawled. Still nothing.

Maybe the shirt wasn't personal enough. He looped it around the wooden valet and pulled open the thin top drawer of the built-in dresser. A padded tray dotted with several tie clips and cuff links lay within.

He picked up a pair of gold cuff links with the initials, WJM. Maybe they'd been a gift from his wife. Clenching his fist around them, he closed his eyes and concentrated. No headache. No vision.

Cody barked outside.

Joey opened his eyes and returned the cuff links to the drawer. The visions had never come right away. Maybe he needed to wear the jacket for a little while longer.

He left the bedroom and limped down the stairs. Think. There must be a logical explanation. He dropped to sit on the stairs, like he had the other night as he listened to Marek play the piano.

The piano! It was the most personal thing in the house. He jumped up and ducked around the opening into the living room. Sliding onto the bench he laid his knife beside him and pushed back the cover exposing the keys. His fingers hovered over the ivories, waiting.

He ran his fingers up and down the scales. Nothing. Maybe this was a stupid idea. So far Luke had initiated the visions. Joey had never called on Luke. Wait, he had the other night when Luke told him to draw.

He had to try. He couldn't shake the feeling that something was wrong.

"Luke!" he yelled at the ceiling with his head tipped back. "Tell me where your dad is!"

* * * * *

CHAPTER 23

AS the last note of his voice faded away, an eerie stillness settled through the house.

It pressed in on him like fog rolling over the fields on a frosty morning, until all around him was misty white. His heart skipped a beat, maybe two or three. He gulped and tried to breathe, waiting for a normal rhythm to return.

Gradually, the mist parted like sheer white curtains transforming the room into overgrown fields, scrub brush, distant trees, and blue sky. The shadowy silhouette of an old shack or hunting cabin wavered near the tree line.

Where, Luke? Where is that place?

Like a movie camera shifting from a wide angle shot to a narrow zoom, the image blurred and wavered. When it cleared, he found himself looking at a rutted logging road.

His eyes ached, dried out from staring. He longed to rub his hand over them, to blink in some moisture, but he was afraid to shut out the image even for that millisecond of time. The vision zoomed closer.

A gray, corrugated metal building came into focus.

It was the maintenance shack near the trestle bridge!

A group of kids sat around outside talking and laughing. Greg Kelly was there with some guys from the baseball team. Jessica Bickman and a couple of her friends. Some sat on an old pile of railroad ties, others on the ground. They passed around a joint and two guys drank beer from cans.

The kids looked up.

"Yo, Luke!" someone yelled. "Did you bring more beer?"

Jessica looked into Joey's eyes, or rather Luke's eyes, and gave a sweet smile.

The image grew opaque and then faded.

"Luke, don't go!"

But the shack and fields were gone. All that remained was the black Steinway and a piercing headache that knifed through Joey's temples.

Closing his eyes, he leaned over the keys and rubbed his forehead.

He drew a deep breath and blew it out slowly.

Maybe he should tell someone.

And say what? There was no sane explanation for what had just happened.

If he was going to believe any of this was real, then Luke's dad was at the shack near the trestle bridge. Joey needed to get there before anything bad happened. He wrapped his fingers around the hilt of his knife, slid off the bench and headed toward the foyer.

Whump!

Joey froze.

The thud had come from upstairs.

Impossible. No one was up there. Except. Maybe. No. It couldn't be.

Outside, Cody barked again.

Unwilling to venture up there alone, he headed to the kitchen and opened the door.

Cody trotted in from the deck, passed him, and made for the front of the house, as if he knew something or someone was upstairs.

The logical side of Joey's brain told him not to follow Cody. Marek had probably returned from wherever he'd been, and Joey hadn't heard him because he'd been lost in the vision.

Yet, the other part, the part that knew Luke was here, sent Joey's feet moving up the staircase. He entered Marek's room and crossed the carpet to the open closet.

On the floor lay the pistol safe. He stared at it while his pulse pounded erratically against the back of his jaw and his stomach turned to slush. He looked up, following its assumed path of descent. On the top shelf beside an orange shoebox loomed an empty space.

Maybe the safe had fallen, because Marek just hadn't pushed it back far enough when he returned it to the shelf yesterday.

Except, Joey knew.

Luke wanted Joey to take the gun. He tried to swallow the lump that had risen in his throat, but his muscles had squeezed too tight. Pulse pounding, he switched his knife to his left hand and rubbed his right hand dry. He blew out a shaky breath and then swallowed.

He stared at the case as if it were a rattlesnake ready to strike. He eased back a step. What Luke wanted didn't matter, because Joey didn't know the code.

Keeping his gaze locked on the case, he eased back another step and froze. Had it moved? No. He rubbed his hand over his eyes and looked again.

The case was now inches from his feet.

"Stop it!"

Cody came up beside him, looking at something beyond the case, except there was nothing there.

"Go yourself! You don't need me!"

Except, maybe Luke did. Joey reached up and tried to take off the jacket, but invisible hands wrestled to keep it on him.

With shaky hands he bent down and snatched up the case. Turning, he threw it across the room onto the bed.

The case popped open.

"Stop it, Luke! I can't do this. Please!"

Cody trotted from the closet and stopped just short of reaching the bed. He wagged his tail.

Joey rubbed at the pain in his head. He blinked as the edges of his vision blurred. This time instead of being transported to another place, he stood in this room beside the bed with Luke.

Marek's Sig 220 lay on the comforter.

Luke watched Joey rub his hand over his thigh, gaze at the floor, and shake his head.

"No, I can't."

"Don't be afraid," Luke urged.

"No, it could go off." Joey's hand came up to rub his chest.

"It can't. The chamber's empty and I have the magazine." Luke held out the black metal clip. "See. Take it."

Joey shook his head.

"Come-on. Just hold it. How else are you gonna get over your fear?"

Joey's head came up. "I don't see you taking up skydiving."

Luke laughed. "Not yet, but I walk over that little bridge on the tracks. And all I'm asking you to do is hold it."

Joey sighed and took the magazine. Luke passed him the gun, keeping the barrel pointed down. "Come on, take it."

Slowly, Joey wrapped his hands around the grip and Luke stepped back.

But Joey's hand started to shake. He dropped the gun and magazine on the bed and whirled toward the door. Luke watched him leave the room, and in his awkward run-hop gait, Joey ran down the hall toward the bathroom.

The room shifted and blurred. Joey massaged his temples and blinked. He again saw the room through his own eyes.

He was alone, except he knew he wasn't.

Inching his way to the bed, he stared at the open gun safe. Inside it, illuminated by blue light, lay the Sig—hard, black, and unyielding.

His stomach churned. He half-expected the weapon to levitate from the case and point at his chest.

"Come on, take it."

Did he really need to take the gun? He had his knife. He rubbed at the pressure behind his temples.

"Come on, take it."

He eased closer to the bed and set his knife on the comforter. Stomach roiling, he lifted out the weapon. He struggled to ignore Luke's persistent urging and focus instead on Marek's voice and his careful instructions for loading the gun.

Finger off the trigger, safety on. Finger on, safety off.

When Joey's world had fallen apart, Marek had believed in him despite the evidence, believed that Joey wasn't insane like his father, believed that Joey hadn't murdered his best friend.

Now Marek was in trouble, and Joey stood there trying to work up the courage to pick up the gun.

He lifted the magazine free from its niche in the foam, weighted now as it was fully loaded.

"I can't do this, Luke. I'm scared."

The warmth of the jacket settled over him, like the weight of a soft blanket. Oddly, he felt comforted to know Luke was here, that he could talk to him, that he wasn't alone.

Almost as if Luke guided his hands the way he guided his feet, Joey clicked the magazine into place with his open palm. Like a TV cop, he slipped the gun into the hollow at the base of his spine, between his jeans and flannel shirt. He then adjusted the oversize denim jacket to conceal the bulge. Maybe with Luke's help, he'd make it through the day without shooting himself in the ass.

Snatching his knife from the bed, he gripped it tight and headed downstairs.

Should he tell someone where he was going? Frank and Lorraine wouldn't believe him. Maybe he should call back that detective at the police station and at least tell him he thought Marek was in trouble.

He set his knife on the table and picked up the phone. There'd be a lot to explain. Detective Cross or Crosby probably wouldn't believe him anymore than Frank.

What about Kraus? Joey slid his hand into the back pocket of his jeans and pulled out the white business card. Before he could change his mind, he punched in the seven numbers for Kraus' cell phone.

It rang, once, twice, three times, four times, five, and went to voicemail.

"Uh, this is Joey Kowalski. I'm at Detective Marek's house. I think something might have happened to him. The house is trashed. There's a broken window, and his dog Cody was locked in a closet. I'm going to the old maintenance shack on the State Game Lands near the trestle bridge. Just wanted to let you know in case. Umm, Bye. And I found that flash drive. Greg wants it back. Bye."

He tucked his pants into his boots and tied the laces. Grabbing his knife, he slid it into his boot between the denim and the leather. He gave Cody a quick pat on the head and left him in the laundry room as he closed the back door.

His first thought was to walk the tracks. It was the most direct route, but walking wouldn't be the fastest. His gaze landed on Luke's truck.

He moved down the steps and crossed the space where Marek's SUV had been.

For a moment a wave of guilt washed over him. Not because he planned to drive without a license, but because it was Luke's truck. Joey was about to commandeer it, as though he had the right.

Would the truck even start? Had Marek taken it out once in a while or had the thought of sitting behind the wheel been too painful?

Joey could drive, though he hadn't driven much. His previous foster placement had been with a mechanic and his wife. The guy used to let Joey help him out in the garage by moving cars in and out. Joey had even driven Luke's truck once.

Last spring Luke had called, and asked Joey to come pick him up at the shack by the trestle bridge and drive him home. He'd had a fight with Jessica. She had left with some other kids, while Luke stayed to finish off a bottle of Johnny Walker. It hadn't been cold or snowy then. Still, it had taken Joey nearly a half an hour to take the tracks and walk out there.

He lifted the door latch of Luke's truck and reached behind the seat for the magnetic box. When he slid back the cover, the only key inside was the extra ignition key.

As he adjusted the seat, the bulk of the gun pressed against his spine. He studied his reflection in the rearview mirror. Luke's presence was so strong inside the cab, that Joey wondered for a moment whose eyes looked back at him.

Shaking off the sensation, he inserted the key and gave it a turn.

The starter whined but didn't turn over. He tried again. Almost, but the battery didn't have quite enough juice to catch it.

"Come on, Luke. Start your stupid truck!"

He turned the key again. The engine roared to life, and the odor of gasoline filled the cab. He cupped his hands over his mouth and blew out a stream of warm breath. Rubbing his hands together, he shivered but didn't turn on the heat. The fan might suck down the battery. He thought about running back in the house for his old coat, but Luke had instilled in Joey a sense of urgency he couldn't ignore. He reached for the visor and hit the garage door opener.

He buckled the seatbelt, shifted into reverse, and backed outside. Daylight spilled across the garage floor. Broken glass glistened beneath the window, removing the last of his doubts that something was wrong.

At the end of the driveway, he turned east and headed up the road.

He slowed, as he passed Nate and Greg's trailer. In front of the crooked front porch where Nate always parked his beat-up piece of junk, there were only deep tracks in the snow.

Several minutes later he slowed again, searching for the narrow, rutted road that entered the state game lands. He glanced at the clock in the dash. Ten minutes had passed. He slowed some more.

Up ahead, the dark outline of a vehicle parked along the edge of the road slowly grew more distinct. Nate's tri-colored muscle car was parked with the passenger side inches from the side of the snowbank.

On the right, a few feet behind the trunk of Nate's car, fresh tire tracks had broken through a pile of icy sludge tossed up by the snowplow.

Joey swung the truck into the left lane and turned the wheel. He hit the snowbank as straight as possible, giving the truck just enough gas to plunge through it. Whoever had broken through the snowbank initially must have also had a four-wheel drive.

Sunlight bounced off the snow, creating a glare that made the ruts hard to follow, but Joey pushed through as best he could. The truck bounced in and out of hidden snow-filled potholes, jerking the seatbelt tight.

Footprints also followed the ruts. Whoever had been driving Nate's car appeared to be headed toward the maintenance shack.

Joey steered through a curve, around overgrown scrub brush, and then hit the brake.

Ahead, stark against the white, was Marek's black SUV.

Luke had been right. His dad was here. Was he in trouble or was something else going on?

Joey's pulse thrummed against the back of his jaw. The weight of the gun at the back of his waist seemed to press itself tighter to his spine.

His hands were clenched so tight on the steering wheel, that his knuckles turned white. He rested his throbbing forehead on the top of the wheel and tried to think as he bounced the knee of his good leg.

His heart pounded erratically against the wall of his chest. He didn't want to be here.

Was Nate meeting Pierson Mott? Maybe Marek had come out there to catch them in the act of something. Joey couldn't imagine Mott walking through all this snow for any reason. If Marek had come to arrest Nate, why would he come out here alone? What was going on?

What if this was just Joey's imagination gone wild? What if none of this with Luke was real and Joey was actually crazy?

No. Marek had believed in Joey, had told him he wasn't crazy.

He turned off the engine and opened the door, shoving the keys in his pocket as he slid off the seat.

The hard weight of Marek's Sig pressed against the small of his back. He didn't need the gun. What was he going to do with it anyway?

He reached behind, wrapped his hand around the grip, and pulled. It caught on something. His belt loop? He pushed against the resistance and tried to turn the barrel in order to pull it from a different angle. Something held it fast.

Luke.

"Stop it," Joey whispered. "If you want to use this gun, you'll have to levitate it yourself, 'cause I'm not touching it."

He heaved a sigh and hooked his hand over the top corner of the door. Luke was getting stronger.

Joey rested his forehead against the denim sleeve of his forearm. "I'm not crazy," he murmured. "I'm not crazy. I'm. Not. Crazy."

Well, he'd come this far. Might as well check to see what was going on, see if Marek actually was here.

He eased the truck door closed and walked to the SUV.

A long, faded-yellow triangular pipe gate blocked the road. Where the two long points of the gate came together over the center of the rutted road, a chain joined them.

Below the padlock hung a dented and rusty sign. *No Trespassing.*

Squinting against the glare of sunlight that bounced off the snow, he focused on footprints that moved toward and then around the SUV.

The person who made them had tromped over a previous set of prints, and a furrow of what appeared to be drag marks moving from the SUV, under the pipe gate, and on toward the shack.

Joey moved around the vehicle and opened the driver's door.

Ping, ping, ping.

He reached inside, pulled the keys from the ignition, and glanced at the seat and console. Everything seemed normal. He closed the driver's door and checked the back seat. Nothing. He then walked to the back and lifted the hatch.

Though the interior of the vehicle was black, sunlight brightened the cargo area.

Two bags of groceries lay on their side, their contents spilled beside a tipped over gallon of milk.

In the corner, a yellow blanket lay folded against the back of the seat and the curve of the wheel well. Was it part of Marek's emergency winter supplies of jumper cables and sand or a blanket for Cody?

It didn't matter.

In the center was a bright red, softball-sized circle of blood.

*****

CHAPTER 24

FROZEN, Joey stared, unable to blink, unable to tear his gaze from the stain. In his mind he was back in his old bed gasping to find his next breath as he watched the blood seep slowly from Kyle's body.

Run! Run!

Run? Joey blinked. He couldn't think about Kyle right now. This was Marek's blood.

Run! Luke screamed. *Run!*

Joey scrubbed his hand across his forehead.

Move!

Marek was in trouble. Marek was the only person who believed in him, the only person Joey would ever trust. He would never have been able save Kyle. He should have gone after Luke. But he could help Marek.

Drawing a deep breath, he closed the hatch and strode to the gate.

"Alright, Luke, let's go."

Ducking into trees and brush that ran parallel to the rutted road, he limped around the gate and inched his way forward.

His boots were soon soaked from punching through the deep powder into low-lying pockets of water. Soon the insides of his insulated boots were damp, and his toes were numb.

His ankle bone hurt, where the top of the knife blade rubbed against it through his sock. The wooden hilt was ready for him to grab.

The gray, corrugated metal maintenance shed took shape between maple and pine trees. He skirted around the back of the building and dropped behind a pile of rusty iron rails overgrown with thorn bushes and covered with snow.

From the front of the shack raised voices stilled the chatter of birds.

"I know you're pissed."

"I'm more than pissed." Nate's cutting tone slashed at his brother like a whip. "I call you to find out where you are and where's my money and my flash drive. Simple questions. Simple answers. But no, my dumb ass brother lost my flash drive, went and kidnapped a cop, and brought him way the hell out here."

"Listen, Nate, I got a plan."

"To hell with your plan. Destroy the flash drive. Let him go."

"I told you," Greg argued. "He knows everything."

"I don't care."

"Do you want to go to prison?"

"I told you Mott would handle the cops," Nate snapped. "He has connections. Now you went and screwed it all up! Again!"

"He won't have to know."

"Of course, he's gonna know, you dumb ass."

Joey crouched and eased around the corner. Hugging the side of the building, he followed the south wall and skirted a pile of rotted timbers. He slid to his knees behind a rusty fifty-gallon drum and took a quick peek over the top.

Mott wasn't there.

Only Nate and Greg stood in front of the entrance.

"No, listen. All the evidence is on that flash drive. Gimp has it or knows where it is. Everyone already thinks he wasted his best friend. Let him take the fall for this, too. I got it all figured out. I used Gimp's name to cover for my friends. Cops will think he owes a shit-ton of money and wasted Marek like he did Luke. He'll go to prison just like his old man, and he won't be able to testify against you."

Nate drove his fingers through his hair and clutched the back of his head. "Damn it, Greg. This is bad. Let him go or I'm done! I'm sick of bailing your ass out of trouble!"

"Don't worry." Greg laughed. He reached toward his brother as if to give him a reassuring pat on the shoulder, but Nate moved back shaking his head.

Greg stepped forward. "Listen, listen. This can work. I can get Gimp out here."

"You stupid shit, he won't come out here with you."

"I'll tell him to bring the flash drive, if he wants to save his cop friend."

"Damn it, Greg. You are not killing a cop!" He paced to the leafless tangle of pricker bushes at the corner of the building.

Joey jerked back out of sight, praying Nate hadn't seen him.

Nate pulled his phone from his coat pocket and whirled back toward his brother. "What are you gonna do next? Kill his partner, too?"

"Yell a little louder, Nate. They didn't hear you in China."

"Shut up! Just shut up!"

"What are you doing?"

"Damn it, no signal."

"Who are you calling?"

"Let me think," Nate said. "Did Marek see you? Does he know you brought him here?"

"I hit him upside the head pretty hard. He was still out when you showed up." Greg chuckled to himself.

The voices seemed to have moved farther from the front of the shack. Joey peeked between the drum and the building.

Nate raised his phone toward the sky, as he moved around in a circle. "How the hell did you have signal?"

Greg stood watching him. "Who are you trying to call?"

"Mott. He'll know how to fix this."

Greg snickered.

"Why are you laughing? Your plan sucks. I wouldn't be surprised if Mott cuts us both loose."

"We don't need him. I'm telling you, this will work. I've got the cop's Glock. I'll put Gimp's prints on it." He pointed his left index finger and thumb at the ground and mimed pulling the trigger. "Bang!"

Joey clamped his hand over his mouth to squelch a gasp. He jerked back, pressing his head between the vertical ridges of the siding.

How could Greg say that so casually? As if Marek's life had no value. As if killing him would fix everything. It was crazy. Like shooting your entire family to keep them together.

"I've got to get away from these trees. I'm going over by the gate. Stay here. Don't. Do. Anything!"

"Come on, Nate, leave him out of it."

"Shut up. I'll be right back. Don't touch that cop. Don't even look at him cross-eyed."

"Who the hell do you think you are, my father?"

"Our father was a drunk and an addict, who used to beat the shit out of both of us. I'm your damn brother. I looked out for you and made sure you didn't end up in foster care like that little piss-ant down the road. You owe me respect. For once in your life, will you do what I say?"

Nate strode off.

Greg followed a few steps and then from inside his jacket pulled out what had to be Marek's service weapon. In slow motion Greg raised his left hand and pointed the gun barrel toward Nate's back. It was just like the vision in the floor tiles.

Run! Luke screamed. *Run!*

Pain slashed through Joey's head from temple to temple.

At any moment he expected to hear the crack of a gunshot echo through the trees. But Greg didn't pull the trigger.

While he appeared focused on his brother, Joey inched around the drum toward the door.

The padlock hung cockeyed from a latch that had been pried off the door jamb so many times a dozen holes pockmarked the wood.

With a quick glance toward Greg, Joey pulled the handle just enough to squeeze through, keeping his hand on the door to stop it from banging when it closed.

He waited a moment for his eyes to adjust. Wedges of light illuminated the floor where the metal siding didn't quite reach the ground. From above pinpricks of sunshine shone like stars through tiny holes in the roof.

A half-wall jutted partway across the width of the room. Shovels and a broom leaned in a jumble against the corner. Bags of cement, torn and spilling gray powder, had been stacked along the half-wall beside a five-gallon pail of oil. A battered drop-leaf table, surrounded by white plastic chairs, filled the rest of the space. The last time Joey had been here, a ratty mattress had lain on the floor on the other side of the partial wall.

Hope and dread churned inside his stomach, as he crept across the packed dirt floor. From the other side of the partition came a soft scuffling sound, like a rat or woodchuck scurrying for a hole.

He froze. Drawing a breath to steady his resolve, he peered over the half-wall.

Detective Marek lay on his side with arms behind his back. Gray duct tape covered his mouth and had been wrapped several times around his knees and ankles. Blood matted the hair around his left temple. It coated his ear and the side of his neck.

Marek's eyes widened, and the color drained from his face. He looked disoriented, as if unable to process what was happening.

The door opened. Greg stepped inside, silhouetted in a backwash of sunlight.

Joey dropped and scrambled behind the half-wall, hoping Greg's eyes hadn't adjusted yet to the darkness. He spared a quick glance at Marek, whose brow was now furrowed in confusion. He must have recognized something in Joey's expression, for the tension in his features eased.

"Run!" Luke screamed.

Joey pulled his knife from his boot and leaned over Marek to saw through the duct tape that bound his wrists.

"I see you Gimp. Come on out of there."

Joey glanced at Marek, who shook his head and gestured for Joey to stay down. But Greg's plan needed Joey to be alive, and Marek needed time to free himself.

Laying the knife on the dirt, Joey pushed to his feet. His gaze locked on the gun in Greg's hand, its barrel pointed toward the ground. His heart pounded and he struggled to swallow.

Something tugged at the back of his waist. He figured Marek had freed himself and reached for the Sig beneath the denim jacket.

Joey shoved his hand into the front pocket of his jeans, pulled out the flash drive, and held it up.

"Thanks for being so obliging, Gimp. Now give it here."

Joey stepped past the end of the half-wall into the beam of sunlight streaming through the open door.

Greg stilled, his face as white as the snow on the ground outside. The gun in his hand shook. "No. It can't be. You're dead You're dead! Leave me alone!"

Did Greg think he was Luke because he was wearing Luke's jacket?

"I. Am. Dead." Joey said the words, but it was Luke's voice he heard. He laughed. The sound rang out exactly like Luke.

Joey's heart thumped wildly against the inside of his chest. How was Luke doing this? He should have taken off the jacket, leaving it and Luke inside the truck.

Something bumped Joey's waist. He glanced down. His breath caught in his throat as Marek's new Sig Sauer, the gun Luke forced Joey to bring, levitated to hover in the air right in front of Joey.

The barrel was aimed straight at Greg.

"Stay back." With a shaking hand, Greg raised the gun he'd taken from Marek and retreated a step. "Stay away from me."

Joey's breath caught in his throat. His stomach trembled as a wave of nausea rose and ebbed. He grabbed at the jacket, trying to tear the denim from his body, but Luke held the buttons tight.

"Luke, don't do this." Joey shot his arms out to his side, extending his fingertips as far away from his body as he could. "Luke, you're going to get me killed. Put the gun down."

Greg moved back. "I'm sorry, Lukey-Boy, I didn't mean to do it." His voice caught on a sob. "Jessica is my girl. If you hadn't made me so mad, I wouldn't have pulled the trigger."

Greg? Greg killed Luke?

Luke had been trying to tell Joey all along what had happened to him. The trestle bridge. The gun held by someone left-handed. The ball cap with the penguin.

Joey had been so wrapped up in himself, that he'd misread everything.

Luke, I'm so sorry. I should have gone after you. I'm sorry I left you alone.

Greg backed away. Before he could reach the door, it banged shut.

It could have been a gust of wind, but Joey knew it was Luke.

The interior of the shed should have been swallowed in darkness, but the brilliant glow of sunshine remained.

Greg's wide eyes fixed on Joey. "Leave me alone!" He wrapped his other hand around the grip of the gun. The shakiness eased as he aimed.

Marek, solid and heavy, slammed into Joey, knocking him to the floor as a gunshot splintered the wooden half-wall beside him.

* * * * *

CHAPTER 25

"GREG." Marek's voice rumbled through the denim jacket into Joey's back. "Put down the gun."

Several quick shots erupted from the gun Greg held, as he fired into the brilliant light where the Sig still floated.

The weight of Marek's arm pressed down on Joey's head, as bullets thudded into the floor and half-wall.

"Luke, stop!" Joey's voice was muffled by the weight of Marek's body. "Give your dad the gun. It's over. We know. We know."

Greg stopped shooting. The sudden quiet would have been deafening, except for the soft sobs coming from near the door.

The Sig that Luke had been holding floated down and hovered inches away from Marek.

"Stay down," Marek whispered in Joey's ear.

He snatched the gun from the air. His weight eased off Joey's back and hips, as he rolled to his feet.

Joey remained on the ground and watched Marek's legs step past him. Several layers of duct tape remained wrapped around the ankles of his jeans.

"Put down the weapon, Greg. Now!"

Slowly, Greg's shadowy form bent over and placed the gun on the floor.

Marek stepped forward and placed his foot on the gun. After sliding it to one side, he picked it up and shoved it in the waistband of his jeans.

Joey rolled to his feet.

Greg slumped to the floor and drew his knees up close to his body. He stared at Joey. "I saw you fall. You're supposed to be dead."

Marek glanced back and met Joey's gaze. "He killed Luke."

Joey gave him a slight nod. "He killed Luke."

In two long strides Marek crossed the room and yanked Joey into a bear hug. He gripped fistfuls of denim and held him tight. Maybe too tight.

At first Joey was content to be held, feeling safe and protected as the adrenaline drained from his system, leaving his legs weak and his knees shaky.

After a minute, doubt washed over him. Why was Marek clinging to him like this? A tiny crack started in the corner of Joey's heart. Quickly, the damage spread, splintering off into more cracks until his heart felt like a shattered windshield and his whole chest hurt from the pain of it.

He pushed against the solid wall that was Marek and stepped back.

He lifted his gaze and searched Marek's face, surprised by the man's puzzled expression.

"I'm not Luke."

Marek's brow furrowed for a moment. "He was going to shoot you." He stepped close and hooked his arm around Joey's neck, like they were best friends. "If anything happened to you, I'd never forgive myself." He tipped back his head and stared at the roof peak. "It's over." He sighed and looked at Joey. "It's really over."

He rubbed his hand over his face and stepped back. "Alright, Kelly, on your feet. Hands on top of your head. Start walking."

Joey darted behind the wall and picked up his knife. He ran his finger over the stickers and then slipped it back inside his boot.

With Greg walking in front, hands on his head, Marek and Joey marched him out of the shed and down the narrow road to the gate.

When they reached the vehicles, Marek opened the passenger door of his SUV and pulled a set of handcuffs from the glove box.

After fastening Greg's hands behind his back, Marek sat Greg in the back seat.

Before the door closed, Greg met Joey's gaze and scowled. "You're not Luke. You tricked me."

Marek slammed the door and turned to Joey. "Now tell me what hell the really happened back there."

"It was Luke."

Marek shook his head. He paced back and forth for a moment and then sat on the front bumper of Luke's truck. He scrubbed his hands over his face. "That was really Luke?"

Joey nodded and joined him, leaning against the grill.

Marek shot him a quick glance and then stared at the snowy ground. "You said that yesterday, but I didn't believe you. Can you see him?" Marek squeezed his eyes tight and pinched the bridge of his nose.

"No. When I put on the jacket, I hear him in my head. I see images, things he saw. He's stronger now. He can move things. He opened your gun safe. Made me bring it."

Marek looked up. "But you don't see him?"

Joey shook his head. "No."

The longing was there in Marek's voice, the aching to see Luke one more time, to know his son was okay, that he was happy. The same things Joey wondered himself about his mom, about Kyle. Were they happy? Were they alright?

"He showed me though. He's with his mom. Your wife. I saw her. She said: '*Come here so I can give you a big hug.*' Luke's okay. He's home."

Marek swallowed. A big gulp that made his Adam's apple bob up and down. He swiped at the tears that leaked from the corners of his eyes. He rose and pulled out his cell phone. "I better make some calls."

He walked off a little way, but a couple of minutes passed before he put the phone to his ear.

Joey crossed his arms and wondered what happened to Nate. Had he seen Luke's truck and decided to get out of Dodge?

A dull headache had Joey rubbing his fingers back and forth across his forehead. The scenery shifted, transforming from snowy ground and barren branches to green grass and leafy trees.

Joey stared through the windshield of Luke's truck as they headed home from school.

"I'll be over after work to help you with your math."

"It's okay, you probably got your own stuff to do."

"Nah, everything's done." Luke pulled the truck into the driveway at Frank and Lorraine's and stopped at the end of the path to the back porch.

Joey opened the door and hopped out. He grabbed his backpack off the floor and stepped away from the truck.

"Catch you later," Luke said, closing the door.

"Bye!"

Luke grinned and waved, as he continued out the driveway and turned toward home.

*****

CHAPTER 26

LEANING into the corner of the couch in Marek's basement, Joey picked a piece of sausage off his slice of pizza. He tossed it to Cody, who caught it with a snap of his jaws.

Die Hard played on the TV. Showered and relaxed in a T-shirt and flannel pants, Christmas Eve was nearly over.

It turned out that Nate had placed an anonymous call to 911, reporting that someone was planning to kill Detective Marek. State troopers were enroute by the time Marek had made his call.

Joey glanced at the other end of the couch. Marek sat with his feet on the coffee table as he started on his third slice. A small area of his hair had been shaved to allow for a tiny line of stitches and a white bandage, which Marek had pulled off as soon as he'd gotten home. The hospital had insisted he stay overnight, and then discharged him this morning.

Detective Lewis had given him a ride home. On their way they had picked up Joey.

Marek met Joey's gaze. "So, what do you think?"

Joey wanted to scream and jump up and down, like a kid who'd just won a huge prize. But he'd been disappointed before, so he tried not to get his hopes up. "Sure. It'd be great to live here, but will they let me?"

"I'll do my damnedest to make it happen. We'll be okay. Trust me."

And Joey let it go at that. Marek would take care of it.

He tossed Cody another bit of sausage.

The movie played for a while.

"I don't understand," Marek said. "You knew I was in trouble, because the window was broken. How did you know I didn't break it?"

Joey shrugged. "You would've cleaned up the glass."

Marek gave a full-throated laugh, a deep rumble Joey had never heard from him. "There are depths to you, Joe. There are depths. You'll make a great detective one day."

Joey laughed for the first time in a long while. In that moment he was truly content. He glanced at Marek.

Maybe they both would be okay.

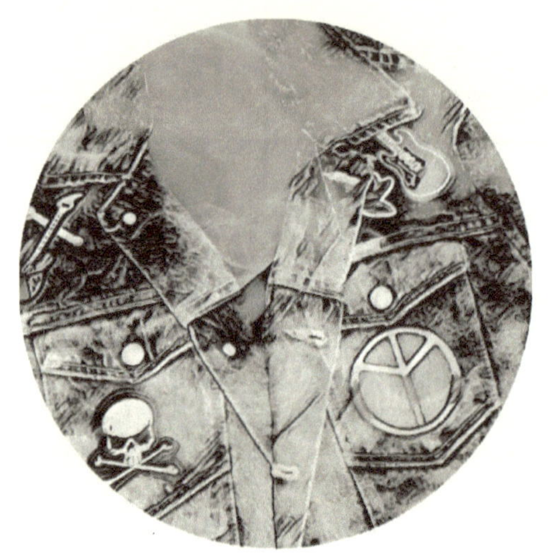

THE END

* * * * *

About the Author

Kathy Otten is the author of historical romance novels, short stories, and young adult novels. She has been writing and making up stories as long as she can remember. A certified book coach, she helps writers bring their story visions to life. She also teaches classes on writing craft, both online and in person at workshops and conferences. When she's not writing, she enjoys walking her German shepherd through the woods and fields near her home or curling up with her cat and a good book.

* * * * *

Acknowledgements

It can sometimes take a village to create a novel. Many thanks to members of Fellowship of the Quill, for your feedback and support. And a special thanks to Babs for believing in this story, when I was ready to toss it under the bed.

* * * * *

www.ingramcontent.com/pod-product-compliance
Lightning Source LLC
LaVergne TN
LVHW050956080826
845145LV00009B/2324